INFERN

MIEKE MOSMULLER

INFERNO

Novel

OCCIDENT • BAARLE NASSAU

Translated from Dutch
by
EvaTombs-Heirman

Occident Publishers
Postbox 306
5110 AH Baarle Nassau
The Netherlands
Telefon: 00-31-13-5077240 / E-mail: info@occident-publishers.com
Internet: www.occident-publishers.com

Graphic design: Martijn Franssen

ISBN / EAN: 978-90-75240-5-97

'This miserable mode
Maintain the melancholy souls of those
Who lived withouten infamy or praise.

Commingled are they with that caitiff choir
Of Angels, who have not rebellious been,
Nor faithful were to God, but were for self.

The heavens expelled them, not to be less fair;
Nor them the nethermore abyss receives,
For glory none the damned would have from them.'

From: Dante Alighieri, Inferno, Canto lll.

Patience becomes insight

I once said to a young man, "Power lies at the center of life. Make certain that you are the strongest, that you have all the advantages. And I don't just mean physical power - you understand. Psychological power is definitely just as important - if not more so." These words have become the motto of my life, they are the very foundations of my success. Perhaps 'energy' would have been a better word than power, but it has too many meanings and connotations. Even hippies talk about energy. My energy is founded on strength, on power, which, if necessary - or even remotely possible - conquers all. Now, they have brought me here. They want me to write down three important events that have shaped my life and given it direction. They call it 'miracles' in here. But I don't believe in miracles. A miracle is something you create yourself, out of yourself, from your own psychological control over other people and over nature. That is how you give direction to your life. Obviously, things do happen that are not under your control. But what you make of these events and what you do with them, depends on you. It must have been about fifteen years ago. I had been suffering from increasing pain in my joints for about a year and the doctor prescribed a plastic bag full of junk. Generally speaking I am a good patient.

My body is my everything, I don't believe in living without a body! Actually, I am not a full-blown materialist either, there must be 'something' more, some kind of power. But I received so many prescriptions, full of anti-bacterials, anti-rheumatics and more 'anti's'. The only effect I felt was a weakening of my own power. They made me feel lame, tired and depressed. So, I rebelled against the drugs and began to look for other ways to treat my rheumatism. For me any kind of help is OK, it can cost money - scientific proof isn't necessary for me - as long as it helps. That's how I came to be in a kind of 'nature' clinic, beautifully situated in the North Italian Alps. The beauty of the surroundings is curative in itself. Here they work with diet, massages, baths in special waters and with a type of homeopathic medicines. 'Extraordinary healing quackery' - I thought it nonsense. But my symptoms just about entirely disappeared! No one need talk to me about being suggestable because I didn't believe a word of it. But that is not one of the direction-giving events that I want to describe. It is about a series of encounters that I had with one of the practising doctors. My then girlfriend was with me when I stayed at the nature cure hotel. It was housed in an old building that had been renovated to the extremely high standard of refined luxury that Italians do so well. From the roomy suite we occupied, the views took in green mountain slopes; the terraces with expensive garden furniture were filled with geraniums and oleander. The rooms had old wooden floors, polished to a shine. The halls, the public rooms and the treatment rooms were all floored with marble. However, I was not altogether happy, it cost a bomb and things had already started to go wrong at reception. The receptionist was impersonal and too business-like. We were given a small room on the third floor, quite nice really, but obviously not good enough for a spoiled guy like me. So, I felt I had to make a big fuss, the manager was called, etc., before I was given the suite that I had actually reserved. And this was how it went on; everyday there was something for me to complain about. I had my first appointment with the doctor, one of the medics associated with the clinic, on the day after my arrival. I don't know if there are people who look forward to seeing a doctor. You do sometimes get that impression when you hear them talking in the waiting room. I definitely don't belong to that group. I loathe it. I find it far too intimate, too close, both psychologically and physically; it is even worse if it happens to be a woman doctor. So, when I entered the consulting room I was already quite nervous. I noticed everything in detail. Before I saw the doctor, I noticed the view out of the window. The amazing landscape; expansive wooded hillsides, steel blue skies, the blistering heat of the sun … a huge light-filled consulting room, no mess anywhere. And then, when I saw the doctor … I had the fright of my life!

'Fright' is not quite the right word perhaps. It was a shock so powerful that it has become one of the three life-changing events in my life - the first 'miracle'. I have certainly never been frightened of people, not even when holding a gun in their hands. But in this doctor, I didn't just see a person: I saw a young God! A real Italian, but as beautiful as only a God could possibly be. By 'beautiful',

I mean physical beauty, but scintillating with strength and power, male strength. I never thought I was a homosexual – but for this boy, you would want to become one. He was just the right height, the perfect weight, with the most beautiful skin colour, a stunning head of wavy brown hair, sparkling brown eyes, muscly arms under a short-sleeved doctor's jacket. He didn't smile when he gave me a powerful handshake and met my eyes with a searching look. He asked which language I wished to speak: English, German, Italian or French.

I never see myself through the eyes of another. I always see the other from my own viewpoint. This was the first time in my life that I felt seen. Just for a fleeting moment I experienced self-awareness, I saw how this young God saw me. That was the shock I received.

At my best, I resemble Henry Fonda: I have often heard that said. But now, through the eyes of this young God I suddenly saw a completely boring middle-aged geezer, hardened by rich living and too much sex with too many different partners, an insolent expression in the eyes - steel blue like the summer sky outside, and ablaze like the torturous heat of the sun from purest egotism.

That's how I want to be, but in that moment, it really didn't look that good, because a godlike gaze was directed at me. In an attempt to overcome my self-doubt, I said in a common accent from the slums in the Hague:

"Can we not just do this in Dutch, doctor?" Of course, that didn't work because the boy didn't understand Dutch, so he missed the dialect as well. But he did answer, still without a smile, in perfect British English, "Can we speak English please? The Dutch all speak English very well." I shook my head and answered him in German, purely out of stubbornness. But 'God' was also completely in control of that language. That is how that miracle, the 'direction-giving event' incarnated, in the German language.

Everything about that fellow seemed perfect. I'm sure you know better than I what the 'golden mean' is? I only know that it has something to do with perfection in relationships in nature, in the rose for example, but also in the human body. Of course, I didn't take any measurements of the boy, but I am sure that his body was created according to the 'golden mean', without a single flaw. Within his genes complete positive chance was in charge at his creation. Everything with him was in balance, in the middle, just right. For an Italian he was tall, but not too tall, he was well developed but not an athlete, and it seemed he lived like that also. The right weight, the correct care.

Now let me stop, it is quite obvious. Just one more thing: he was friendly, but not too much so.

I sat down on the chair he indicated and I was annoyed by seeing myself as I really was. The boys who are trained by me, I teach them never to think about themselves when presence of mind is required. Your waking consciousness needs to be fully focused on the other person so that you can anticipate before it happens. My practised eye saw that this young man naturally possessed this quality. And I, the teacher of learned presence of mind, sat opposite him and observed my own person in all its impossibility. All self-assurance disappeared, the 'mastering over yourself and the other'. This time, the other had the power. How did he do that? I didn't know, except perhaps because he was God-like.

"What is the matter with you?" he asked, while his godly gaze rested on my imperfections, with some mildness I must admit. Completely thrown off course I answered:

"I feel unwell, doctor, I have never felt like this before."

"What is wrong then?"

Silence; I couldn't utter a word. My learned presence of mind was based on the model of a predator hunting his prey. For that to happen, you have to be completely at one with your passions, your sense organs must be honed and kept sharp and awake, you cannot let go for a fraction of a second, every part of you needs to be focused on your goal.

You cannot have thoughts; just as the lion has no thoughts … everything is instinct, passion, power. But this fellow had touched me before I had armed myself with wakefulness; he had attacked and thrown me out of myself, like a knight jilted from his horse. That knight now lay immobile in his heavy armour on the ground and only waited for the death stroke to come.

"What is wrong then?" rang out his clear and musical voice once again. His friendly eyes shone with sympathy at my powerlessness. I wanted to curse wildly, rage and scream: *'Away with this 'God'!'* But instead a shiver went through me and I answered,

"God only knows, doctor. God only knows."

"Surely you know with which problems you came here, with which diagnosis?"

Aah, that is what he meant with his question.

"Yes, yes, rheumatoid arthritis. For the past five years I have been feeling more and more broken. I keep myself going with intensive exercise but the pain is unbearable. The medicines make me feel like an old man, in every way. I am only middle-aged and really cannot do with all this. I hope you can do something for me here."

He nodded, not in answer to my question but to affirm that he understood. He asked some more questions of a medical nature, looked at the medication I had brought with me, was silent for a while and then asked,

"What do you think is the cause of your ailments?" I had by this time come to my senses and felt I had something to prove. I said,

"You are the doctor."

Unfazed, he nodded his god-like head with curls, raised his mighty shoulders and laughed for the first time, and I noticed his teeth: perfect, strong teeth, of course. The human being is the most self-centered of the animals, because he is capable of refining his instincts with his intellect. There isn't a grain of goodness in this king of the animals, who over-reaches the lion because he can consciously, with complete intent, be false. Was I sitting opposite Nietzsche's Übermensch, was this Zarathustra? Could this Über-being become even more Über? I didn't think so. Calmly the 'King' spoke,

"Do try to answer my question. You know yourself and your body better than I do."

"That's true, of course, you have a point there. I live under a lot of tension, a lot of stress; maybe I am stiff from anxiety, doctor. But I am not afraid, not even of the devil himself. Well, maybe a little of God, and then also of you."

"Why?"

I had let myself be tempted by replying with stupid answers. Now I had to give him another answer. I avoided this by saying the following:

"Furthermore, I have drunk a lot, smoked and eaten too much. Not much sleep, many women, much coffee. That might also be the cause?"

The boy stood up and said,

"I would like to do a physical examination. The examination room is through there, I will be with you shortly."

"Should I undress?" What did you think? But the boy said patiently,

"You can keep your underwear on."

He was young, but he was an experienced doctor. Observing, listening, percussing, sensing … it all went quickly and professionally. I was allowed to dress again and was sent away with the information that he would write up a treatment plan which we would discuss tomorrow. Today I still had a day off.

I walked out and went to sit down on a bench in the shimmering, dazzlingly beautiful gardens. I felt exhausted, but also somehow strange. As if that boy had transplanted something within me that I now wanted to remove – though at the same time it also seemed essential to my life. I swore silently, in the hope that 'God' would vanish, but he stayed, if it was indeed him. I had never felt like this before,

I felt panic-stricken but also positive. It started to make me cry, because I felt so alone … and again I swore. I was becoming an old maid damn it! I jumped up and started walking fast, as fast as my legs would carry me. But I had to sit down again as I was overcome with that same feeling. No, it wasn't a feeling, it was something more real, it was as if an actual organ had been implanted which made itself felt, half unwanted and half desperately needed. I wanted to escape from it, but it had united itself with me, so that wasn't going to be so easy. If now, fifteen years or so later, I had to say what it was, then I would call it "*Goodness*".

If you, like me, detest flies, and one lands on you, then you will immediately swat it. This wasn't a fly, and it wasn't on you, but in you. I wanted to swat it away, but it was inside and I had to put up with it. It made me feel desperately weak, I wanted it gone. Still, there was also something desirable about it, like a mirage in the desert, this illusion of possible goodness – which you never wanted, never sought, never knew – that suddenly nestled itself inside you, like a swelling with its own rules. Something you are aware of will start to overcome you, you know, will start to digest you. Still, you don't want rid of it either! Like your own impossible child who demands all your energy, but who is still your own flesh and blood.

That evening at dinner I sat opposite my girlfriend. She was twenty-five years younger than me, a girl still. She was a thoroughly indulged and spoiled child. Indulged by her wealthy parents, spoiled by the desires of her indescribably beautiful body and her extremely lazy and unpleasant character. Only older guys possessed enough tricks to satisfy her desires. I was number who-knows-what who was allowed to show her off for a while. I was hopelessly in love, completely dedicated to her and pretended I was the boss over her – because that is what she wanted. Cindy she was called, but she certainly wasn't Cinderella. Work, she absolutely could not, loveable she wasn't either. She was beautiful and she made herself count.

"You are so boringly quiet," she said with an unfriendly tone.

"I'm not looking forward to tomorrow", I lied. "I really don't much like all that medical stuff. But, needs must."

She lit up a cigarette, a bit of a curse in these healthy surroundings. She inhaled the smoke slowly, deep into the very finest alveoli of her lungs, and slowly exhaled. Her behaviour awoke an intense indescribable lust in me, which collided with that strange new part of my being that I had acquired that afternoon.

The following morning, I crawled, completely broken, out of bed.

Cinderella had waited for her prince and I had thoroughly done my best. Now I had to hurry to my appointment with the doctor. 'Everything will have been a dream. At the desk there will be just a normal young doctor, who will just treat me, nothing more.' Confident that that is how it would be, I entered the consulting room. He would not affect me, I was armed to the teeth with my powers, ready for anything! But, if you want to look straight at the sun, you will be blinded - that is just a law of nature. What should you do if the sun himself in all his bright shining glory sits waiting for you at a desk? You will still have to greet him – and then you are lost. Did every patient experience this? Or was I a little crazy? I didn't know the answer to that. Again, I was completely taken out of myself and as vulnerable as before. The power, warmth and clarity of that boy hurt me, it gave me unbearable pain. In a flash I understood that this is how I wanted to be, would have wanted to be – but a large gap between the reality and the ideal was just about incomprehensible. In fact, something like that you really don't want to acknowledge about yourself. Surely you especially live to *not* feel something like that? With all my power I tried my hardest to find the strength to engender and bring up feelings of hate – it didn't really work. I heard myself say:

"I'm going home doctor, I can't be here any longer."

The doctor was silent, but kept on shining and warming. He heard my words without judging – and I already regretted them. I said:

"Oh well, I'm really not sure. Do you see the point in it?"

He began to smile and there came the music of his voice, in that German with the South Tyrolean accent:

"Of course, I see the possibilities to lessen your complaints. But the decision is yours."

"Then tell me what you have in mind for me," I mumbled, powerless. I don't remember anymore what he said. I found it impossible to concentrate on the contents of his words. I was thinking of the words of the old Goethe, who says that the rays of the sun *resound.* Not that I know much about Goethe, but I do have a good memory and remember what I hear now and again, so that I can make a good impression when it is necessary. Here, across from me, *resounded* the shining sun, and the sounds had many colours but no meaning. 'I need to go to the psychiatrist', I mocked. Would this god-like being know what effect he was having? I waited till he had finished speaking, the concert had ended, was finished. 'Now you have to stand up and applaud … what an idiot I am!' I sighed deeply and said:

"OK, doctor, I place myself in your hands entirely." Again, that friendly laugh appeared - the one that knew no ridicule. He said:

"You will only need to come and see me once a week. The rest of the time the treatments will consist of injections, massages, baths and music therapy."

Now I did understand that, and with revulsion I exclaimed:

"Music? I don't like music at all!"

"Precisely, that's why."

He stood up and I was allowed to go, towards the freedom of my normal self – apart from the positive/negative swelling, that place inside me where power was wanting to be *goodness…*

Day by day I improved. I caught myself counting the days till the next consultation with the doctor. Every day was beautiful; we swam a lot, lay in the summer sun, and enjoyed the meals. Cindy was allowed to eat and drink what she wanted, but I was placed on a meat- and alcohol-free diet. The chef had so much imagination that I never missed the meat. The alcohol was another story. I would gladly have drunk myself silly, but I had to stay sober and suffer watching Cindy disappear into that delicious state of inebriation. It was a wondrous time of rest and rhythm. We had to rise early, the treatments started at eight o'clock in the morning. Thankfully Cindy made use of the siesta time in the afternoons, but I hadn't the patience for that. I went walking in the surrounding countryside and, yes, one afternoon who did I meet coming towards me but the young God, also alone. He just looked like a normal young man. He was wearing jeans and a tee shirt, quite strange for God. When he noticed me, he slowed down. It was obvious that he didn't just intend to pass me by with only a "Grüß Gott" and so I also stopped in my tracks and greeted God … We were standing in front of a café with a terrace in the village and on impulse I invited him to join me for a refreshment. I expected a polite refusal, but he said 'yes' and we went and sat down on the terrace. I only noticed the outside of the boy, I realised that very well - looking back. I saw his very attractive body and the beautiful head; I had no idea of the personality – except that it left something behind with me, something oppressive. Completely inaccessible he was – and I now know that that was because he wasn't afraid of me.

"Tell me … " I asked, "Why do you work here? Why not in a real hospital?"

I already began to feel warm. Was it like shame, that feeling of warmth? We sat close to each other. He looked at me, and laughed his happy laugh and answered:

"It's for a short time. I am waiting for a training position in a normal hospital, such a 'real' hospital as you call it. This seemed like a pleasant diversion to me, and it is proving to be so. Maybe this will change my career for good, the work I do here seems much more effective than what I have experienced so far."

"How long will you be here?"

"One year. I have been here for three months now. And you? What is your profession by the way?"

I turned away slightly, didn't want to make myself vulnerable.

"I'm in business."

"That could be anything," laughed the young doctor.

"Indeed. Everything."

"Why did you not choose the 'real' hospital then? You don't strike me as a man who goes in for alternative therapies."

"You mustn't say that … . I am pragmatic. If it helps, I believe in it."

The conversation was about nothing. We drank a lager together and I was surprised by his peacefulness. I thought he had said 'yes' to my invitation out of politeness, but he remained seated and ordered the next round. I relaxed and suddenly started laughing.

"The doctor forbids alcohol damn it!" I shouted out. "I had forgotten – and so had you!"

"Back to the regime again soon then, hey?"

We drank our beer and he asked,

"Where do you come from?"

"From the Hague. Do you know where that is? By the North Sea, Scheveningen. I was born in the slums of the city. It has now become a dangerous place to live. I am a self-made man. With us there is a saying that '*you can never become a quarter if you were born for ten cents*'. I did - I have become a whole Euro, at least! My drive to make something of myself has propelled me over all the obstacles in my way. I now live in a villa in Scheveningen, I own several houses abroad, a boat, a Jaguar, and for every finger a good-looking girl – if I want."

I should have known that my bragging would not impress him in the least. I looked sideways and he looked at me, but I had not made an impression, not a fraction, not a millimetre. Instead, he was affecting me, with his whole damned '*good-intentionism*'.

"Lucrative business ventures, then", he concluded. "Have you ever been in jail?"

I was astonished. I had thought that I was shameless. But God even won that one. With a steely expression, I said,

"No, never. I am much too clever for that, my boy."

"That is an interesting answer, very illuminating."

I was silent. I did not want to share anything more with this churl. The 'human' is a totally bad being. Why would this boor be any different?

But when I was walking back to the hotel on my own I had already changed my mind. You can spend as much time thinking as you want, reality cures all your illusions. The reality was then that I could feel something growing within me, something I had never felt before, and every time I met the doctor it grew, like an embryo. And I knew, even though it hadn't yet come to full consciousness by then, that what I then felt beginning to grow in me, that that same thing was fully developed and in its full glory in that young man. That is why he made me think he was a god, the very first second I met him. So, I must know God then, although I absolutely did not believe in him; in power and energy, yes, which is more than just physics of matter … but not in God … The God phenomenon of the young doctor developed for me into a huge mystery. I knew very many people and I thought I had acquired quite some knowledge of human nature. I strove for omnipotent power and then used that people-knowledge. That's how I knew how to gain the upper hand in situations. During the power-play within a human encounter I could easily understand the opponent and what they were made of, and use that for my benefit; and after every encounter I felt satisfied. I did not have a sense of guilt, or scruples. Such a girl as Cindy, for example … . She was sweet or tedious, mostly tedious, but she was so beautiful that she could get away with a lot. She wound me around her beautiful fingers, but not any further than I allowed, obviously. I let her be, because I wanted to – and let her think that she had some power over me. Whatever, she was an open book for me, a person of flesh and blood, with some strong sides and large areas of weakness. She engendered lust, but I was in control of that. I did not do that for her, but for myself. Make sure that you never lose the power over yourself! That is the first rule in the book of power.

But with God, all these little human rules meant nothing. Nothing was making any sense anymore. I had absolutely no power over him; in fact, it was the opposite, he was gaining more and more control over me. I had no idea how he did this, he seemed completely innocent...

The thought of the next appointment filled me with a mixture of happiness, anxiety and terror ... though some degree of confidence had developed and I no longer shrank with shock when I encountered him.

"Today I want to ask you to give me a biographical sketch of your life, Sir. In the first week the emphasis of the therapy was focussed on the physical body. But there is more than that that needs attention."

I nodded, but I said,

"I will only do that, if you also tell me something about yourself." I used the informal 'you' intentionally. In German this has quite serious consequences, that's why I did it. But he didn't bat an eyelid and cleverly took up the gauntlet by saying,

"Because it's you I will reveal some of my hidden secrets." His radiant warmth poured out over me with his laughter – and again I was put out of myself and observed myself for the 'shite' that I really was.

"Good," I said calmly. "I was born in the Hague, as you know, the second of three children, with an older and a younger sister. My father worked in the building trade as a bricklayer. My mother often worked evenings as a waitress. They were common people. My father was a real bastard, if, indeed he was my father, which I doubt. He was an alcoholic, and when he came home drunk he beat my mom to a pulp. He never hurt us, but she had to protect us from him. He was always jealous – and rightly so, I think. But I must admit that I don't understand how the body can endure all that. What he did to her… I always escaped when he started on her, especially when I became older. I was scared that I would kill him. When I was seventeen, there he was, suddenly, dead on the floor of the living room. Mom found him. I did think … but there weren't any signs of violence; he probably had a heart attack. What a relief that was! I whistled as I buried him, in a manner of speaking."

"What kind of boy were you? How did you get on at school? Tell me something about yourself?"

"Arrogant, insolent, aggressive, always and everywhere the boss. The whole neighbourhood was my terrain and I was in charge. I was only satisfied when everyone was frightened of me. I had no appetite for learning, so I went to a school to learn trades. Furthermore, I was born before the war, so those early years were not particularly happy or without worries."

It wasn't unpleasant to tell him about myself. That is the danger of a well-intentioned good listening ear; you easily give away too much. So, I asked in return,

"Now you. How was your childhood?"

"I was born in a region near Merano. When my mother was pregnant with her first child, that was me, my father died in a car accident. So, I never knew him."

"Ooh … " I felt truly sorry for him.

"My mother had to carry on running the farm. My father had been a small wine producer. From early childhood on I worked hard there. But I was good at learning and she did everything to support and foster my education. She still lives there and I visit her weekly."

Why did this little story affect me so much? What was so special about a little boy with a mother? In my mind I saw the sun on the mountainside. The dedication of the child for the mother – and vice versa. That was it … it was something beautiful. I gave a little cough and said,

"She will surely miss you. My story is really not that nice. No Italian sun shining on the hillside where the grape vines grow. More grey, dull days, eyes fixed on the totally normal Dutch pavements and the tarmacked roads. I was a street urchin, loved football, took part in the street riots of the football club. Except never, never ever touched the women. That is at least something that I learned from home, through negative example.

I joined the army and that was like coming home. There I felt good and improved somewhat. I developed order and discipline within myself and it became clear that I did have some talents. I earned myself a high school diploma, was a good leader and climbed up the ladder as far as possible in that situation. By then I had had enough and I didn't sign up for a second tour of duty. At that time, with a good army report in your pocket, it was possible to get a job almost anywhere. The perfect civilian life lay before me …"

I was silent then. What the hell should I be telling him next? I didn't really want to reveal anything else.

"You say something else now," I said, to gain some more time. I had been lured out of my comfort zone. Time to beware!

The boy opposite me laughed and said,

"I am twenty-five. There really isn't that much to say, everything still has to happen. I studied in Bologna, I graduated six months ago. I don't have a wife yet, nor a girlfriend. I have been offered a position in a hospital to specialise in surgery. But since I started working here I am a little unsure about doing that. That's about it really."

I could not even find a way into his life story. Into his childhood yes, but the adult man remained a stranger. What should I be telling him? I could of course invent something. Lies posed no problem for me, they fell like ripe fruits into my fantasy. But, lying to God … not possible. I said,

"In the army I made friends and when I left there I set up a business with two of them - an import and export business. It was in the sixties when everyone still had the wind in their sails when it came to business. The time of the Beatles and Toon Hermans, but you don't know him of course. I earned good money and I still don't do too badly."

Not a lie was uttered – just a lot left unsaid. I remember that meeting with the young doctor in the minutest detail. When I think back to those weeks I see exactly how it all went; also, the feelings I had, they all come back again. He sat there, at his desk and I saw his scepticism. He wasn't stupid, that boy. Everything about him was balanced, even his judgements. He was not easily taken in but he was uninhibited. He knew damn well that I gave less than half what was due. He asked,

"And your private life; are you married, do you have children?"

"Yeh, yeh," I mumbled. "But that all went wrong. I don't like to look back at that. I have two sons I never see. I don't even know where they live. My ex died of cancer a few years after we divorced. You know, I don't mind admitting that I wasn't exactly the faithful husband. I always had a few women on the go, I was born in the wrong culture. I still do have several girlfriends at a time, they could poke each other's eyes out. Cindy here is my favourite at the moment, she is quite boring though, and if she finds out about the others I will lose her. That will then be a relief, you get it?"

I saw myself through his eyes and that was very annoying.

Never before had I had a conscience. Now I heard it speak. I could push it away from me, which I did, but it was there for the first time. Well, actually, maybe I had had it as a child also, maybe ... There was really no point in telling this boy about my life. What was most important, I could not speak about. It remained surface chatter.

"Do you know what I want to say?" I asked sharply. I could feel the hardness shine from my bright blue eyes, but it didn't faze him. Untouchable? "I want to say that you are sitting opposite a criminal, someone for whom nothing is too bad. Not in the past, and not now."

Still I hadn't affected him. He gazed directly back at me and said,

"I don't want to be your confessor."

"No, you are a doctor and you are asking me about my life story. My whole story is worthless if I don't tell you that I'm a criminal."

"What kind of criminal?"

The brown eyes rested on me, filled with great warmth. People never have that look. They are always scared or jealous or insolent…

"Every sort, my boy. In life, everything is always about power and money. Those are the two central connected principles and they are what I live by. I have no other starting point, they are everything I live for. But I'm not the executor, if you know what I mean. I am the commissioner. It doesn't really matter what I do, exactly. It matters that I know precisely what I want to achieve and that I achieve it no matter what or how. Preferably by legal methods, if possible. But if it isn't, I have no moral qualms about using whatever path it takes."

The boy nodded his head to show he understood. He asked,

"Have you ever loved anyone?"

I shivered. 'You', I wanted to say. Was it love? This strange feeling somewhere around my heart? I shook my head and said, while looking into the goodness of his eyes,

"No. Love? I don't even know what it is. If you ask me, it doesn't exist. It is an illusion, a fabrication."

But I felt something like tears, in my eyes, in my heart.

"Has anyone ever loved you," he asked kindly.

I wanted to escape, to run away. But I didn't, I stayed sitting there and answered him, while thinking, 'yes, you',

"Maybe my mother, my wife and my children. I don't believe in it, but they were dedicated, yes. Women do have something, sometimes. And I must say, you also have something special about you. God knows what it is, maybe it is love … ."

Satisfaction leads to resignation

Fifteen years have passed since that amazing meeting, which I still haven't stopped talking about. Since then, I haven't been the same. I was unshakeable before that, a man who could not be unbalanced, a rock; rock-hard. Think about a nice antique set of scales, with on each side a bowl ... in one a weight, in the other bowl the object to be weighed – then you see what balance actually is. It is essentially unstable, it will easily tip if any changes occur on one side of the scale. Not in my case then. I had solidly screwed down the balance point of the scale, so it would never wobble again.

Everything was so tight that I could keep my balance in any situation.

The first gaze of that young man, that Italian doctor, wrecked that screw. He *was* balance, in every way. Except that in his case, the balance was there by the control he had over himself, as young as he was. Power yes ... but not over others. That is what I felt then and didn't understand any of it. What became very obvious however, was that I was now raging and out of control. A state of chaos developed within me which spread out and caused my whole self to flounder. I could no longer be the person I had always been, and this continued. What had always been my strength became an empty powerlessness. First, only in meetings with him, but over time this effect spread out to encompass my relationship with others too. My power slipped like water through my fingers, my grip was deteriorating rapidly.

But I will go back to those first weeks and explain how it developed. I began to fall in love with that boy, with his beautiful external masculinity, but even more with the complete power he had over himself. He was by nature like a predator whose awareness is instinctively completely focused on its prey, in control. He could not be moved in any way but there was no trace of hardness in him. I began to understand that this was what I had been striving for, but somehow I had achieved the opposite. I burned with admiration just for this quality in the boy and I did have some difficulty in separating that feeling from actually being in love. I kept having to remind myself that I didn't feel the need for physical contact, that I actually only desired to be in his presence. I wanted to see how he did it and to enjoy his perfection. From the gentle warmth in his beautiful brown eyes, from the sudden breaking forth of merriment held in balance with a deep seriousness. From his muscled body with the delicate doctor's hands. It was a being in love but of a psychic nature. It was more than a love a father has for his son as there was no blood relationship, it was just that fascinating balance, by which he could walk through the world completely unhampered.

The ambivalence of the situation I found myself in, tore me apart. I felt love developing within myself but at the same time a destructive disgust. How could this young fellow be like this, without any effort on his part, without any training? Was this a freak of nature? Was this the result of a unique genetic configuration? Or did he just make better use of the characteristics he was born with? And how come he could do that, and I could not? I constantly tested him with difficult questions, bad behaviour and hidden threats, but he never faltered, not for a fraction of a second. If it came to a fight, you would always be the loser, in a duel you wouldn't stand a chance against him. Everything he did or said had a faultless certainty about it, making any attempts at undermining him seem utterly pointless. I kept on trying, however, and became so stupidly ridiculous that I became seriously frustrated.

"What on earth is wrong with you!" complained Cindy. "I always thought you were a strong guy. But here you walk around in a daze, deep in thought and achieve absolutely nothing. When I speak you don't even hear me."

"What do you mean by 'strong guy'?" I asked.

"Well, at least not such a cry-baby. Have you been hurt by something; by me?" she asked. I uttered a mocking laugh then was silent. I found her boring, her beauty repelled me. I stood up and walked away.

I was always hoping that I would run into him. I knew his routine and when and where I might bump into him on his rounds. Then we would have a chat and, if he had time, a drink. We discussed everything but not my 'work'.

In the third week of my stay there we went for a walk in the mountains at his suggestion. He seemed to know every route, every path. When we slowly started to climb I asked,

"Do you do this with all your patients? To see if your treatment is working?" I could feel my ankles, knees and hips. He stood still and looked at me searchingly and answered, "No, I just very much want to go for a walk with you. You can do this, you'll see. It is an easy route."

"OK, OK," I mumbled.

Nimbly he walked ahead. He wore professional climbing boots and ¾ length trousers. I noticed his muscled calves. I was in good condition but twice his age and I did have, though healing well, rheumatoid arthritis. I felt myself to be an old man. But he halted often to point out the fantastic views and I delighted in his company. That, too, was a new experience for me; till then I had only ever experienced pleasure in myself. Then we reached a level country road with distant views all around. The mountains were less high but we could still see dales and valleys below us. There was an inn with a simple terrace where we could eat and drink something.

"Do you believe in God?" he suddenly asked me.

"I'd better not then believe in him. I haven't exactly served him well up till now," I replied.

He threw up his hands in the air.

"Does God exist? Apart from what you might or might not like?"

"You are asking me this at the right moment. At this moment, here in the sun, on this mountain-top beside you … yeah, there must be a creator of all this. I am not a materialist, not at all," I replied.

"Aren't you afraid of him then? Do you not fear him?" he asked.

"Why?"

"Well, you did tell me that you were a criminal? So how will that go then?"

I burst out laughing and said with cynicism,

"Do you worry about that?"

He remained serious and answered,

"Yes".

His 'Yes' was like a hard punch in the face. This is how he loosened the screw of my inner hypomochlion, my balance point, and made me lose my balance completely.

"What do you care, you aren't a carer of the soul, are you?" I said.

"I care a great deal, as I'm your friend," he replied.

Friend ... that tile I saw, on the wall in the toilet in the bar, with that little verse by Toon Hermans... 'if you have someone who laughs and cries with you ... then you have a friend.' Sentimental nonsense really, but I tripped up over those words. I fell into an abyss of loneliness. I could not utter another word. He could though. He said,

"You never told me what it is that you actually do - maybe better not to, I don't even want to know. Maybe I see in you the father I never had."

"Nice father -" I protested.

"Don't you have everything? A healthy body, strong, beautiful. A stunning face, a strong soul..."

"And a dreadful personality. Man, you don't know me at all!"

What on earth had happened to me?

"I do know you," he insisted.

"You are mistaken, you think you see something in

me that you have yourself. Only, I acquired this quality through a very special route; where, with you - well yes, I don't really know for sure. I never think that deep – and I certainly never talk about it."

He was silent. Maybe somewhat disheartened. Our coffee arrived with a bottle of mineral water and a bread roll. Maybe this was the most beautiful moment of my whole life. A cloudless sky with the sun above and, beside me, my friend. Was the love mutual? He said,

"Maybe that is all true. My interpretation of your character may be incorrect, I haven't clocked up that much people knowledge. But the feeling of a bond between us is no mistake. Don't you feel it too?"

I nodded hopelessly and he continued,

"Therefore, I am concerned. God exists and he will judge you, believe me."

"You Italians are so emotional, so over-dramatic."

"My mother tongue is German, I was born in Sud-Tirol."

"You are a real Italian. Theatrical."

"If you mean that I have emotions, then, yes you are right, I do. You are a real cool Dutchman; me an emotional Italian. And I am concerned about you."

"What do you want? Should I go and confess?"

"No, you need to reflect, and repent. Reflect on yourself and on your life."

At this point an unbearable feeling of powerlessness rose up within me. I had to shut him up!

"For God's sake, shut up. Behave like my son then, and be quiet!"

He was quiet.

A bird of prey menacingly circled overhead, probably over its next victim...

Self-reflection is a seriously life-threatening occupation for a man like me - clearly becoming more obvious by the day. But every meeting with the young Italian put me in such a good mood that I longed intensely for our meetings. Cindy was beginning to get bored, so I took her to the airport. For myself, I extended my stay at the spa hotel for another four weeks. My symptoms vanished and the frequency of the meetings increased. For one reason or another he liked hanging out with me.

"To what do I owe the honour of your interest in me?" I asked him, during a dinner in the hotel's divine gardens. He put down his knife and fork and looked at me with some surprise and a peaceful yet powerful gaze. He said,

"You are a very interesting man. Moreover, I miss a father as I already told you."

I answered him uncomfortably,

"Well there are better fathers around! Interesting? Well..."

"You have had a lot of experience, even though you don't want to talk about it. You know life, I don't. I have undergone a training of course, that I have. I was at the Waldorf school in Merano, really a very good school. There I learned so many things. But about the world ... no, I only know about the world from a cultural and agricultural point of view. Politics, power relations, business - I have no knowledge of these at all. You've already got all that, I like that. What is life worth without wine? That is what life would be like without you! I never appreciated that side of life before you came into my consulting room. You are alert, cynical – a bit aggressive. There are more people like that. But when I spend time together with you I experience a whole world, a new world."

I felt extremely unhappy. This young man was in love with me because I was a dick; a man who denies everyone else all happiness and gets his 'kicks', his own power, from that. He was learning about the evil in life from me, and I had the dubious honour of being the object of his hunger for knowledge.

"So, you hang around with me, damn it all, to acquire knowledge of the wretchedness in the world!" I exclaimed.

He shook his head, picked up his cutlery again and resumed eating. He was my superior because he never ever seemed to lose his balance. He also didn't appear to have that human need for other people to like him. That actually gave him power – while I just became shakier by the minute. Silently, he finished his plate of food and only then began to defend himself.

"No, Gerrit!"

He could hardly say my name. "I did not say that, do not put words in my mouth. You are a true 'man of the world', that is what I mean. I never said anything about evil - that is your own conclusion – and that is not relevant at all!"

I was defenceless. I said,

"I do know myself a little, I know who I want to be, my boy. I am a no-good because I want to be no-good. As to 'evil' - you really can find out about that from me. I was trained to be a sniper in the army and have used that skill on many occasions later on."

He didn't even blink an eye and looked straight at me. "Nowadays I teach this art to young guys who, just like me, can't earn a living in the normal way. I no longer work out in the field, if you know what I mean. I send out the boys. Yes indeed, I do know the world!"

"What is it you really want, Gerrit? Are you trying to frighten me?"

I replied with a sneering guffaw,

"I am under no illusion that that would be possible. What I learned in my training, you have by nature. You don't need all those crutches. You have no need to prove yourself, to make yourself seem stronger than you are. You don't need to do anything at all. You just are who you are, just like 'God'..."

I was weak, thoroughly weak. Cupid had shot his arrow and in a moment of confusion had hit his target, straight into my heart. The old Gerrit was dead, the new one was desperate. There was absolutely nothing I could do about it now. I learned about this love because he had put it in me and I could not get it out again. It grew bigger and bigger, like a swelling that breaks through all boundaries. I wanted to take him home with me, or to stay with him. He wasn't my lover, he was too noble for that – no, he was my son, like he wanted to be. But, sooner or later father and son must part; and with trepidation, I felt that moment coming ever closer.

I felt that I had the right to a good life. I had had a horrible childhood and I hated everyone who had a better life than me. Moreover, I didn't trust anyone who deigned to be good and high-minded. I thought them weak, those people in whom nature with all its beauty and power had been subjugated for silly ideals. From time to time the hate flamed up in me with such intensity that I needed to let off steam - sometimes as violence, sometimes sex. Now I had met someone who was the opposite of a weakling. Someone in whom nature displayed her highest, most beautiful, most powerful works - but at the same time also displayed all those characteristics that I so admired in myself. Without any effort, without badness, without the hate. Be that as it may, that wasn't even the worst of it. What was even worse was that something real streamed out from him and entered into me, something I could not shed. I have not been able to shake that off and it has ruined and destroyed my whole life. I have been stripped of all the power and strength I was so proud of. I became the weakling I so hated. A whining, whimpering old maid with uncontrollable desires, with irrepressible feelings of shame and unreconcilable guilt...

After I left Italy, at first, it wasn't so bad. We said our goodbyes but we would keep in touch. He was coming to The Hague and I wanted wanted to do another course of treatment - even though he would be far away, we would certainly meet up. It was like a teenage holiday romance, full of hope for the future. We'll meet again! Once back home though, nothing made sense any more. I lived in a perfectly decorated villa, had the use of a housekeeper, a gardener, my agenda was full of appointments, both business and private. But I could not incorporate that new 'growth' within me into my daily life. I felt myself to be emotionally disturbed. My house felt ugly in all its perfection, the park-like garden was artificial - a park in the dunes! I found the incentives that drove my business partners now pointless, the advances of my girlfriends made me puke! Golf was so boring. I had lost the desire to go hunting, expensive dining in fancy restaurants made me feel nauseous and beer had no flavour any more, expensive wine was now bitter and sour. The only thing that was even remotely of any value to me now was the sober grey beauty of the North Sea on the blond beach; that brought some elements of joy. Everything else was shit, nothing, void! The only thing that was continuously missing - the presence of my Italian son – became an unbearable burden. He didn't make contact and I couldn't reach him by phone. After a few months I came to the conclusion that his Italian blood cooled fast, he had forgotten his fatherly friend just as easily as he had impressed him.

I became totally unbalanced, it became ever worse. My GP prescribed antidepressants, which didn't do anything. I abandoned my work to others, but without me they were worthless, and they took unsafe risks. So then I interfered again but could not bring up the sternness needed. I was totally broken, as was everything I had built up.

At Christmas I received a card from Italy. A card with a pre-printed Christmas message with a hasty signature underneath. Convention, perhaps, but still... My whole life long I had kept grief at bay, now here it was, as if it had been lying in wait just under the surface, growing ever bigger till this moment. Like the genie in the bottle - now uncorked - it would overwhelm me. With the card in my hand I went to sit down at my desk, grabbed a fancy sheet of writing paper, my gold fountain pen and, with a handkerchief for the tears in my other hand, I began to write.

The Hague, 25/12/1990

Dear, dear Friend...

Those three words epitomised the whole of my new existence. I felt how the wife I had, long ago, had loved me. I experienced how the children I had been given, two little boys who called me 'Daddy', had absolutely not affected me. I had found her love irritating, their dependence a nuisance. Now I cried, because I was at last experiencing what I had actually felt then but had repressed with my own choice to be hard. Where were those boys now? About the same age as him, to whom I was writing 'Dear dear Friend'. I would go and look for them, those two - in the new year. She, I could not find again, she had died. Dead ... one day one will die. 'God exists and he will judge you'. That's what he had said to me during that first long walk. He was already judging. Because of his love he had condemned me to a hell of longing. Longing without lust ... longing for him ... longing for my children ... longing for her ... longing for my lost life. You can achieve everything, until you are gripped by self-awareness. Never let light shine even one ray upon your deeds – you will be lost, powerless, a slave to that thing called love. Dear, dear friend. Seven times I began again. Then I thought: Damn it! I will just write what I want to say.

'Dear friend,' I wrote, 'really, I never thought we would not speak or not see each other. I left full of trust but the weeks have turned into months and I must admit to myself that it is over. I am a broken man, not only because of the parting. Especially because you have brought me to my senses, young man. For the first time I see myself from the outside, maybe through your divine eyes. And what I see is nauseating, I cannot live with that. But I won't end it all, because imagine if God is there!

All best wishes for the New Year.

Gerrit'

Within a week I received a telephone call from him. I never dared hope for this, so his voice hit me like a lightning strike. He didn't stand on ceremony but barged straight in with,

"Gerrit, I apologise. I never realised that our friendship had such an effect on you."

"I was under the illusion that it was mutual," I replied.

"That is true. But life, with its strong currents, dragged me along. A few days after you left I met the girl of my dreams. You will understand how that has taken up quite some of my attention! Then I received a request to start my internship half a year earlier than expected due to the illness of one of the junior doctors. So I took that opportunity, even though the work at the spa hotel was pleasant enough. So now I am working eighty hours a week - and I also have a girlfriend. But, when I received your letter – today – I realised that I had neglected something."

"And?" I asked.

"Well, I can't do anything. I really don't have time for anything, Gerrit. I just wanted to let you know that I really appreciated our encounter. And if I thereby woke you up to self-awareness – well, that is a good thing, isn't it?"

With sarcasm I said,

"That good thing is destroying me! I have to go on, I think I'll manage that too."

I was of course too proud to let him see my despair – which was of his doing - or my desire for him. It would have to end. I would go in search of my real sons; maybe they would fill the void.

Courtesy becomes heartfelt tactfulness

They asked me to describe three life-changing 'miracles' now and they are not even wanting to hear about my whole biography! The first 'miracle' I have already described. The second occurred seven years or so later and is closely associated with the first. It really is only one miracle – but never mind. I had to find three. What occurred in the seven years in between, I will leave out. We are now in 1997 and I have passed my sixtieth year. I had spent much energy on the forgetting of that 'God', with the help of many artificial interventions - I may need to reveal more about this later – I had more or less succeeded. These had been the worst seven years of my life, in every way. On that Spring evening, when the devil just happened to be away on holiday, the phone rang – like it often did. I never say my name, I just say "Hello". "Pronto!" sounded that voice that I will never forget. Even when I'm dead, I will know that I still exist in the memory of that voice. "Hey Gerrit, this is your Italian friend."

For seven long years I had painfully been working on re-establishing the tightness of the screws on the balance within my soul – and in a fraction of a second it all came loose again. Damn it! I should just hang up, forget that guy! Damn it! Instead I heard myself say,

"Hello, Gerrit here."

The 'miracle' I am alluding to, was the effect of what streamed out of the man. I didn't even see him, we hadn't spoken for years – yet immediately that 'tumour' feeling was there again. I did know that it was still there within me, but I had very consciously turned myself away from it. It now seemed that it had grown within me without my realising it. He had also grown, I could hear the development in his voice. Like before, he came straight to the point. He said,

"I am coming to Leiden for a conference. If you like, we can meet up?"

"Where are you staying?"

"In a hotel."

"Do you want to stay at mine? The Hague is close to Leiden."

"Yes, please,"

We arranged that I would collect him from Schiphol in precisely three weeks.

"We will talk more then."

A few polite greetings, and he was gone. I should have shouted "NO!" This was all wrong. You never give an alcoholic a beer, do you now? But I had already sensed the smell and seen the fresh foam. It couldn't be helped and it hit me hard! I arranged for a room to be made ready for him and discussed potential meals with my housekeeper, just to be on the safe side, and went to the barber to have my hair cut. And I waited. 'He will be seven years older. He must be thirty-two by now,' I thought to myself. But his beauty had increased so that he radiated confidence. His hair was just as thick, he was better dressed, his gaze, when he looked up at me, pierced my heart. Not a youngster any more but a divine young man. Surgeon in Florence in the hospital there. Handsome, sporty, educated and, above all, completely natural. I felt myself a worn-out, underdeveloped thug – all I could offer him was courtesy and hospitality. So, that is what I offered. It was one of those exceedingly rare beautiful afternoons and I had arranged to have the table set for lunch in the garden. He had freshened himself up in his room and appeared at the table without his jacket. Finally, we were sitting opposite each other. Before me sat the embodiment of what was destructively growing within me. And I loved him like nothing on earth. Oh boy, did I love him! With one well-placed thrust of the lance he unsaddled me by asking, in that manner of his,

"How are you, Gerrit?"

I remained silent.

"Why don't you say something?" I looked at him for a while, and then said,

"What should I say? Good? Bad?"

"You could tell me something."

I was angry at him and I was going to show him.

"Shall I tell you something? Seven years ago, I met you and I let you know, in no uncertain terms, that your existence had disturbed mine - uprooted mine, even. After that - you just dumped me! With much effort and pain, I have finally managed to find some inner balance again and, yes, you guessed it! Here he is again to throw me back into confusion. Probably just to disappear again for seven long years – or maybe even forever?"

I paid close attention but the only reaction I noticed was a kind of sadness in him. He didn't get upset, he didn't get angry. He just felt bad. He said,

"You only see it from your own point of view Gerrit. Try seeing it from my perspective. I was only twenty-five. I did feel a lot of love for you, but what of that? I didn't know what to do with that. And you were not wanting to let go of anything, you were constantly sparring, wanting to see who was the stronger of us two. That is not how it works with me. I couldn't care less who is stronger. I can tell you that wholeheartedly. But, apparently, that was just what made me the stronger one – and it was that that brought you down. Well then, it was better that you went your own way then. No?"

"OK, good, fine" I said stubbornly. "So far, so good. But then I don't understand what you are doing here, now? What are you actually doing here? Pulling the rug from under me again?"

This is where he should stand up, grab his things … That is how this works. But not at all, he remained sitting peacefully and looked at me with a deep desolation. A look that contained the triumph of power.

"In the first place, I am older now - and therefore stronger. I now understand more, and don't just feel it. I have finished my post-graduate studies and am settled in surgery and I have experienced quite some things, believe me. I can't say that I thought about you every day, but weekly, yes, without fail. I prayed for you regularly."

"Yuck!"

"What, then, did you expect of God?" he retorted wryly.

"I prayed for you regularly and then I experienced you, who you are and all that you do."

"Are you clairvoyant?"

"Experiencing is different than seeing."

"Well, and?" I asked, irritated.

"Well, I never forgot you, and I was waiting till I felt myself strong enough to continue our friendship."

"It was quite convenient, then, that you just happened to have to be in Leiden."

He answered me calmly,

"This is already the fourth time I have come to Leiden."

"Well damn it!"

"Just stop it, Gerrit. You are going against yourself here. You wholeheartedly want this meeting – and now you are trying to chase me away!"

I helplessly nodded and sank down in my chair.

"That is how it is, exactly," I admitted, "that is how it is."

"How are things with you Gerrit?" Unperturbed, he started again. I sighed long and deep and thereby let go of unwanted emotions from deep within me, and then began to talk.

"I have never yet loved anyone, my boy. I know that now. But that is because no one has ever really loved me. Many other kinds of emotions, but not love. I love you - yes. But that is logical, because I can feel your love. And I don't get it – what in heaven's name brings forth love – I know, for sure, that it exists. I cannot use any love, you see. It doesn't fit, it has totally the wrong effect."

"I'm not convinced. I think you are mistaken."

"What is happening to me would only make sense if

there was an eternity, and if God did exist. But he doesn't, so it is pointless cruelty."

"Still, you want me to stay."

"Of course. For seven long years I have yearned, not weekly, but daily, three times per day even - sometimes twenty times per day - I have wanted to see you. You awoke something in me, something that feels like my life's purpose – but I have lived as if that purpose was a nonsense. I can forget it all, but with some difficulty. But now, here it is in the full glory of reality – he is sitting opposite me. You are it." He lowered his eyes and was silent. My son.

After the meal he withdrew for a siesta, that peculiar Southern custom. I felt myself somewhat unhappy. That awful feeling of guilt I only ever experienced when interacting with him. This was the first time that I felt I had actually had an impact on him – it was not a pleasant feeling. Like hitting a baby. Well, normally, that wouldn't affect me with feelings of guilt, maybe even the opposite – but that was just it. In my interactions with him I seemed to experience the flip side of things. Would he really be sleeping? I could feel his presence in my house. That evening we would be dining together and I would try to behave myself.

I was so proud of him sitting opposite me that evening, in the restaurant. Such a beautiful Italian young man whose beauty depended wholly on his equilibrium, and beyond that, his kindness in every situation. He had donned a smart jacket, a decent tie and his gold watch, indications of a well-filled wallet. All the while he remained humbly and naturally straightforward. We celebrated our reunion with Champagne and I asked,

"Aren't you angry with me?"

He didn't avoid my question and said,

"I found you annoying, yes. Very, very annoying even! You only ever think about yourself, isn't that right?"

"Probably. I mean that I think a lot about you, but most likely just from my own point of view. Isn't it the signature of evil that it only serves the ego?"

"How is that with you, Gerrit? Do you really want to pursue evil, or did it just go that way by itself? You can make a very good impression you know, why don't you just be nice?"

"Because you don't achieve anything that way - at least I don't. I like power and strength. Men who look for something different are weaklings."

"Isn't that because you are really terrified?"

This 'nice' young man had some spunk!

"Well shit!" I swore. But then I controlled myself and said, "That is probably the true reason but I can't see it myself. My best students are the scaredy-cats. Courageous guys like you are never amongst them. They get their courage from their weapons and do not have courage within themselves at all. That fear is useful, you can mould them to your will. But do I myself also have that problem? Well, maybe so. I gladly let myself be governed by you..."

"That was not my intention."

"Since the time we met you have done nothing else, my boy! Not with lessons, but, by the affect you have on me. What is so nice about me anyway?"

"'Charm' is maybe a better word for it. Because you are so hard, the moments when you're friendly are very charming. Women will probably fall for that. And as for me, it is your fatherliness, your preponderance, just your overpowering strength is so impressive to me. No one I know has that, not one of the surgeons I know, though many are power hungry."

I smiled in my 'nice' manner and said,

"The amazing thing is that you possess everything that I would want without all that effort of intimidation and the invoking of fear, and without all the hard work of having to make yourself into a predator. I would want to be a lion in the human world but most likely I am a scorpion with a venomous tail. You, on the other hand, lift yourself up with huge wings, like an eagle, above all that difficult stuff. Oh my, if I could only understand what it was all about!"

"Where did you come by all that wisdom, Gerrit? You must have come across some occult knowledge?" he asked.

"How do you figure that? I have my eyes and ears open." I poured another glass of Champagne and evaded his question with, "Come boy, have another glass."

During the day he went to Leiden and lunched there with his colleagues. We spent the evenings together. He was very loyal, didn't let himself be tempted to arrange anything else for the evenings. He was 'home' at half past six on the dot, withdrew for an hour and appeared, perfectly turned out, for dinner. I enjoyed our hours together tremendously; the only drawback was the certainty of the short duration of this happiness.

"Help me think about about something other than myself. Tell me something about you, about your private life, your work and such."

"I married a girl that I met after you left the sanatorium. She has given me three children, two girls and a boy. We have a fantastic relationship, completely open and trusting. I don't see that anywhere around me. I spend long days in the clinic, but I feel such a strong desire to be with her that she never complains. My work is good, though I frequently wish for a deeper meaning to my work. Surgery is satisfying in itself, solving problems - even rescuing and redeeming people. Still, something is missing, something that was present when I was still at school. Depth is what I miss."

I could not envisage what he was talking about. He was my friend and therefore my personal possession. Still, he had a girl who he daily desired, he had three children with her, which indicated that he slept with her. For seven long years he had been busy with many different people, but not with me – and now, here he was, giving the impression that I was the only person that was important in his life. My jealousy made breathing difficult. The only true reality seemed to me to be this moment, us two, at the table in a restaurant or at home. Later, together on the terrace or in the living room. Together, in bed, I would have liked to have tried that too. With him I could share my whole life, every hour of the day would be interesting and exciting. Had I become gay? Not at all, just in this very special case it could happen, if I could just hold him so that he would never leave again. But that was not how it was, at all.

"Why are you so quiet?" he asked.

"I am thinking about all the rest of my days without you."

He shook his beautiful head.

"Why do you attach yourself to me so, Gerrit? We could just be friends; don't you have other friends?"

"Nope," I mocked. "Friends don't exist. Just you."

"Can't you be satisfied with the status quo? Does everything immediately have to belong to you? Does it have to be your own personal possession? Your own property? That is the problem."

"Don't you say 'your' wife and 'your' children?" I asked.

"That is the convention. I don't actually experience it like that. We are all people on a journey and we travel some of the way together, sharing love and sorrow, without becoming each other's possessions."

"I don't believe any of that. That is not possible. Nice words those, learned from some philosopher or other, no doubt. The reality is different."

He shrugged his broad shoulders.

"I have no wish to try to convince you of anything." He was adjusting himself to my way by being subtle and pliant. Oh well, it was only for a few days. I would dearly have had deeper conversations with him, but I didn't know how, couldn't find the words or missed the right tone. I felt a growing desire for something other than physical presence. He had more to offer, but I wondered if he even knew that. After four days I took him back to Schiphol airport. We shook hands vigorously. We promised to phone, but *really* this time. I watched him walk away! Strong, self-confident, athletic. He looked back once and raised his hand.

I don't know how long I stood there, the image of him etched on my retina, and thereafter in my imagination. I stood there crying and couldn't stop. This was the first time I experienced what saying goodbye really meant. The beloved is with you and then he is gone from view and there is no guarantee you will ever see him again. Probably not. What on earth does that young man want with such a clingy old codger like me? Just get out of here in a hurry. Breathe a sigh of relief that it is now done. Great to be going home, to wife and children, young and beautiful and innocent as the Spring.

But, five hours later he phoned to let me know he had arrived home safely. Hesitantly he mentioned,

"I left in a very low mood, Gerrit. We forgot to do something, though I don't know what. You wanted something and we acted as if that wasn't the case. Or am I mistaken?"

I welled up and said with a shaky voice,

"No, boy, you are right. I have told you before that you are a kind of embodied reproach to me, that also is total ... love. Loving reproach. That works on me like a mirror; I see myself. And what I see, I cannot endure. I need a priest, not a doctor, I think. 'Confession' they call that, don't they? I would want to tell you everything but cannot do that to you. That is why our conversations are not what they should be and I was left with a broken-hearted sadness. You cannot do anything about it, boy. Just forget it. You go your way, you have other tasks, higher probably. I'll manage, really."

There was silence for quite some time, I could feel the

change in his mood. Then he said,

"Well, I'd better go. I won't disappear from your life again, Gerrit, I promise."

"OK, bye-bye, my boy."

I hung up and cried bitterly. It wasn't sobbing anymore, but real human crying with floods of tears and wailing...

The effect of this encounter on me was different from the previous time. That is why I call it the second 'miracle'. The first time something odd had remained behind in me, something had developed that had completely thrown me off balance. This time it felt as if he had taken something away with him, back to Italy. I had lost Gerrit. An emptiness remained behind, maybe that sensation I had experienced as an 'inclusion' had now been taken away, like a hollowing out. This manifested within me as a gigantic unfulfilled desire, a desire for ... Gerrit. Gerrit was gone, I couldn't find him anywhere, he must have gone to Italy with his young friend. And I was left behind without a friend and without myself. Without access to myself I could not carry on with my work. I stopped working, and the days became endlessly long. I had, in the meantime, made contact with my two sons, though the meetings were rare. One of them was a representative in a software company, the other had continued his studies and become a PE teacher. To facilitate the relationships, I gave them money from time to time, once for a new car, then for a trip abroad - or something like that. They gratefully accepted these gifts, in exchange for allowing me to have some time with my five grandsons occasionally. Not all at the same time, but usually in twos. We played football or went sailing and such.

Because the emptiness was unbearable, I went to visit a psychiatrist. The GP had had the antidepressants ready, so I looked higher up for help. But the shrink didn't have anything new to offer, either. "You are going through a grieving process. You want to deny that your youth is gone. That your friend finds other things more important than your friendship. That your work is no longer as challenging as when you were young. I agree with you that it isn't a depression, but, it could well become that."

He made a series of appointments for consultations. I had no desire to continue with this drivel, but agreed and filled in the form. Later on, I cancelled the appointments. I phoned Italy. By now it was mid-summer and we had had brief telephone contact about once a month. After the much loved 'pronto', I asked,

"Could I come and visit for a few days in the autumn? I can stay in a hotel and see you occasionally ... there is something that I want to discuss with you."

He answered without a moment's hesitation, thank goodness,

"Of course, Gerrit! But you must come and stay with us. My wife would love to meet you and I look forward to offering you our hospitality."

Somehow, I would survive the rest of the summer. There were plenty of beautiful young women who allowed a guy like me to charm them. This old Gerrit could still do that despite his grieving!

At the end of September, I flew to Florence. And the second 'miracle' repeated itself. I learned what hospitality is, what courtesy is. I had often opened my house to guests and I regarded myself as a hospitable person. I would have a room well prepared and they could eat with me, and so on. But otherwise, life just went on as normal. My guests could enjoy free luxury accommodation and that was it. This is what the Dutch are like. We also like to be left to our own devices.

He came to the airport to collect me, he had taken a week's holiday off work to ensure I was well looked after. It is very difficult to put into words what happened next. He was there but that wasn't all. He really received me, his life made space for mine and I was made to feel that my arrival had been very much anticipated. It is was a celebration, my arrival, a high point in the life of the whole family. There was nothing to suggest that my arrival might have been a bit of a chore. Nothing like that. His wife was a calm girl, just as natural as he was, maybe a little shy but extremely friendly. All of my potential feelings of envy fell away because of the ease with which she granted him to me for the week. That he would devote all his time and attention to his guest was a matter of course. They accepted life as it presented itself, and celebrated it. Even the children gave me the impression that they had been looking forward to these days, as if I was a very special uncle from the far away Netherlands coming to visit. I should have brought some gifts, their absence pained me. Oh well, I would make up for that.

They lived in a villa on the outskirts of the city, a beautiful house – not as fancy as mine, of course – in a garden with palm trees and oleander bushes. Here in this house, with these people around you, happiness could be yours...

But, I did want to talk with him, that is why I had come. He hadn't forgotten that, for when we were sitting at the counter of a café next morning, drinking our espressos, he asked,

"What did you want to discuss with me, Gerrit?"

With a movement of my head towards the terrace I said,

"Let's sit there and we can talk."

I sat opposite him, in the shade of the awning. I took a deep breath and said,

"Look here, son. I have talked about this a bit already. Now I want to speak more openly. I don't want to burden you with my style of living. Who knows, one day I might even confess to you – I wouldn't trust anyone else – but at this moment I can't see the point of that. It would only burden you. What I do want to say is that I can categorically distinguish between a life before, and after our first encounter. I have developed awareness of my unscrupulousness. Believe me, I know that road through and through. No one has ever managed to divert me from that path, truly. Then, one day I walk into your consulting room and, hey, it is achieved! Completely. From that very first second, I am no longer who I was before. In the seven years that we haven't seen each other I have managed to pull myself together - with much pain and effort, but my life has never been as it was. In that very first second, something slipped into me unnoticed, and it started to grow and grow, like a cancer. Even when it doesn't hurt it is still growing. It is really something positive ... but a bit like when an asthma patient can't tolerate pure air – that is how this Gerrit cannot tolerate his own growing self-awareness. Now my question is: Was this your *intention*? Did you do something to me? Do you know what you have done? Or don't you know that either?"

I could see that he was moved, and it took a little while before he spoke. I waited patiently.

"You know what, Gerrit, I was twenty-five then. I was just, well, quite young still. No, I didn't consciously do anything, but since you ask me straight out, I do know what it is. At least, I think I do." He stayed silent for a time and I waited. "I remember 'that second' also, very well. You came in with a certain aggressive air about you. Generally, I know your type. You are hard, domineering, on the attack, without considering who you confront. Do not think for one moment that I did not see these things or that I did not, for a fraction of a second, know that I could have been intimidated. But my own presence of mind was slightly stronger than that." I raised my eyebrows. "Yes, that is how it was, I caught the spear you threw before it could hit me. In the martial arts it would have been normal to throw it back, but, by Jove, I can't do that. Precisely because by catching it and holding on to it, a certain strength was released in me. In that one fraction of a second, I 'saw' you, Gerrit. Believe me, when you have truly 'seen' someone - and that happens to me from time to time - then the love streams forth without end. That must have been it ... that is what you experienced, and what remained with you."

A disaster overcame me, there beneath the awning of many cheerful colours on a terrace in Florence. In full public view I burst into floods of tears and I did not know how to stop. He just sat there staring at me, at a complete loss as to how to proceed, as well. The truth penetrated more deeply than ever before. The totality of my sins appeared before me and filled me with horror. Everything I had ever done appeared in front of my conscience and I judged myself so hard that I had to totally crush myself. I just kept on crying, people around us looked away, they probably thought someone had died or something. Eventually he stood up, placed his hand on my shoulder and said,

"Come, Gerrit, let's go for a walk."

We walked and walked. From time to time I felt his hand on my back to support me. He didn't say a word. My tears dried up and I walked with after-sobs, like a child beside my young friend who had seen me as a father figure. My crisis of conscience was now joined with a deep shame.

"Let's sit here for a little while," he said. We arrived at a sunny town square. On the opposite side stood a church or a monastery. I felt myself empty but I still trembled from excessive emotion. We sat down, the terrace was still quite deserted.

"Gerrit, Gerrit," he said and I felt myself beaten. I was sitting next to a young man, a good thirty years younger than me, who possessed all that I would have wanted to have – much of which I had also achieved by murky means. But he had it as a positive where mine was negative and he had it by nature. And with him it had not come out of a blackness, but from the coloured palette of God. I hoped, of course, that God did not exist, but, because of this friend,

I was beginning to doubt this. I did believe in strength and power, in sub-conscious processes that could be strengthened and cultivated ... nothing divine about that, though.

That, in fact, was what had happened to me due to our having met; I had begun to doubt the existence of God – in the opposite direction. I no longer regarded the reality of God as impossible, indeed it seemed probable that he did exist as I detected his workings. Where else did these previously carefully eliminated guilt feelings come from? That shamelessness that had been turned upside down into this deep feeling of shame? Here in Florence I had been given a crushing insight. Maybe helped by the religious piousness present here. Though that did not count for me, as I was not sensitive to that. Perhaps with this blessed youth beside me – my point of view had become untenable.

"We shall go and visit the monastery in a little while, when you have calmed down. I want to show you something."

"I can't take much more."

"It is necessary."

"What is it you want from me? I've been completely shaken to the core."

He leaned back and looked at me seriously, then said,

"It isn't me that wants anything, it is you, you wanted to talk about this. Now you have the opportunity to realise what it is that you have done."

"I have done?"

"By living as you have lived. If you repent before you die then you can be saved."

"What are you talking about! Are you one of those pulpiteers?"

"You know that I am a surgeon, Gerrit. But within my passionate Italian blood pulsates God. I feel him in every heartbeat. My nationality gives me the passion, but God who pulsates within my blood rules way beyond nationality and peoples. I want to bring you back to Him, Gerrit. There is enough affinity between Him and you..."

"Your optimism is admirable - maybe you are a fantasist. If only you had left me in peace, my whole life is in ruins..."

He shook his beautiful head and said,

"There is much to accomplish, we aren't finished yet."

I could feel the emotions welling up in me. I could not face another episode of weeping. He saw this and said,

"Come Gerrit, we will go across the road. Man up!"

"What is that on the other side?"

"The monastery of San Marco. In the Middle Ages the man, after whose beatitude I have been named, created the most beautiful paintings. I would very much like you to see them."

"What is his name then?"

"Beato Angelico."

"What does Beato mean, then?"

"Blessed and blissful, beatific."

"That is definitely you, Beato."

First, he took me down to see the cells in the basement where all the walls are painted by Fra Angelico. The blissfully religious images with their soft but clear colours affected me deeply in my fragile, wounded state. I let myself be pulled along and affected by the pure beauty that would normally not mean a thing to me, but that now caused me razor-sharp pain. The deathblow was next. He took me to an apparently world-famous masterpiece created by that same monk, the Guidizio Universale – the Last Judgement. Like a child I stood before a childlike image about the destiny of the human soul who chose either the bad – or on the other hand, the good. The contrast between the two is rather enormous and it is all very beautiful if you can believe that you find yourself on the right side. If not, well then, you better not look - or just not believe in it. But here I stood. Not believing wasn't an option any more, and not looking ... it was too late for that. He, my blessed friend next to me, really wanted me to look. He wanted to rub my face in it! Hadn't I asked for it by wanting to come here? A cosy chat over a beer was not his way of doing things. I wasn't crying any more. The deathblow was the complete turning upside down of my erstwhile fear. The fear I had overcome by following my murky dark path ... which hadn't returned initially, when the strange feeling planted within me had settled and started to grow. But, which now, with the beholding of the torturing in hell awaiting me, was suddenly appearing again. I whispered,

"Beato, do you know what you are doing? Can I, can we, manage this?"

He was giving me a 'praegustatum in mortis examine' as he called it; a foretaste of the ordeal of death. Or to be precise, a foretaste post mortem, after death. I did learn a few Latin words from the man who let me taste hell before my death! I did enter into a hell - and it was going to take a long time before any enlightenment happened. He showed me all around Tuscany and Umbria, took me to see all the religious places and wherever possible he confronted me with images of the Last Ordeal. As a surgeon he was accustomed to wielding the knife and ruthlessly opening festering wounds. The sun shone. The images around me – landscape, buildings, art – were brilliant, but I could only see with half an eye. My festering mind had been cut open and filth came pouring out, nothing but foetid emotions and thoughts.

With Beato all was in balance, and so my balance was also safe in his hands. In the evening as darkness fell, we sat outside with the whole family under the starry heavens and enjoyed with much pleasure the most delicious dishes. I never ate out once the whole time. The lass, Chiara, the woman of the house, insisted that I join them and share their meals. She prepared the most amazing dishes with assistance from her home-help. I am not particularly fond of children, but these three were well brought up and had plenty of respect for me, *the old bastard* … In Italy, meals are very important, as it is in France also. But in Italy it is more of a social occasion, if I understand it correctly. The heart-felt hospitality made the food and the wine taste even better. The wine came from his mother's own vines which gave it an extra special aroma. Before the meal Beato said a prayer, the Lord's Prayer, or something. I didn't understand a word, didn't know it even - which made it much easier to bear. A kind of beauty sounded out with his strong voice and the Italian – Latin words. If I were ever to start over again I would be a catholic priest in Italy, such were my thoughts. At the end of the day when I slipped between the sheets, all on my lonesome, I was content and fulfilled. The kind hospitality, the interest, the love these people demonstrated filled me with satisfaction. And so I slept like a baby till early the next morning. I awoke around six o'clock and in the full light of the morning Hell erupted within me once again.

"You must not think that I don't understand," he kept repeating on one our sightseeing trips in the car.

"I don't think anything anymore. I just feel shit, cheated."

"I mean - I don't judge you, Gerrit."

"I know that, obviously. Otherwise I wouldn't be here, you know; I won't let myself be judged."

He was silent and I knew what he was thinking: 'when you are alive you can escape judgement, after death it will irretrievably overwhelm you'. But he answered,

"And if I understand it correctly, God will surely understand. You do, however, have to achieve some kind of insight and feel repentance," he said.

"How on earth is it possible that you, as an educated guy, over thirty, can have such a childish faith?"

"It isn't a faith. But that you won't believe, of course." He grinned, then became serious again. "Why do you feel so aggrieved, if it is all nonsense?"

"I am divided into two beings. One of them doesn't believe a word of it, the other suffers greatly. That suffering indicates that, indeed, it all rests on reality. So now I don't have a moment's peace, during the day, anyway. During the night I am in heaven, boy. What a wonderful family you have, really fantastic! If I had been born as your child, I would have become a priest in one of those beautiful monasteries like San Marco, or maybe Assisi or somewhere. As it is, I stand before the images of Hell - like the last one you showed me in Pisa – and in San Marco. Beato, what should I do?"

"Penitence, Gerrit. That is still to come. You cry because you are afraid – and because of hurt pride."

"You are such an old-fashioned type of guy, Beato. How is it possible!"

"Maybe they knew better how things really were, back then. I am not old fashioned, I am post-modern!"

"What is that?" I asked.

"In the modern day everything to do with God and the spirit is rejected. I am a man who came after that. I believe, because I know."

"That'll be right," I sighed.

"So, now you have managed to bypass penitence, father." He enjoyed teasing me, mainly because I have no sense of humour. A professional comic can make me laugh, but in real life there is nothing to laugh about. Then I said,

"I heard you. But I don't recognise penitence. Penitence is different from guilt. First there has to be an awareness of guilt, and then maybe you have to experience that you've done something seriously wrong. That, I do not have, you are right. I am much too proud for that. I do everything right, I am the best, I can't be bettered. And I mean that." Silently we drove on. I could feel the images of Hell suffocating me and I asked,

"Beato... does repentance in Hell even make sense?"

Compassion leads to freedom

I left Florence after a week, completely satisfied, replete even.

Satiated with the beauty, the truthfulness and especially with the goodness. It had all become a bit too much for me. I don't know if other people feel that way, but for me I can't take too much of all that. Most likely because you have to take it all in even though you don't have much in the way of those qualities yourself. It is quite difficult to give much to me. When I look back at my feelings from that time, I must admit that revulsion was not that far off. The strangeness that had unsettled my life was still there, it was being overpowered by hate and jealousy. I hated Beato and his whole damned life, his averment of the supernatural, the supra-human, the godly. I didn't want any of it for myself and I begrudged him the right to it with all my godforsaken strength. I could have had him bumped off, but something held me back; I sensed that he would then really gain complete ownership of my soul. I loved him with all of my soured shrivelled heart, but now that I had tasted his life I could no longer stand him. That sweet, kind little wife, full of resignation, those adorable perfectly raised children, that catholic life in Italy! Revolting, that sunshine over all the piety. Disgusting! He must be obliterated - but I loved him too much for that and in any case, he was untouchable. You can't murder God even if he does present himself in the image of a weak, mortal human being.

Back home I cursed and swore at my staff, I remonstrated by sitting and playing with my revolver in full view when they walked into the room. I hated the whole world, except myself; and I couldn't see how to free myself from my own emotions. Smashing my Chinese vases didn't give any satisfaction as they didn't cry. Causing other living beings to suffer was no longer an option for me due to that damned 'something' within me which got in the way. I could still get excited, but the images of Hell that roamed about in my memory, made stepping out of my present comfort and life of luxury somewhat unattractive. For the first time in my life I got in my own way, as it were, and could not move the obstacle. I went to play golf and smashed my club in two, then another and the next. I went swimming in Scheveningen, round the pier, where the currents are very strong. But my strength overcame that and all my troubles found me again once I returned to the beach. With boxing I beat every opponent, even the younger ones, with a knock-out. I went hunting and shot a perfect bullseye, drank litres of wine and gin and stayed as clear-headed as glass ... I was invincible because all I really wanted was to be conquered.

At that time the luxury of 'caller display' didn't exist yet, or if it did, I didn't yet have it. So, when the telephone rang

I was never sure whether to answer it or not. When my secretary was there she answered the phone then I could say – if it was Beato – "Let him call back!" But in the evenings, I answered it. It was inevitable that the moment would arrive when I would have to hear his voice: loved, and so hated!

"Pronto! Beato am Apparat, Gerrit!"

If only my heart would stop or I could just collapse. But no, nothing doing, Gerrit was fit and well; nothing to complain about and youthful for his sixty-two years of age.

"Hi," I said, subdued.

"You are avoiding me. I have phoned at least ten times trying to get hold of you."

"You could have given up. Maybe I don't want to be contacted."

"I get that but I feel your pain. We are connected, aren't we Gerrit?"

O no, not that too. Sympathy through connectedness.

"Yes, yes, of course." Damn it. I felt tears welling up. Love won't be suppressed even by the strongest hate. I then said hoarsely,

"You have shown me a side of life that I have tried my utmost to avoid. I thought that I had overcome it, but I have become powerless. I can *do* everything, anything, but I am nothing. Everything is so conflicted. I like you very much my boy. But I cannot cope. I am furious, wild, I hit out at everything – and don't achieve anything. I had better forget you and your damned piety altogether."

Silence reigned and I thought: well, I'd better hang up. But just when I was about to do that the holy one did say something.

"Gerrit, I am so sorry!"

"What are you sorry about? This was what you intended wasn't it? What you worked so hard to achieve? I don't expect falsehood from you."

"You don't understand. I find it terrible that you cannot make something new out of the chaos. Surely you can start anew at any time? I can stay beside you? In the background just in case?"

"If you became my partner, I would say 'yes'. Then you would be there for me totally. I wouldn't share you with anyone and every word you uttered, every deed, would be curative. Love from a distance means nothing to me, I want all of it. Or nothing. I guess it is nothing then."

"I have understood Gerrit. I am sorry, really sorry." I hung up and was furious. Furious in despair…

I poured cement into my heart and built a bunker on these foundations. There I holed up. Me, they would never touch again and whoever came near was immediately showered with bullets.

This is how I lived for a number of years and I never heard from Beato nor did I make any attempts to contact him. Love is lost on me. I haven't a clue how to react to it, either.

This is how I came to the experience of the third 'miracle'. It takes place in the present. The circumstances are quite horrendous but it is a miracle none the less. Two years ago, I was diagnosed with prostate cancer. I won't go into the details here, but suffice it to say that I was treated in a university hospital and it didn't take long before the outlook was declared quite hopeless. Metastasised in my bones. Because of the hormones they castrated me, and I underwent every medical intervention possible. That is why I am still alive, but I suffer tremendous pain. Even though they tell us that pain is no longer necessary, I do want to be a little bit awake and that isn't an option with being pain-free. Death is getting closer, that's for sure. That's true for everyone, of course, but in my sixty ninth year I see him very close by.

Just before I started with all this misery I had a new lady friend, this time a somewhat more mature woman with an interest in spirituality. She didn't abandon me, even though we didn't have a permanent relationship. She was also the one who gave me the address of the clinic where I am now. They cannot cure me but they do know how to lessen the pain somewhat, in one way or another. I do now have something resembling a life again, even though I know that I will die here. I am confident that this will be my last residence. So, I have said goodbye to the Hague, my place of safety behind the dunes. I will never return there. My villa I gave to the boys, they can do what they want with it. My bank accounts and my investments, my stocks and shares remain mine till my last will and testament becomes operative.

I have driven here in my own car, with a tiny bit of happiness within me. It is Spring and by chance, for a change, a beautiful day and this has given me the good feeling of leaving my past behind me once and for all. I did think about Beato, naturally. Should I phone him, ask him for help, his attention? I didn't, in the end.

In the past I could have made that trip in one day. This time, I stayed the night in South Germany. Two sleeping pills helped me sleep a little and after an early breakfast I continued on my way. I felt myself a pilgrim on a journey to a place for dying. When you have to die, your senses instantly become so clear - everything is suddenly so beautiful, so light, so safe. You are already homesick before you have even departed! Slowly I entered the mountainous landscape where I would find death. My friends tell me I should not be thinking about death because everything can still be turned around. But what they don't grasp is that Death is thinking of me and that I can feel his breath on me. There is no way back, not for me.

The clinic is quite a big place, newly built and of the best kind. I was received by a kind little nurse who approached me in the most friendly manner. That was the first part of the third 'miracle' of my life. This time there was no lack of interest, no cold objectivity, but genuine laughter visible in her eyes. She phoned the doctor straight away, he wasn't long in showing up. I knew that a couple of Dutch doctors worked here so I was not surprised that the doctor spoke my own language. I saw a broad-shouldered man, with winter sun-tanned skin and pitch-black hair. He was surely well over forty, but I didn't notice a single grey hair. I looked into eyes darker than I had ever seen before. "I will personally take you to your room," he said, and I liked him, "so you can rest a bit, and then I will call the doctor whose ward this is. I work in outpatients and treat people who come in from the outside." I was sorry. I would have liked him to have been my doctor. He walked with a powerful gait ahead of me, and carried my suitcase as if he were the youngest hotel porter, and opened the door to my last place of residence. It turned out to be a sunny room, decorated in soft colours with much wood and a large window that looked out on to the mountains, the tops covered in snow.

The pure beauty of it hurt my senses somewhat. The doctor said,

"I had that too, when I first came here. It is so beautiful that you have to start doubting your own Godlessness, don't you? I do hope that you will start to feel at home here. I will leave you in peace now." And, with a laugh: "In a minute the real doctor will arrive!"

What I did find very thoughtful was that the 'real doctor' didn't interrupt me with a visit, but that the nurse came to tell me that he would come at five o'clock. I still had just under an hour, enough time to sort myself out a bit, to unpack and to lay my medical papers on the table ready for perusal. At five minutes to five I was ready and sitting in a chair by the window. Still somewhat nervous of the doctor - despite my previous experience - my heart beat a little too hard and fast ... I thought about the other clinic, fourteen years ago where I had been for treatment for innocent rheumatics. I thought about Beato, and felt an unbearable desire for his sympathy with my suffering. With his well-balanced strength he would deplore what had befallen me. I heard a knock; nervously I jumped up,

"Come in!" I called out. And in the doorway stood not Beato, but another God, a Greek or a Germanic one, who spoke perfect Dutch. A handsome man, in his fifties, and a totally different type from Beato. With my clear senses I saw his golden hair and his blue eyes, just as blue as mine but with a depth that encompassed the whole universe. He didn't wear a white coat, but a jacket; well-polished shoes … He looked like health itself and I felt very, very small. The only thing that could ever intimidate me – apart from Beato – is scholarship. This I do not possess at all, and when I am confronted with it I am nowhere. This doctor, who appeared as the epitome of health also possessed the demeanour of the scholar. He sat down with me at the table. I handed him my file, but he said,

"I spoke with your oncologist from Leiden, I know him well, he trained with me."

"With you? Ooh, you are the professor from Amsterdam?" He nodded, leaned back a little and asked kindly,

"How do you feel?"

"I have been travelling for two days, in a relaxed manner. Not too bad. I have become used to the idea that I will die soon, maybe this is my last Spring – probably yes. It is strange that something like this eats away at your body while you still feel yourself to be intact. Only the constant pain makes you think about it."

"Do you have any particular expectations?" I laughed cynically out loud at his question.

"That I will die, yes! Expectations of you, here? I hope that you can do something about the pain so that I can die like a human being, otherwise you'd better just shoot me dead like a dog." He didn't move a muscle, only his gaze became cool and grey.

"It might be better for you to control your thoughts

about death somewhat. It is also possible to think about the life you still have left."

"With such horrendous pain you have no life, doctor." His gaze changed to softness and sympathy again. He said,

"I understand. We'll do our very best. I just have to let you know that I won't be treating you myself, I only supervise here. At the moment the doctors aren't here; next Monday you will meet the doctor who will accompany you through the treatments." I was kind of sorry, I did like him. I said,

"OK. I hope that they live up to your expectations. I have another question: What else should I be doing here? I am not really sick, am I?"

"In the main building is a restaurant, a sitting room and a library. We organise all kinds of things. But in the town through which you came, there are also many restaurants, there is a walking group, swimming pool, tennis courts and more. Only golf is not possible here." Laughter lines wrinkled up around his eyes. "I don't think there is a gun club either – and the shooting season is closed."

"You do have knowledge of human nature." I said. We shook hands and I remained behind very much alone.

No, a miracle was not to be expected here. This doctor had, it is true, left something with me, a deep impression or something like that. But, some very lonely days lay ahead, everything so strange – and in store, a lonely dying. But I was not to think about that anymore! The days had way too many hours. I could not comprehend that I had ever been too busy. Here the day starts at eight o'clock with breakfast. That takes care of half an hour. And then what?

Walk around a bit, explore the surroundings, nod 'hello' to strangers. Reading, I don't like, so a library is useless for me. TV watching – well, it's always the same. A walk is nice, but it ends again. An outing in the car to the little town, more like a holiday village. Window shopping on Saturday, on Sundays everything is closed. Back 'home' to have a sleep, that makes time go a bit faster...with resulting insomnia and hours of sleeplessness in the night, tortured by intense pain.

A phone call to the boys, to my girlfriend, after which loneliness feels even worse - as you know that they are involved with other things more interesting than yourself. I haven't made an impression on anyone, I thought sombrely. No one will cry when I die – "away with those thoughts!" But I do not want to live any longer either. What must I still do? Everything just bores me...

On Sunday evening I became overwhelmed by a mood I had only ever experienced through contact with Beato and had since surreptitiously managed to avoid. I do not know how it came about. Maybe a moment of inattention when I let the beginnings of this feeling creep in. Maybe the boredom and the excess of free time had left me reflective. I experienced my life as it had unfolded and I experienced a dreadful feeling of recrimination. Beato had once warned me that, after death, there was no possibility of avoiding self-awareness. I had pushed the fear of this happening away from me and buried it under tons of concrete ... but now this self-perception was springing up through this concrete. Maybe this was an after-effect, caused by the professor with his deep blue eyes. He had power, that man, just like me. But he had used it positively, whereas I, as hate and antipathy. I felt remorse that I hadn't done better. At first it was just a general change in mood. But in the course of a few hours everything became differentiated, I began to see images, pictures of what was weighing on my conscience. Was I already dying? Physically I didn't feel all that bad, so that wasn't it. It came from within and it couldn't be stemmed.

Monday morning at ten o'clock the doctor assigned to me, would come. I was completely broken by the hell of the experience of the night with my conscience. Worse even than the bone pains were these torments, because they had to do with me as a person. At ten o'clock on the dot there was knock on the door and I shouted,

"Yes!"

It was as if the film was played slow motion. The door opened very slowly and when I had received the first glimpse of the doctor I knew that a miracle, a wonder, was being played out. That God was merciful, that he had sent an Angel to stand by me during the impossible task I had become aware of during the night. The task of acquiring remorse before death of my wrongdoings and misdeeds. In the doorway stood, a little older but in full glory of his godly balance my everlasting love, my friend and my enemy: Beato. Blackness enveloped me and he caught me in his arms. I hugged him, clamped myself to him and heard his beloved voice in his South Tyrolean German as he said,

"Gerrit! I asked if I might treat you. I heard about your

illness."

He didn't reject my embrace but caught me up in the full power of his love. I started to cry as I had cried in Florence. I moved away and sat down, sobbing. It was as if it just occurred to me for the first time what was wrong.

"How can it be that such a bastard as I can experience this! It is a complete God's-wonder, a miracle, it cannot be true! How do you happen to be here!" I shouted, while the tears streamed. He came to sit by me and said,

"I frequently think about that first year of my career, about the Spa clinic where we met each other. Well, I wanted to change my job anyway, work in another city – I took a year off so that I could be here for a year. So, I am really taking a year off, a break in my career. I have only been here for two weeks, Gerrit! Last week I noticed your name on the patient-list – I think it's really awesome."

He placed his hand on mine, attempted to catch my eye and said,

"You have a friend now, Gerrit."

I could barely endure his words, felt his goodness and his love which had become even more unendurable than before. In the past it would have driven me mad and crazy. But now I could no longer escape it. I had to acknowledge his hand, accept his friendship – and trust in his skills without a trace of doubt. I felt like the child who is with one of his beloved parents – not a feeling I had ever experienced. I was the child receiving here, even though having misbehaved, and the feeling of not deserving this was my first experience of remorse. He stayed with me for an hour. He went through my medical history or 'anamnesis' as he called it, discussed the history of my illness with me and listened intensely to what I had to say. He had matured a lot. I could feel a confidence that hid great wisdom but also a strong practical side honed from much experience. He was a scholar of a different sort than the professor, he was dextrous and a man of action.

"I know I don't have any chances left, Beato. I have to die, most likely before your year here is out. I don't mind, you have to die sometime – and I am sixty-nine, that's not too bad. I have come here to learn to live with these pains, so I can die like a man, in full possession of my faculties. But, in the meantime I haven't forgotten your admonitions, those images of Hell you showed me. I don't believe in all that - and somehow, I also do. Can you understand that?"

"You don't want to believe it - and I understand that, fine. But by that 'not wanting it', you do still experience the reality of it."

"And that is your fault. Before I met you, I didn't doubt for a moment."

"It's probably better that you acquire some conscience before you appear before the judge."

"Are you still so religious, Beato?"

"Much more so, Gerrit. I have experienced a great deal."

"Me too. There is a lot to talk about." I sighed, and the days already seemed much less long.

When he had gone, I felt for the third time how something had entered in to me, something from his presence. Something that, despite my rejection of it, had just seemed to have continued to grow. I used to think of it as a swelling but now as a positive force, a piece of light that had developed and grown into a sun, shedding light on my life, on my personality. I had not wanted to feel it, nor see it – and now it was undeniable. It was like an imprisonment within a cell, with no means of distraction. I had never been in prison but I could feel the similarities. A short or a longer time awaited me before my death in which I would have to face up to what I had done. Yes, I will now have to acknowledge who I am and what I have done. I knew that I would tell him everything, I would confess all. To keep the balance, I would ask him to tell me his life story as well. Not the condensed version as before, but all the details, as much as he wanted to.

I have found true happiness. Though I may not think about the end, it is particularly death that is making it possible for me to conjure up the strength to be able to carry that happiness. There is one man, the best one in existence, who has given me his love, who cares about me. The price I have to pay is self-knowledge. That gives me a very strong experience of the pain of sadness. It isn't just that I had been negligent, it is all much, much worse than that. If I hadn't been standing here before death I would have made my escape again. Now I think I am able to find the strength to let in the happiness and the suffering. He often discovered me in tears and in deep despair. He wouldn't try to comfort me because he was realistic – and a hard taskmaster. But I love every detail of his whole being. What he does and what he says, for me, it is always just right.

There is another life possible for me to live, even now, even though it may only last a few months. If I had had such a human being around when I was child, a different Gerrit would have grown up. Maybe that is my only excuse – that there was no such person.

"Where are your wife and children, Beato? Where are you living?"

"We figured out an intermediate solution. They live in a house in Ticino, where they speak Italian. It's easier for the children not to have to switch languages and they can go to school there too. On Fridays I go home and early Monday mornings I return here. I have a room here. It isn't all that easy but it will have to do."

"Why on earth do you want to work here for a year?"

"They practise spiritual science here, precisely the type I am looking for. Such an opportunity has to be grasped when it is presented. Besides" - he laughed out loud - "I have to be here for you, Gerrit, don't I?"

"I don't believe in coincidence anymore," I agreed. "I don't know what you mean by 'spiritual science', but whatever, I do feel very, very good here. One is really cared for here, not just by you. It's all about the individual here, about the person. Usually you are there as a patient for the doctor, for the nurses, for the hospital, the protocol, the lecture by the professor and so on."

"Have you had any contact with the other patients yet?"

"Not me. I am a-social, anti-social even. Just leave me in peace."

"Well, you could make small talk?"

"That is a possibility. It would have to happen spontaneously, though, I am not on the look-out."

"Gerrit, are you prepared to tell me about your life? In all detail and honesty?" That question engendered a feeling of solemnity within me. As if I was in a church and had to reply with the 'yes' words. I answered,

"Yes, Beato. If you will entrust your life to me also..." He looked at me straight and nodded in accord.

When writing something like this it all seems quite easy. It is, however, very difficult to express the emotions in words. All I can say is that they were very intense and powerful. I landed, as it were, in a totally different life-stream. As if I had already died and then continued on after. Not that I can actually imagine what that would be like or that I even believe in that ... well, yes, I do, because of Beato, I do believe. Just that is the essence of the new life-stream. It is the conscience. And if, like me, you begin to listen to the whispers of conscience, when you no longer silence it, you will come into contact with some very violent emotions. Il Guidizio Universale. I had a foretaste of it and Beato assured me repeatedly that everything is still possible and eternal hell fire is not a forgone conclusion no matter how bad a life I have lived. From here on in I was able to gather enough courage to step into that other life-stream and let myself get swept along to what I absolutely could not yet feel: remorse.

It is true that I found it terrible to realise that I was not a particularly great personality but a miserly little man who managed to make something of himself by sheer greed and violence. That is not remorse, that is more like revulsion. In my whole feeling life there wasn't a spark of remorse to be found.

"In any event, Beato, I am not a weakling. You recommended I get a copy of Dante's Hell from the library to read. He described the weaklings as the most completely meaningless creatures in existence. Not even worthy of a place in Hell, because they could make the inhabitants there feel superior to the weaklings, and rightly so. A feeling of superiority is not permitted in Hell. So, a weakling I am not! Unless – and I ask myself this in my more frightened moments – my whole life's path rests on the impulse of weakness. That is a possibility. That I wanted to grow up in an easy manner. Big, feared and rich. But still, I don't believe that, as a small child, I was already not a weakling. I had guts and was a wee fighter. I always wanted and had to have the lead and got it too. Sometimes after a big fight, but in the end always! If you ask me for my very earliest memories then I think about my granny. She – my mother's mother – was a widow and stood on the market with fruit, with a fruit cart. The market was at the edge of the neighbourhood where I grew up and I could walk there from home easily. I must have been a toddler. She ran her stall with two boys and they were always very busy. Attention to me was not much in evidence, just a kiss on arrival and departure and now and then a yell. "Keep your paws off!" she would shout, if I wanted to taste a strawberry. But then she would give me three anyway! That I do remember and it was, I think, the only warmth I received as a child. Three strawberries from my screaming, scolding grandma. And then also – but that must have been later – a confrontation with the nursery teacher. I just hated that bitch. Yes, well, you look offended, but she really was God-awful. If you did something that she didn't approve of, you got a rock-hard slap, right in the face. That would be punishable now. Maybe it was then also, but it happened. Every day I received a few of those and she was quite handy, no way could you avoid her hand. Every day I hated her more and eventually I kicked her in the shins as hard as I could. I received slap, slap, around both ears and was sent away from school. At home I didn't say a thing, because you never knew what would happen. So, I spent a long time – can't remember how long – hanging around on the streets during school time. A young boy or four of five years old! Till I was picked up by the police. Then my Pa went to the school and gave that rotten wife a serious cursing and telling off and I was able to return to another class. Yes, yes, you are surprised, Beato? Did you know Gerrit was like that? That smart rich gentleman, who hasn't earned all his money in the most honest of ways – but still a nice guy? You need to brace yourself as this is just the beginning..."

"You misunderstand my bewilderment, Gerrit. I know you better than you think. What surprises me is the anger that still rises up in you when you talk about it. Once you are a bit older, you really should be able to forgive and become somewhat milder. That's the side you show me, particularly in our friendship, not that anger and revenge."

"I am an eternal curmudgeon," I mocked. "I have complained and moaned so much with so much passion that it is now part of my make-up, it's in my bones to moan." Beato shook his head and I could feel his steady, open-hearted compassion.

"Tomorrow we will continue," he said with conviction and left me and my nasty emotions alone. That last comment about forgiveness and mildness stirred my conscience. Remorse I did not experience - let me reiterate that clearly. But the events that occurred in my life and their descriptions came to be seen in another light and I will try to describe how I began to see them that evening and that night.

I saw my granny, who during the threatening pre-war era ran a market stall; she had to make herself strong to survive the competition and to earn a living. The little boy, that was me, underfoot. Wanting to touch everything and eat everything ... she had no time, no money, for little children, but she did know the feeling of remorse that follows the shouting at such a little boy. I was a pest. The nursery teacher had a class full, forty such pests, those urchins, boys and girls, mostly uneducated, neglected and therefore wild as little animals. What else could she do but use her hands if she wanted to remain in control? She had no option but to use physical means to maintain the upper hand, so that is what she did.

I now had a completely different relationship to those events I had told Beato about. Was it his magical workings that caused this change in perspective ... that caused the light to shine not only on my own misfortune but also on the world around it ... that caused me to feel that it was my own doing, that I had wanted the world to be like this? I hated the people from my youth, my 'educators'. Was there anything to be thankful for? With the best of intentions, I could not find anything; still, I did feel a certain mildness. It was the mildness of Beato, that was within me ... just as with every meeting, a little of his goodness seemed to enter into me. What kind of wonderful thing is that? Can good attributes be contagious, like an infection? Whoever plays with pitch will be tarred – whoever handles gold will be lit up and warmed by it? I lay awake with the pain, but also with the feeling of alienation from myself. Again, I had been placed outside myself by Beato. But with death imminent I couldn't care whether he had gained the upper hand. I was too exhausted to start another power struggle like before. A certain energy was released that did not, this time, turn into a hunger for power. I lay there, examining it, and felt amazed. Gerrit perceived Gerrit as he could have been, as he could still become. 'This day is the first day of the rest of your life'. That 'rest' may be short, there wasn't any 'rest' as yet. Twenty days, fifty, a hundred-and-fifty? A whole series of days in which another Gerrit could appear on the scene, one who came out of the periphery, not from his centre. With a sudden jerk I stood up out of bed and said out loud,

"Now you are going crazy as well!" I took two sleeping pills and after some tossing and turning, near the morning, I did fall asleep. With that, I have described three 'miracles', it's miraculous! Understanding it I cannot, but writing it down helps. Organising your thoughts and feelings on the paper, which doesn't answer back. So, I will continue to write till my hand is united with the other hand on my chest for all eternity...

Unselfishness leads to catharsis

I am made of negativity. I am somewhat like rock; compressed revenge and anger. I hate the whole world, except myself. I'm the only one who can meet my own standards. Well, OK, of course there is one other living being who also meets these standards, in fact who rises way above them. I cannot raise myself above him and that is the reason why I am often so angry with him. That is when I treat him badly, don't answer him, sit opposite him sulking. If only he would let himself be affected by that! But no, he just gets up and walks off. Sometimes even without uttering a word, sometimes he says something like,

"I will come back when you can be more civil."

Then I feel like a naughty child and become quite lost. Still, I am too strong to end it – or too weak perhaps. I have a talent for seeing the worst in others, that is the reason I survive here. Otherwise I would be destroyed by the images of perfection all around me. I am surrounded by kind, well-intentioned people, who really make an effort on our behalf, they do their very best and support each other, too. I wouldn't be able to endure that if I couldn't also see their bad sides. But in Beato I can't find anything to deprecate. The worst thing is his innocence. He doesn't seem to have any knowledge of his own qualities. He is just Beato and he is - just by chance - perfect; not his fault or his doing. I have never found him to be annoying in any way, there is only envy when I feel anger. I see him four days per week, sometimes together with another doctor, mostly on his own.

Then we talk if I feel like it. This morning he arrived in my room at exactly 10 o'clock. His eyes radiant as always, his cheeks were fresh, from the spring breezes in which he had walked, or from goodness knows where...! Spring enveloped him in any case. I had visions of cherry blossom trees and flowering roses … and also of cumulus clouds and the scent of a much-needed shower of rain on dried-up land … *This man would turn you into a poet!* He looked at me searchingly, and then said,

"Thank heavens, you seem somewhat more approachable today. For shame, you certainly know how to spread horror around yourself."

"Sit down, Beato. It's a pity that nothing seems to affect you. Nothing touches you, now does it?"

"It does touch me, don't you worry about that," he answered.

"Well, I know … You wouldn't be perfect if you had no feelings," I replied.

He shrugged his shoulders. His beautiful broad shoulders.

"Ah well, perfection! I know a lot about turmoil, confusion and desire … " he said.

"For sure, but as pure emotions. Then they fade away surely, as soon as they have come. No?" I suggested.

"Yes, they fade away … How are things today, Gerrit?"

"Lousy," I replied.

"Pain?" he asked.

"The confusion hurts more than my bones do. Your treatment in that respect is patent, my boy."

"What kind of confusion?" he asked unperturbed.

"The chaos that develops when you lose your orientation. When nothing makes sense anymore like it used to. Why does God bring chaos instead of order?"

"God?"

"You."

"Don't talk rubbish, Gerrit."

"I'm not. I have no image of God, but if I do have to visualise him, then he has your qualities, only mightier, larger etc."

"Then you will also understand why there has to be chaos. Tell me some more about your childhood, Gerrit."

I really did not want to go on, I had postponed it by sulking – but now I had no choice. Should I be honest? Was that a possibility? Or should I make something up?

"The war began when I was five years old. Later I learned that my father had been a sympathiser with the enemy. We were regarded as outcasts, but I paid no attention to that. Pa was an NSB-er, that is what it was called, a Nazi sympathiser. I think my mum was a whore, but I'm not sure about that. She always worked nights and, as you know already, she was always beaten. I think it was something like that. I also don't think Pa was really my father. I don't feel any bonds of blood, I do with my Mum. She completely neglected us but still I feel for her when I think back. But Pa was a real shit of a man, a weakling through and through. If you have to prove your strength by abusing a woman! I don't think I will meet him even in hell because he is too low for that." Beato listened quietly; when I was silent for a moment he asked,

"Is there nothing that could redeem him in your eyes?" His question shocked me to the core. If I had to say 'yes' then my whole life was standing on very thin ice. Had I not built my life on the foundations of my hate for my father, who most likely wasn't actually him? Was that not the only source of my strength?

"No," I said. "I wouldn't know of anything. If he had only been bad, I would have valued him. But he wasn't bad, he was weak. A nothing, a zero, only comprised of muscles, fists and a dirty angry red face."

"What if he had not been your father, or the husband of your mother? If he had been an outsider, would you then also judge him so severely?"

I had to digest all this. The unbridled anger, the hate - and maybe also the fear of the physical superiority of that wild man from my youth.

"I don't know, Beato. I am speaking the truth when I say that I cannot see how? As far as I can make out, he was an empty nothing who filled the void with rubbish. I am not like that, you understand. I may even be worse than him, but at least I *am* somebody."

"Have you never seen him in a moment of weakness? In a moment of self-blame? Of regret?"

Beato always knows how to hit his mark, and flawlessly. He targeted the core of the matter. Precisely. Within a second it all came flooding into my memory, in all its sordid glory. I had suppressed it, forgotten... An enormous wave of fear overwhelmed me and I begged my friend to save me…

That day I could not speak any more. Beato tried to comfort me and eventually left my room with the promise to return tomorrow. We would then see what followed.

The storm of the confusion of anger had subsided somewhat and I had to think. I am capable of that; I am a strong personality, after all. I realised that I owe my strength to my capacity for keeping silent. That is an ancient law: Silence creates power. As soon as you start to talk, your strength seeps out and you weaken. That is the great danger here, there's too much talk. You are seduced into it, it is pleasant to talk about yourself, to experience someone else taking you into himself. Especially when that person is Beato. Or one of the other holy ones who walk around here. Silence gives power. It is a form of self-renunciation albeit one that greatly empowers the self. A sort of payment in advance. But now the lighting on the scene of the play has changed because I am close to death. Do the same principles apply, I wonder … Death itself does seem like the great everlasting silence, but maybe there is, hidden behind that silent everlastingness, a living, absolute power? Who can say? I have always regarded death as the end. Through death you can make an end to the threatening unrest and all manner of twaddle and danger to your own life. In that respect I have made use of death to turn things to my own favour. But it hasn't escaped me – and it has been pointed out to me – that death has more power than just the bringing-to-an-end of a life, to peace, to stillness. The one who remains behind, gains in power and strength, and that is a fact. That is why he who actively works with death cannot easily be a materialist. Materialism – I mean the point of view that only material things, and not magic, exist – is something for weaklings and scaredy-cats, for the bourgeoisie. Real evil knows magic, and the deeper the knowledge, the worse the evil can be. So, you aren't dealing with a petty thief here, Beato, look out!

I spoke in my mind the words I did not want to speak out loud. But there was more, there were words that I didn't even want to mention in my thoughts, as my power would then be affected. Gerrit is indeed an interesting guy. But the fascination is based on his power which he has very consciously developed and which he keeps intact. The question is always: do the same rules apply when facing death? Does it make sense to start serving that other Lord when you feel you must enter his domain soon? Haven't you already absorbed a bit of His Kingdom by going around with those 'blessed ones'? Did He place an emissary on your path because He wants you to be saved? My thinking was not free from sarcasm but also not from earnestness. It was a mix of black and white like a chess board. As was my mood: full of anger, trembling, depression, but also shot through with positivity and a kind of happiness. The real question is: When the Great Silence makes its appearance will you still have any power?

If that were true, if any power at all remains after death, then I would choose to increase that power – in whatever way possible. This is what I did during life, and after death

I would also want to do that. But I anticipate with trepidation that there will be no question of a change of heart. The more power possessed during life the more powerless after death? I would have to face that possibility if I truly wanted to turn myself around. If I didn't want to reflect on myself I would be a weakling, a man who couldn't face the consequences of his actions. I can see death standing there, not too far away. The professor here may well tell me to push those thoughts away but that doesn't ring true with me. I must face death in truth as my life has been quite unusual. Just like the professor have I lived both with and for the magic. White and pure in his case ... in my case as black as death itself. Remorse I cannot feel as I have cancelled that capacity, destroyed it. Or not? Is there a small kernel of it left behind that could be brought to fruition by Beato perhaps? Is that the small chink of light that is growing in me? I want to investigate and examine this. I do not want to confess before I have had a chance to do that...

Beato knows me well, and so he didn't ask any further about any humanity my father may or may not have possessed. I left it at that - that there hadn't been any ... he was a nothing, a weakling.

"He hated the Jews, that I do remember very well. I'm sure he was a traitor. So, I defended every Jewish boy and girl who needed my protection. I was only ten when the war ended, but I was a scoundrel who enjoyed fighting. Everyone could expect to get a thrashing - except the girls or the Jews. I didn't really understand that much about it all, just that I had this urge to do just the opposite to what my father did."

"Such a nice boy, actually. That Gerrit," Beato said with a smile.

It was making me sad. Maybe it had been just like that and maybe it could all have turned out so differently … .? But I said, while shaking my head,

"Ach... I had an unstoppable streak of self-assertiveness. I still have that. Except that in your presence it becomes lame, that's why you think I'm a nice guy. I was wondering if it would make sense to move to the other camp, now that defeat is in sight."

"The other camp?" he asked.

"From black to white. From angry to no longer angry. From darkness to light," I explained

"Just because you fear defeat?"

"Do I fear the defeat? Had I never met you there wouldn't have been anything to fear. The magic works beyond death, the black one does too. It is black because you have chosen it. It isn't a question of being bad by accident, it is intentional, chosen. During the war I probably experienced more of that than I remember. In any case I am not going to get myself excited over a defeat. That doesn't exist if you remain true to your original choice."

"Just think about the Last Judgement?"

"That is a children's fantasy. I'm sure you can be a leader on the other side."

"It is characteristic of the devil that he convinces himself that he can still win."

"Please don't interrupt! I wanted to say that through your intervention I have been won over. With a minuscule chink of light, a white spot in the black, a glowing point of 'good', a fraction of self-renunciation. Before that, I could cuss and swear as coarse as they come – and I had meant it. Now that's no longer possible, particularly now, fourteen years later, long years in which that minute creature has grown into a real being that speaks and so forth."

"Well, why are you doubting, Gerrit? About crossing over to the other camp? Surely that has already happened?" I caught his eye and said,

"I'm not joking, boy. This is a tragedy, a drama. I am in no-mans-land, don't belong anywhere any more. After death it will also be so, most likely."

"Maybe you should read Faust."

"I know that story. No, I am no Faust. He did have upright moral striving and fell temporarily into the wrong. Not me. It looks bad for me, I do know that."

"What do you imagine it will actually be like, Gerrit? I get the impression that you know a lot more than you have hitherto led me to believe. You have put yourself forward as a 'criminal'. A black magician is really something different. Which is it?"

Was he unsure? For the first time? But he said,

"You didn't catch me out, Gerrit. I 'got' you from when we first met, I know we know each other very well – I feel your destiny ... that touches me - not your whining."

"Are you angry?" I asked him.

"Yes. I find it desperately annoying that you keep attempting to bamboozle me. It won't work, Gerrit. The devil lost long ago; just give it up."

"You are a strange one. A man of the world, educated,

successful, with all possible talents imaginable – and then talking like an Italian village priest."

While you could have expected him to get up and walk away angrily, he just began to laugh – his irresistible sunny laugh. He said,

"And you just love that sun-drenched village with the kindly priest, don't you, Gerrit?"

I threw my weapons down on the table for the umpteenth time.

"Just tell me how this continues," I moaned. "I will do what you say. Shall I offer my services to King Arthur?"

He answered, smiling,

"The victor determines what the loser has to do, that is the code of chivalry. You just go and see the Master now. See what he has to say..."

Were we playing a game of knights, or was this for real? Sometimes I lost the plot. In any case the days were interesting and they flew by. Maybe I still had the same amount of pain but my awareness of it was being diverted. Now I had to go and visit a 'master' of some kind! I dreamt about white elephants on an oriental backdrop. When I woke up, in the morning, I was afraid. The Westerner has a screen in front of his eyes, you can appear in front of him without him seeing you. The Easterner – particularly when he is called the 'Master' - is open and attentive and awake and ... ruthless if necessary.

I knew the 'Master' by appearance. I have been here now about four weeks and feel at home. I still have not really met everyone who works here, including the 'Master'. He set up this centre some thirty years ago and he was the leader till he handed the sceptre over to the professor – maybe I should say: the flame.

Since that time the air here has been distinctly European though still mixed with Eastern promise. And that promise comes from the Master. He is a real Indian, not Tibetan. He is beautiful as only Indians can be beautiful. The men become more handsome when they get older. Well, old ... he is probably about the same age as me. He usually walks around in funeral clothes, an old-fashioned grey suit, sometimes anthracite, with a white shirt and a grey tie. Grey socks and black lace-up shoes. His head, on the other hand, is gorgeous, noble and lively, constantly in movement, he is completely himself, but inscrutable. That is what I find so scary about Orientals, they appear to have a kind of incarnate mystery about them – and you never really know what lies behind that friendly smile.

I had an appointment with him in his office in the main building. You never see him in the actual hospital – at least I have never seen him there. He lives in a Swiss chalet, a bit further away in the grounds. I had a chalet like that in my better years, I used to go there in the winter to ski. In the summer I preferred sailing on the sea in my yacht ...

It was a sombre day, low hanging clouds threatened rain. I reported myself to his secretary and he kept me waiting for at least half an hour. That is a well-known tactic to make you feel small - but perhaps he had genuinely been detained. In any case he arrived, hurrying a bit through the hall, stopped when he reached me, stuck out his hand and apologised, "I am so sorry to have kept you waiting. Please do give me another few minutes, I don't want to feel rushed when we start our conversation."

I nodded and sat down again. It took five minutes for him to 'un-rush' himself, after which, with a friendly gesture he invited me into his room. Now I had become nervous and so I observed every detail. The window with a view to a meadow with dark clouds above. A small writing desk, the emphasis was more on the armchairs in the corner by the window. Frugal, almost no books, but also no Eastern atmosphere. He conveyed that... We went to sit down in the armchairs.

"Would you like something to drink? Coffee, tea, something cold?" he asked courteously. I could certainly use something; so, coffee. Silently we drank coffee. He crossed one leg over the other and leaned back, relaxed. It was as if to indicate that I had nothing to fear.

"Il dottore asked me to have a look at you," he said, with a twinkle in his eye. "Intended as punishment I think! Many people are frightened of me, because of my penetrating gaze or something."

It was certainly a very strange start. I was dumbstruck - I kept silent and just waited to see what came next. That way I gave him every opportunity to look with his 'penetrating gaze'. What did he see? I could not fathom it. In any event it was unpleasant. Maybe I was stripped naked, maybe not. He was somewhat paler than when I had first come in. He moved forward somewhat and said,

"Is there something I can do for you? Do you have questions?"

Shrugging my shoulders, I said,

"Beato thought it necessary - he probably gave you a list of questions?"

He nodded.

"But you, sir, have to give your permission."

"Please call me Gerrit!"

"Good, Gerrit."

"I don't mind anything. Look as much as you like. I do appreciate your reticence to undress me without permission. So now you have that."

That cleared that up. The atmosphere changed completely, and I did regret giving him my consent. Of course, if you not really believe a word of this then it made no difference. But immediately I was cured of my disbelief. He sat completely dead still, but something started to move that touched me deeply. Similar to the effect Beato had on me, but more so, more intense, frightening. Did I experience myself? Did I feel what he saw? He kept being silent, silent and silent. Apparently, he also knew about the rules of power.

A storm broke out and I saw an angel with a flaming sword. That sword struck my individuality and set me on fire, the only thing that survived was that point of light given to me by Beato. I had nothing except a minuscule piece of light to which I clung. All the rest was ruthlessly judged.

"Praegustatio in mortis examine." He spoke, sitting opposite me. "A fore-taste of the ordeal of death. If you had not gotten to know Il Dottore you would be totally annihilated at your death. Now the ordeal awaits you."

That is what he said, or had it been a vision or an hallucination? Was I going insane? I could not move a muscle; my body didn't function any more. Was I already dead? Died of fear? Come on arms and legs! Obey my will! Move!

I could move again as normal. I breathed. I was alive. The master kept silent and watched, kept still and watched.

"Say something for God's sake!" I shouted out. He nodded, got up, walked up and down the room several times, sat down again and began to speak.

"I don't have to tell you what I see, sir. You are very capable of self-knowledge so you are aware of what you have made of yourself."

It sounded stern and was undoubtedly meant to. This man did not want to understand me. I nodded and asked,

"And my illness?"

First, he kept silent, for a few minutes perhaps. The he looked straight at me and said,

"Your body is riddled with it."

"With the illness."

"Yes."

"So, you also don't see a chance of a cure?"

"I would never say that. In life everything is possible, as long as death hasn't entered in. But a strong process once set in motion won't turn around of its own accord. You would need an impulse of similar, or better still, stronger movement potential to turn it around."

"And you don't think that is a possibility." I stated. He shrugged his shoulders, almost with indifference.

"I don't know if it is expedient, sir."

This made me angry. What did this little manny think? This underdeveloped immigrant?

But he perceived that too, smiled, and said,

"I do not judge you. I am in search of a solution."

"What for?"

"For the deadlock in which you are stuck. I have in fact seen something, one thing ... that you cannot know about. But it is precisely that one thing that is the cause of the imbalance in your life. Of the loose screws."

"What is that then?" I asked brazenly, I was curious. He took a deep breath in; on the out-breath his devastating words sounded out,

"Your father was, actually, your real father."

I have often slapped people and naturally received some slaps in return. But I have never yet been overwhelmed or beaten. Never. Not even by Beato. Even he could not win the good fight – and he never wanted to. This small, soft, brown man, who I had only seconds ago relegated to being an undeveloped immigrant, brought me the coup de grâce. I do not remember how I managed to return to my room, but here I am. Even though I am completely destroyed, I remember every single detail of my visit to the 'master'. He despises me, that is for sure. He would have wanted to pick up the sword and chop off my head. No, there is nothing in me that he would understand. Well, so be it! What do I care what he thinks? But psychologically he took that sword and conquered me by declaring that my father was actually my real father. I believe him, I have to, his power comes from his contempt of my existence. Beato and the professor also, still regard me as human, because I appear as a human being. This 'master' knows better ... he knows the origin of my ways. That is made obvious by his comments. The best I can do now is to end it. Or do I have to look at myself seriously? I ruined my own soul, in the clear light of day. Absolutely intentionally. I felt I had the right to do so – and, it seems that I did not have the right to do that. That right has now been taken away from me for one reason or another. Or, in other words, my judgement about that doesn't tally. I have to think about all this carefully and then take matters back into my own hands...

Beato always comes in the morning. But now here he was at my door at five pm in the afternoon. The master must have sent him, or so I thought. But he said,

"I didn't want to wait till tomorrow after all, Gerrit; I am uneasy. Maybe you shouldn't have gone to him after all."

I let him in and said,

"You, uneasy? But I'm glad you came. Gerrit has been completely dismantled by a soft duffer. How is it possible? With one stroke I could have floored him – and I let myself be tempted to listen to his deep unfathomable voice as he pronounced the last judgement. The shit-bag."

Beato sat down and suggested I do the same. Yes, he can suggest, and because of his complete harmoniousness, you do what he says. So, I sat down. Beato said,

"Listen up, Gerrit. In this situation you are the shit-bag, the duffer and the weakling. The master is a noble man, very intelligent and strong. Keep your gob shut, or you can immediately grab your stuff and depart."

I was way much too offended to rise to the challenge. So, I just left it and said softly,

"Good, good. That is how it is, I know that. The apple is rotten to the core, Beato. The rot does not come from the environment but from the core, from deep inside."

"Ach well, life hasn't been particularly easy for you. So, some things have come from outside also. What is it that affected you so, Gerrit?"

The pain in my bones had increased, I also felt oppressed and claustrophobic, as if my lungs would not fill with life-giving air. I groaned and said,

"I don't think I have much time left, my symptoms are getting rapidly worse. I will answer your question. That geezer, the one who beat my mother again and again, I assumed he was just a guy she cheated on. He was her husband, but not my father. I always thought that he could absolutely not be. I was a growing boy and I wanted to kill him, honestly – unless he had been my real father. It was damned complicated. I wasn't strong enough, he was massive, strong as an ox, a real rat, all hard-bone-strength. Just imagine, Beato ... with that power he hit my Ma. Not that she was particularly sweet or anything, she was a bitch. But this was really terrible. My hate towards him is the source of all my hate. It was autumn, I was seventeen and there had been another one of those riots at home. I went for a walk, took the bus to the dunes and walked through a 'no go' area, where you needed to have a pass to walk. It was peaceful, rainy and a bit sinister. A man came up behind me, I found it a bit unpleasant at first ... those footsteps in the tracks of my father. But he caught up with me, began to walk beside me and started talking. He was wearing jodhpurs and tall riding boots; a short jacket and he carried a bag in his hand. He was probably about forty, quite handsome and very talkative.

"Why are you roaming around here, young man?"

"I like walking here. There is never anybody around, there is a good breeze and soon you will see the sea, with its wild waves and a grey sky above it. And you?"

"I love nature. I love the forces within the plant world. I always come here to look for edible mushrooms. Shall I show you which ones you can eat and which ones not to?" He gave extensive instructions on how to determine which ones were edible, which ones a bit irritating and then he showed me the downright deadly poisonous ones."

I was silent, overcome with the memory. I tasted the salt in the sea air, could feel the dampness in the gusts of wind, the runny wet nose without an available hanky, the ice-cold fingers without gloves. The memory invoked a kind of trance, within which the voice of Beato woke me up.

"Did you poison your father?" he asked surprised.

"I didn't know he was my father. Our life improved a lot after that. I had to, didn't I?"

"What did you feel, Gerrit?" he asked sharply. I felt sick. I said,

"You have asked me if I had ever noticed anything human in him, remember? Well I did, when he was dying. His fear, his helplessness, his dependency ... were human."

"What did *you* feel, Gerrit!"

I looked at him and tried to make my gaze as hard as

possible. That was hard to do with him right there, difficult because I was facing death myself. But a remnant of the old Gerrit did surface and I said,

"What did I feel? Pleasure, Beato, my good friend. It was the most beautiful moment of my youth."

I had said this with some pride and I again experienced that feeling of pleasure. Except for now a few seeds of doubt had crept in. Perhaps that shit-bag had been my father after all. And then what? Is that worse, murdering your father, patricide? That thought did seriously detract from the pleasure of the experience. But, had I finally managed to shock Beato? No, no way. He sat there opposite me in the balance of his golden mean. Oh, I am sure he found me despicable. But he could feel the pain of that without losing his emotional stability. He found it awful but it did not scare him or make him feel insecure.

"Don't you feel any regret, Gerrit?"

"Regret? No, why?"

"Never thought that perhaps you shouldn't have done it? Or felt any kind of sadness?"

"No, I would do it again in a flash."

"Why then are you so affected by your visit to the master?"

That I had to think over, he had a point there. Why?

"Because maybe it was actually my father. That changes everything, you understand. None of it makes any sense any more. I don't regret it, but I do ask myself should I be expecting some repercussions, after death I mean."

"Your feelings are more important than your actions in

this instance. If only you could feel repentance."

He really was concerned about the well-being of my soul. I felt 'lightning' strike within my bones and I sat up.

"I have to take something," I said as I took a tablet from the strip and a sip of water. I sank back down into the chair.

"What a fucking day." I looked into the soft, warm but clear bright brown eyes of my young friend.

In those eyes I saw myself, as God sees me.

I cannot eat any more, everything is against me. I feel bad, very bad, every hour of the day and night. Only a short half hour of life left to live when Beato comes. He cares about me, even now. He should have been a priest, he reads to me daily from the Bible. I am rebuked, reprimanded, urged – I only hear the half of it. Sometimes I think: 'Pathetic Italian! Just stop!' But then I am also grateful for the unusual sound of that voice of his when he, in his mother tongue - South Tyrolean German – reads to me. Sometimes it is like ear-splitting thunder and then again soothing and comforting music... It always ends again and then he asks,

"Gerrit, do you feel remorse?" I won't lie, so each time I staunchly say: 'No.' Then we talk a bit more. But today I remembered something, and I said,

"You have never yet told me anything about yourself! You haven't yet said a word!"

He checked his watch and settled in and began to tell me his story.

"In the region where I grew up it is never really winter. It rarely freezes, that is why palm trees and oleander bushes can grow there. In the autumn God himself comes very near the earth, you can see him if you are sensitive enough to such things … First, it is his countenance which arrives, which paves the way, so that all the demons that have chosen to inhabit the earth in spring and summer are swept away, before He himself takes up governance in the Etheric realm again. As you know, I had no father, he died before my birth. But in the autumn God was very close to me and he stayed close the whole winter long. Have you seen the mountain hillsides drenched in autumn sun covered with vineyards and apple trees? The way they take on a golden hue in the mild autumn sun? Do you remember the effect that has, as it enters your being via your eyes? The melancholy of dying nature and, within that, the coming glory of the resurrected Christ? As a small boy I could feel His presence and I asked my mother who He was. She said,

"Das ist unser lieber Gott, mein Sohn (that is our dear God, my son). He moved His Kingdom to our earth, only our eyes aren't opened to see him." But I did 'see' Him, although not with my eyes. Mama taught me how to pray, Ave Maria and Pater Noster. That was also sung on festival days in the little Church or in the Church in Merano."

I was beginning to get irritable and to feel terribly unwell so I asked,

"And, have your little angel feet never yet landed on the ground, then?"

He raised his eyebrows in surprise and said,

"I thought that you wanted to hear something about me?"

I nodded.

"Sure, I wanted that. About how you played dirty little games with your little pals and such."

He shook his head laughing. Never out of balance, never!

"That, obviously, I never did, Gerrit!"

"Fighting then? Or being beaten up by others?"

"Also, not."

"Teased? By nasty little beasts like me?"

"No! You don't tease me either, do you?"

I sighed deeply and said,

"Do continue tomorrow, Beato. This is more than a man can take."

Still, I was glad he had come by. The shock that the Indian had delivered had been somewhat absorbed by his visit. Usually I ate my evening meal in the dining room in the main building. It was high season and there were many guests; you had to reserve your own table to be sure of a place. I always sat alone, because I didn't like to make any more contacts in my situation. Sometimes I spotted one of the doctors; other than that, I knew no one. But this evening I had a strange warmth in my breast. Most likely an after-effect of Beato's presence hitherto. Maybe I felt something of his good fortune. How would it feel to be Beato, so unshakably good? For me just ten sentences about his religious upbringing were too much to bear. But how would it be to be like that yourself? I knew for sure that I did have something of that in me and that that was what was giving me that warm feeling. Warmth in a cold heart, a heart like a grave...

From out of that warmth I nodded, unawares, to a girl, eating alone at a table. Normally I would never even notice girls like that. She wasn't good looking but not ugly either, badly dressed and far too shy. But I had accidentally caught her eye, it gave her a fright too, and she blushed. I stood still and said in English,

"I am alone too; can I join you?" I may be an old geezer but I can still be charming. A well-dressed older man with, because of the weight loss, a somewhat severe presence! She didn't dare to say no and I could easily have intimidated her but there was that warmth in the recently discovered 'grave' which made me feel sympathy for this shy child. She appeared to come from Belgium, she spoke French and a few words of Dutch. We spoke in English. She looked better because of the blushing and we ordered a bottle of wine.

"I have seen you here before." she said, to have something to say.

Casually I tasted the wine and answered her when the waiter had gone,

"I usually eat here. But I keep myself to myself, I have a desire for rest."

"This is your idea," she defended herself.

It made me laugh. The warmth grew, with help from the wine.

"What are you doing here?" I asked, and I was genuinely interested.

"I'm not sure, really. I can't find my direction, don't fit in in the world, in life. Maybe here I will find the answers to my questions. And you?" The English language does not distinguish between polite and friendly forms of the word 'You', but she spoke with great respect for my great age. I felt the urge to scoff at that, controlled myself and said with some gravitas,

"Child, I am here to attempt to bring my life to a decent end. You are looking for a way through life, I am trying to leave my life's path. I want to die with dignity, that is one of the reasons for my being here.

"There is another reason that has attached itself to that: I am searching for a kind of confession, a last sacrament, or whatever it is called."

With huge expressive eyes she stared at me.

"Are you sick?" she asked.

"Very sick, yes. Condemned to death."

"That's not possible!"

I smiled.

"Why not? Everyone dies and I'm already almost seventy."

"You look so well! What are they doing about it here?"

"Everything, but with no promises of a cure."

"My father died last year from cancer. I know how bad that is. He was just sixty."

I suddenly had an intense feeling that my life was over. I could start a conversation with this lassie, but not a relationship. Even a friendship was not fair, imagine if she started to have feelings for me. But she said,

"But you can't just accept your illness like that! Why don't you fight to become better?"

I shrugged my shoulders.

"Why should I? What is so interesting about living longer?"

"Don't you have any family?"

She could awaken feelings, this child! First, I felt the end of my life and now - total loneliness. I kept silent. She didn't give up though!

"There must be someone who binds you to this life?" she asked.

"Yes, something, dear child. Fear of God. I want to remain alive because I fear God."

"You believe in God?"

"The fact that I am so scared that He does exist makes me suspect that he is indeed a reality, yes."

"What a negative way to believe in God!" she said, baffled. "Is it not the normal fear of death? Fear of the unknown or of the 'nothing'?"

"I am not afraid of death. I have known death long before today."

She shivered. It is a beautiful thing that people experience so much more of each other than what is visible on the surface. The girl felt the emptiness, the black hole in my soul. I asked,

"What's your name?"

"Sophie. And you?"

"Gerrit. Short for Gérard."

I could feel her innocence. So very different from my girlfriends. You would not want to possess her, you wanted to ... offer her protection. So open and blameless in a world full of hate … it would indeed be almost impossible to find your way, being like that. She needed a knight in shining armour who could be a shield for her.

"Do you have a profession?" I asked.

"Well, profession... I have a passion. I am a violinist and live in poverty, as there is hardly any work."

"Don't you have a man, or a friend?"

"Sometimes. I can only find boys who are so shallow. TV, computers, film, pop music – and sex. And, of course alcohol, smoking and drugs. A conversation like this, isn't a possibility."

Why did I feel my lost life so strongly? In all its aspects, lost. How would it have been if, I as a boy, I had met a girl like this? Ach, I would have blindly passed her by. When later on I was lying in my bed I made the resolution never to, ever, touch Sophie. That was my first intention. The second was just as firm: I would show her the best side of me. I wanted to let her see how to find her way in this threatening world – without falling into the traps that I had walked into…

"Gerrit," I said to myself, "you cannot die before you have done something good. A good Gerard you will be for her, one who knows through and through what the world has to offer and who - even if it happened in a bad way – still managed to acquire some wisdom. "

I awoke differently. The night's rest had indeed been interrupted, but for the last few hours I did manage to sleep well. When I became conscious of myself, I didn't jump out of bed like a trapped cat, but stayed horizontal for a while to experience that feeling of warmth and happiness. The warmth came from Beato, the happiness from Sophie – or rather from the good intentions I had extracted from that warmth. Weaving throughout all that, was another feeling. It had already made its presence felt yesterday, it was here again now, but more pronounced. I felt regret for my life, regret that I hadn't searched for what I had now found. Not remorse, that is something else. I regretted what I had not done.

"Yesterday something happened to me which made me forget myself for a moment, Beato. Just go on with the story about your life, I don't want to come back to myself just now."

"OK, Gerrit. Yesterday you had problems with the golden vineyards, with Our Dear Lord himself walking there, visible to the young Beato."

"I would really like to hear that now – in moderation please."

He laughed, and I felt so much affection for him.

"You asked if I managed to touch the ground with my little angel feet. As far as I can tell, you have established that it is so. It just happened by itself, without 'dirty little games' and such like. I found learning easy but I had the good fortune to have been in a Waldorf school in Meran. That way I did not get trapped in my frontal lobes -"

"In what?"

"Only in my head, my intellect. My hands and feet were always taking part in the learning too and that is how I arrived peacefully with both feet on the ground. Not with a bang, nor too carefully."

"Tell me something about your harmony!"

"I know sadness well, obviously, Gerrit. I missed my father. I really missed him terribly. And I wasn't really understood. Everyone liked me, I can't complain about that.

They did find me a little odd. I was open and spontaneous and talked about my clairvoyant experiences with my mother and sometimes also at school. When I did, everything fell silent, which taught me to keep quiet about these things ... So, that is what I then learned and I was lonely in that respect. Not within myself of course, because there I had all those 'beings' around me, but in the everyday world where all that had to remain a secret."

Because I loved him his words moved me. Within my mind's eye I saw that beautiful small boy holding that secret that nobody wanted to hear. I asked,

"Have those 'companions' remained with you? Or did you lose them as you grew up?"

"No..." he said hesitating. "It is a complicated process, Gerrit. The older I got, the more the experiences receded into the past."

"That I don't understand."

"After I became twenty-one a memory came up from my life before birth, and that memory expanded, became more encompassing, more intense and clearer..."

"I can imagine a deep silence falling when you say such things."

"Do you also think that I'm mentally disturbed then, Gerrit?"

"I know you too well to think that! You don't have any defects. But if you had told me this when we had just met ... well, then, that would have been the end of it. Now, continue with the story."

I felt heat rising from shame. Why shame? Because of the fact that he disclosed such intimate experiences to me? I noticed he was moved and I also knew that the cause was not external. He had a vision or an inner sight of something. Now, at this moment, while sitting opposite Gerrit.

"I will tell you later what I have learned about life before birth, yes, even before conception."

"Is there still a 'later' possible for me?"

"Let me say, 'all in good time', Gerrit. But first I want to tell you how things continued with me. I did not really embrace real intellectual thinking - not like other boys of my age did. I had the capacity to do most things but I lived and floated in the content, I also experienced myself at the same time in that living and weaving. I know fine well where that sensibility 'sits' and how to get access to it, but I seldom have need of it."

"I haven't a clue what you are on about, sonny. You speak in riddles though I hear and understand the words, of course."

"Well, here you are then. You are a Dutchman, but not an intellectual. Maybe you know some of those soberly abstract thinking gents, who don't experience things?"

"Sure." I replied.

"Well, they see the world via their sense of understanding. Through a kind of intellectual pair of glasses which conveniently calculates and categorises reality for them. Your Linnaeus is an example from history, your government ministers are often examples from the present day."

"Well, what of it?"

"That way, all contact with a living reality is lost, leaving only a lifeless image that can be construed in very complicated ways. This is how we get our natural science. That,

I also have absorbed, of course, but from the other side."

"From the other side?"

"By living in the reality and by weaving with my thinking. That is the way I learned everything – I never realised that it can be done in any other way. But later on, with self-knowledge, it all became very clear to me."

I didn't understand any of this – yet somehow, somewhere, I did. Something tickled me within my sick bones, very deep inside as if I could feel the marrow move. I had to change my position and shake my arms and my legs to get rid of that horrible sensation.

"What are you doing?" he asked in surprise.

"Your stories make me nervous," I grinned. "That's the maximum dose for the day."

We talked a bit more about my complaints and then said our goodbyes.

"Tomorrow it's your turn to talk again," he said simply and he left.

For the first time since my arrival I had to hurry; I had a lunch date with Sophie. We were going out to eat in a little restaurant in a village lower down the mountain. I hardly ever went there because why would you on your own?... Here I was, in my posh car, snaking down the roads with speed, accompanied by a lively, healthy, young creature. I don't know if the approach of death gave me new capacities, but I could really feel her youth and her health. Her trust in me moved me deeply, and again I wanted to bring about what was best in life for this young person … .

"May I call you Gérard?" she asked. "I don't really like

'Gerrit' and I can't pronounce it very well."

"No problem, kid. I am starting a new life with a new name. And a daughter. Or a granddaughter even? How old are you, anyway?"

"Twenty-one." So, she could easily be my granddaughter.

"Do you have grandchildren?" she asked me.

"Yes, a couple of boys. Sons and grandsons. No girls."

"I'm sure you've had many girlfriends. One can tell."

"How?"

"You aren't the father or Grandpa type – you're a man." I parked the car in a large car park. She was already out of the car before I could be a 'gentleman'. I proffered her my arm and said decidedly,

"With this man you need have no fear, Sophie. I'm looking for something else now..."

She laughed happily and, as if reborn, I stepped forward on my diseased bones.

My liver function was bad, I constantly felt sick and eating is not easy. But, here I sat opposite Sophie at a little table for two, covered in a crisp white table cloth and set with silver cutlery. Despite my nausea I looked forward to the watercress soup, the oven-baked salmon and the coffee served with a chocolate - from the lunch menu. The memory of how something like that could taste was stronger than the physical dilemma of the moment. I was delighted with the love this child brought with her and by my own newly awakened and unexpected happiness. She wasn't good looking, the lass, but her generosity made her beautiful. She was badly dressed, cheap and in poor taste, but the costliest robes and jewellery couldn't match her beauty, in my opinion. She was happy, enjoyed the luxury, and she was honest – a feature I had never yet encountered in a woman. Never? Well, maybe with Beato's wife and his children...She was totally not sexy, she had no airs and graces, was actually not at all desirable. But, a swan would certainly rise from this duckling, one day, long after I'd gone!

"How on earth did you end up here?" I asked her.

"A girlfriend of mine told me about Johannes. About how much he knows and all the things you can learn from him. The reality is even greater than her stories, you know. I don't think she really understood that much about it." she replied.

"Who is Johannes?" I asked her.

"The man in charge."

"That professor?"

"Yes, him. Haven't you met him?" she asked me.

"Yes, briefly. As doctor, not anything else." I replied.

"It is a bit strange coming across such a great man teaching total strangers in such a remote place... I feel totally unworthy, actually. But it doesn't seem to bother him. What's the story with the clinic? Can you remain there?" she asked me.

" I have a room there... I can stay till my death. We won't have to wait ten years for that, Sophie."

"I can't imagine that. You are so full of life – you are enjoying eating a meal – how is that possible?"

"I would not touch her; no eroticism must appear. But I did want to share my emotions. I briefly laid my hand on her pretty little hand and said,

"You are a sweet child, Sophie. It makes me very happy that a child like you exists!"

She blushed and mumbled,

"I am not a child."

She was a child, a girl who skipped next to me when we went shopping later. I bought something for myself, that I absolutely did not need, but which made it possible for me to buy a few nice sweaters and some trousers for her. She didn't object, accepting without a word, which also touched me. Apparently, the thought of having to reciprocate in some way never occurred to her...When I dropped her off at the car park later on, I was totally exhausted.

"You have to go and rest Gérard!" she said concerned and shook my hand. "Is there something else I can do for you?" Downhearted, I shook my head. I must stop all this, it could make her too attached to me, and me to her.

"Why are you now so sad?" she asked, while she stood there. "We can just follow our hearts, can't we?"

"What do you mean, lass?" I asked, surprised.

"You think that it might be better not to have a friendship, because it may bring sadness. While we both hunger for friends ... let's just be honest and just go ahead and do what we want to do!"

I felt the tears welling up; one rolled shamelessly down my sunken cheek. I wiped it away, sniffed a bit and nodded.

"It's all good Sophie. I would want to see you every day of my life – but it scares me..."

"I can take it Gérard ... Gerrit." She was the wise one - I

the child that still had to learn everything.

"Good. What shall we arrange?"

"I am performing in the big hall this evening. If you come and listen we can have a drink afterwards."

Violin music did not interest me in the least, but that was of no consequence now!

"I will be there and I won't miss a single note!" I shook her hand once again and walked in the direction of the clinic. I needed to cry terribly. During my relationship with Beato I had become aware of my past which caused me pain and, slowly, I began to learn about conscience. The meeting with this girl caused the past to fall away. Only the future seemed relevant; carefully this must be nurtured and formed, out of love, out of goodness... The black was forgotten, replaced by gold. I rejected the idea that it was an impossibility to make such a turnaround. After all it was actually happening...

Steadfastness leads to faith

I slept a couple of hours, didn't go for dinner and was sitting in the second row at half past seven.

By now I had been at the clinic for a good four weeks and hadn't taken part in any evening events at all so far. The 'great and the good' sat in the front row, amongst them sat the scary Indian, who had after all, triggered something in me. The hall slowly filled up and, to my surprise, by eight o'clock, there were more than a hundred or so people. Classical music does nothing for me, I don't have the ear for it, I have no affinity for it whatsoever. In my hand I held a little pamphlet with the programme. It didn't mean a thing to me and now I am writing this, I cannot even remember what was played. And sung. I saw, and heard, obviously, that Sophie played together with a pianist and also, that twice a singer joined in. But I barely heard the piano or the singing, I only heard the violin. She was dressed as a professional, a long black dress with a low front. Though it was a bit shabby, she definitely looked better, the make-up also helped. They have a very particular way of doing things, these musicians. The way in which they catch each other's eye when they are about to start playing, the manner in which Sophie holds the bow on the 'attack'. But then she started to play, and I still get goose bumps up my back when I think about the superiority that she demonstrated. She rises high above the complexities of mere violin playing. It is as if she were riding a bike and whistling happily at the same time! I let myself be carried along by what she did; her movements, the quick fingering, the proud bearing of her head, the expressiveness in the work. A child, a girl, yes. But, with a huge talent, at age twenty-one already quite well developed. It was a kind of melodic force of nature, an expression of great physical accomplishment, expressed in sound. It grabbed me completely and I was lost in it; I had experienced who she was, this child of mine…

In the interval I remained seated and everyone left me in peace. I didn't have the strength for small talk. I had to endure till the end, because then I had a date with her … . When it finally ended I just remained seated – in the hope she would come to me. I was totally finished. Everything hurt, my mental state more than anything. I didn't even join in with the applause, it was too hard. Eventually she entered the almost empty hall and came to sit beside me.

"How's it going Gérard?"

"Not good," I whispered.

"What's wrong then?" she asked, sounding frightened.

"It will be the approach of death, my dear child. Everything seems to affect me much more deeply. I am overwhelmed and can't handle anything. But, now you are here, everything is all right. You are an acrobat, an artist, an athlete! And you bring forth shattering sounds with those acrobatics. How on earth can you learn to do something like that?"

"With a great deal of practice and a modicum of talent."

I genuinely felt better, I straightened myself up and looked into her gentle, radiant eyes.

"A certain amount of talent, yes, yes."

"It is a passion, I am driven, Gérard."

"You totally forget your shyness. And then that dress! And what happens next?"

"I had wanted to go for a drink but you can't, can you?" I stood up and said,

"Oh yes, indeed."

She wrapped her stole around her shoulders, picked up her violin case and said,

"Let's go to my room."

I dragged myself up three flights of stairs, she went in front to enter her room. It is a relatively old-fashioned attic room with a large bed, an old wardrobe and a desk. And then, of course, a music-stand and piles of music books. And two kitchen stools, one of which she indicated for me to use.

"Well, they haven't given you the best room," I said sourly. She put her things away and said,

"I have no money. I am staying here till the autumn in exchange for these concerts. Hardly anyone ever stays in the room above here so that makes studying good. For me this is perfect, better than at home."

"And you are satisfied with that?"

"Why not?"

I grinned and said,

"My intention was usually sex, money and power, Sophie. This is pathetic, unworthy."

She then sat opposite me on the other stool and looked me right in the eye. Today's youth is nothing but straightforward! Then she said,

"I have to tell you something Gérard – Gerrit. I sat there, there in the dinner hall, alone at the table just like every other evening – I watched you coming in, like so many evenings before. You never noticed me. I did notice you. You do have a notable presence, you are, as it were, quite out of the ordinary. A wealthy gentleman, developed, chic. You intrigued me, people like that are rare. In films maybe. But not in real life. I wanted to get to know you. But from the very first moment you spoke to me, I realised that you only ever think about the man-woman relationship."

"That's not true!"

"Let me finish. I realise that that is exactly what you don't want, but that 'not wanting' or 'not allowing' or 'not able' occupies all your time. So, it's all you think about. We can't have a free relationship like that. Not a cell in my body thinks about sex with you. Not because you are so old, or because you are dying, but because it makes no sense to think that way."

I grinned and interrupted her anyway.

"Whenever I see a female, I only ever think about sex. I have never had any other thing to do with women, what else could I think about? Well, I don't want to do that to you - and so I think about it."

"That is exactly what I mean, can I not be a human being here?"

"That's exactly what you are, my dear child. That is why this is all so new for me and I do not want to think about sex."

"Do you feel desire then?" she asked me.

I lowered my head so as not to look at her beauty. There she was in her worn-out evening dress with her shoulders bare, her lovely neck, her shining eyes. She wasn't good looking, but she was a girl with everything such a child had. I said softly,

"You must excuse me. You are young, your skin is perfect and soft ... and so on. I am doing my best, I won't touch you, honestly."

"What a drama this is!" she exclaimed. "You make me constantly aware of my physical body. I just want to be friends ... surely that should be possible!"

"It is, Sophie. It already is, I have fallen for your character, your behaviour, your wisdom. Truly. Also, for your innocence and your vulnerability. Your very capable fingers on the violin. Your supremacy there and over me, I, who cannot do anything other in life than strive for power."

"Can you just admit that you have a problem, Gerrit?"

"Power develops in the silences, my dear Sophie. I am not in the habit of being honest! But you know where the key lies ... to my heart? My soul? Being?"

Here I was with a girl of twenty-one in a sort of student room having deep psychological discussions. Is this how the young people interact with each other? Did I miss out on something? Have I lived in a different dimension, excluded? I shook my head and looked at her,

"Why are you suffering here with such an old guy, Sophie?"

"Age only matters with sex, not with friendship. You are a striking, interesting person, Gérard. I would very much like to own a little of you. And what's more ... I want to comfort you, because you have so much sadness in you … Would you like to have something to drink? I have quite a choice here."

We drank a bottle of red wine between us and then she took me 'home', concerned, due to my unsteady condition. It was a warm and windy Spring evening, even this high up in the mountains. We stopped and stood at the door of the clinic. She laid both her little girl hands on my shoulders and gave me three kisses on my cheeks.

"Thank you so much for this terrific day, Gérard!" She said and turned around. Quickly she walked away into the night.

"Shouldn't I be taking you home?" I called out happily. She turned and waved.

Completely confused, I found my room and my bed.

"The strangest things go on in this place," I said to Beato the next morning.

"It was indeed quite odd to see you at the concert," he grinned. "But today you have to go on talking about yourself."

"The past seems less important now, somehow. As if the door to Heaven is slightly ajar … . maybe that's an illusion. I shall tell you some more." I transported myself mentally to my younger years and began.

"Killing another human being creates a terrific strength, Beato. Especially when you know how to keep quiet about it and when no one finds out. Maybe it's like heroin. Once you've used it you keep craving the effect. I have never divulged my secret. In the army I met a fellow who knew a lot about such things. He taught me many things, but even him I never told my secret to. You are the first. Well, actually that Indian guy is the first, but he saw it for himself. Maybe there have been more people in my life who could see that, but I don't know about that."

"What did that fellow, you met in the army, teach you?"

"He possessed ancient wisdom, Beato. 'Power-technique' you could call it. Like Machiavelli, but with more magic. He taught me how to keep myself 100% unaffected. How to make and keep the other impotent and powerless. These are psychic techniques of intimidation. With that, I also learned how to disengage my heart and to paralyse conscience. There are well-known methods for these things. I'm sure you know this, after all, you know it all! No one could enter, it was one-way traffic with me. No exchange, all power was executed by me alone. With those skills I went into business. Particularly in the arms trade; often illegal but under a legal façade. I functioned on a government level, Beato, internationally. Not openly, not on the big stage, but behind the scenes. These dealings worked just the way I wanted them to and I never experienced any opposition."

"Sorry, Gerrit, maybe I am somewhat naive, but such dealings always fail sooner or later, don't they?"

I stared at him for quite a while. He never wavered, of course.

"Naturally it went wrong, Beato. The moment that there is even a fraction of a second of insecurity the whole house of cards tumbles down. Then you get a free ticket to jail, immediately."

"So, you have been in jail?"

I laughed, sarcastically.

"Of course not! I never had a moment of insecurity – never! As long as I live no one will ever dare to try anything against me. Still, it did go wrong. The moment I walked into your consulting room in that clinic in Italy, for a fraction of a second, I saw myself the way you saw me. You, absolute perfection, a young God, impervious to my black activities … You managed to achieve what no one else could. You managed it because you are so unbelievably kind, literally 'dis-arming'. All my weapons clattered to the ground and in my vulnerability, you grabbed me, boy. And you put something good into my badness. From that moment on, everything went wrong, although I did manage to salvage a few extra years. Sex and money are stimulants but the real prize was 'power'. The big bosses of evil in a James Bond film are idiotic fantasies from a writer who doesn't get it at all: striving for power doesn't need hungry piranhas in swimming pools or underground laboratories... Striving for power needs simplicity, the simplicity of black magic technique. But love is pure poison - one drop of light is enough if it is a drop of white magic light. Don't you think that at the root of all this search for power is a desire for love? Total unrequited desire for love?"

Now I stopped talking, totally exhausted. I had confessed, and at the same time, come to the realisation the penitence I had to perform. Love was the penitence. Beneath the concrete poured into me by my striving for power, love germinated. And love you must not want to have, but want to give. “Do you feel remorse, Gérard?”

Beato remained stubborn in his pursuit. I asked the question of myself. Do you feel remorse Gerrit? I shook my head no.

“I still cannot feel that, Beato. I do feel sadness, because no one taught me that I could have used my power to do some good.”

“Then there would have been powerlessness, poverty and chastity, Gerrit.”

“Aren’t those the vows of a priest?”

“Obedience, yes. Obedience, poverty and chastity.”

“Now, for that I am obviously too weak. That gal, the Belgian, Sophie ... has brought it to my attention that I only ever think about sex when I’m with her. Which I demonstrated, by saying that I absolutely didn’t want sex.”

Beato burst out laughing.

“Many a priest will have that same problem, thinking he is completely chaste. But remorse, Gerrit. It’s all about remorse.”

“I just don’t feel it. I’m not just going to invent nice words.”

“You could strive for it.”

“Why should I strive for bad feelings?”

Beato stood up, smiling gently, and shook my hand vigorously and said,

“Till Monday, Gerrit. Then it is my turn again.”

“Greetings to your wife and children from me, Beato.”
He left the room - the absolute balance.

Remorse, what is remorse? I have tried to experience

what it is, but conscience itself is missing in me. I think that remorse is the expression of conscience as it speaks in our feeling life. But that is just what I have tried to exterminate with decades of practice, preferably root and branch. But Beato has been sowing and in these fourteen years something has sprouted and grown. That is why I noticed Sophie and want to bring her all good things. I did say that 'love has to be the penance'. That little bit of love, for Beato and for Sophie … is a form of remorse. I do want to do it better still, in these last few days, weeks or maybe months. Out of that 'wanting to do better' I will have to look back to the past to learn to feel what remorse is. But, for an arrogant upstart such as I, that is an almost impossible task. What will remain of my power? I already have to renounce the sex, despite still being a desirable fellow, that women look at, beautiful women. My money I can give away: give it to that scary Indian for his enterprise here … or to Sophie … or to Beato. Maybe dirty money will be cleansed this way. Washed clean and not for the tax man. Oh well, never mind all that, I don't need it any more. But that power is somehow inextricably interwoven with my personality, that is what I am. If I have to give that up - nothing will remain, only that thinly flickering flame of love. Maybe that is all I get. Is it worth more than 'powerfulness'? The fact that I am thinking about it is a beginning of reflecting. On the other hand, I have no idea how I will stop the struggle for power. It is interwoven with my 'I', it is me, myself after all. Even if I already wanted to, I still would not know how to go about it.

"Do tell me Sophie, what is it like to be a woman?"

She started to laugh.

"A metamorphosis of that obsession with sex - this question seems to me to be. Don't look so cross, I'm just teasing you a little. I don't regard myself as that much of a woman, you know. When I am with you I do, I feel that I have a female shape – really! But most of the time I am not all that conscious of my gender. I think that I live in my soul more than in my body. I live in the music, in harmony and disharmony, in tempo, in rhythm. You awaken my femininity that's how I know that you are so sexual. You are a good-looking man, and an intelligent man also."

"Who's talking about sex now?"

Again, she laughed and I felt the physical attraction like clouds on the horizon.

"It's all your fault. In music it plays no role, as long as there aren't any words anyway, no song. Perhaps it is possible to express masculine or feminine in music, but the music won't be affected by it."

"So, what is it like to be a woman in contact with a man such as Gérard?"

She sighed and said,

"Well you certainly are persistent! I feel silly, naive, inept. Frumpy, unkempt, uneasy. Very small, sometimes too respectful and too submissive."

"That doesn't add up at all!" I exclaimed.

"I'm doing my best," she giggled, "to let my humanity rule."

"You have so much wisdom, Sophie. Totally not silly. You are exceptionally accomplished. You could, of course, do something about your appearance, you could be much more beautiful. But submissive you are not!"

"I did say that I'm doing my best. I don't want to feel that either, it is below my dignity. You are a bit of a cavalier, Gérard. You know life and I know nothing. I don't belong in your world."

"What 'world'?"

"Of rich, successful, smooth people. If you weren't so sick you would not even have noticed me!"

"The nice thing is that you are open, Sophie. Your heart is an open book. I have never yet encountered that. Women are dishonest creatures, lazy and seductive. You are honest."

"And totally not seductive," she said sourly.

"Is that what you want to be then, Sophie?"

She thought a little while.

"No. Desirable yes. Let's abandon this line of thought or you may end up seducing me!" she laughed.

In the evening we again ate together in the dining hall. Perhaps people had started to gossip about us. Such a well-preserved gentleman with such a very young girl … We couldn't care less, we had a good time together.

"I have a similar question to one from this afternoon, Sophie. What is it like to have no power?"

"Who says that I have no power?" she asked, in all seriousness, and her question confused me no end.

"Let me ask it in a different way then. Do you recognise the feeling of power, Sophie?"

"I don't think that that feeling itself has much purpose. It's about … *do* I have power or not?" she replied.

"You are very intelligent today," I stated.

She ignored that and went on,

"I believe it is a moveable feast. Sometimes you do have power and sometimes you don't. Just now I did definitely have power, it caused you to falter. Then, after a while, you get it back again, it can't be helped. It's all about the balance, I believe."

"And what happens if you meet someone who is greedy when it comes to having power, Sophie?"

"That would only work if I became scared."

Suddenly I found her very lovely and said,

"I don't believe that that is a problem for you. Indeed, fearlessness disarms."

"Believe me, it can be a problem for me, Gérard. But, I can overcome my fear. Immediately, straight away, usually ... I have told you that already, before. I do feel that I am a nothing, but I also try my hardest to let go of those feelings, to straighten them out, to overcome, you name it."

"Then you are constantly fighting with yourself?"

"Something like that, yes. Exhausting but also satisfying. A power struggle it is for sure, but a necessary one. And you Gérard? How do you deal with these things? With power and with powerlessness?"

I leaned back in my chair and said in such a manner that she wouldn't know if I was serious or sarcastic,

"I read 'Mein Kampf' and applied all the rules. Or rather: 'how an idiot became the most powerful – in any case the most feared - man in the world.'"

She possesses some of that unshakeable quality that Beato has, my little Sophie. I was silent for a while, but she did not avert her gaze when she said,

"You're pulling my leg. You are a pain."

"A pain I am for sure. But I'm not pulling your leg! I acquired memberships of two very significant brotherhoods. I shouldn't be mentioning a word about them, but since I am dying anyway, and I regret my actions – I thought that I'd just warn you."

"What about?"

"About me."

Her eyes began to fill with tears. I was ashamed of myself. What I could, and wanted, to tell Beato, I had to hide from her. She was young and inexperienced and was a little in love with me. Quickly I said,

"I'm so sorry, my child. I'm speaking crap. For you, I am completely trustworthy. For you, I will convert. I wish you only the very, very best. Also, all the very best that that old Gerrit has to offer."

She wiped away a tear, sobbed a little and then she said,

"How do I know what is true? Are you being honest now or are you making fun of me? Were you being honest a minute ago?"

I placed my hand on hers. A thin worldly-wise old hand … ,

"I'm always honest. In reality, I am a shit, truly. But in this shite, there is a small point of light. You found it and it will grow, I promise you that, Sophie. I really do promise that!"

Her young, still innocent, girl hands grabbed mine. I could feel her soft warmth; how sweet she was. She said softly,

"Then I will only look at that Gérard. Only at that."

When I got out of bed on Sunday morning, because of the constant pain in my bones, a look in the mirror revealed that I looked sallow. The thought 'Things are rapidly going downhill!' shot through my mind. It was the first time that I felt a sharp pain with the thought of the end. I did not recognise these emotions; they are, after all, the inevitable consequences of love – and 'that', I had avoided like the plague. After taking two painkillers I went to sit down in a chair by the window. The sun was up already - it promised to be a gorgeous day and I was in awe of its beauty. She was as beautiful as Sophie, this Aurora. No, Sophie is even more beautiful. She has spirit, that lass. Maybe Aurora does too, but she doesn't speak a word to me … whereas Sophie does. I felt a tender warmth inside, a concern for Sophie. Within a few days I had fallen in love with a human child, just because she is as she is. A blossoming rose, but for me, for the first time ever not specifically physically desirable. I loved her - yes, but what actually? Her soul. At the same time my departure looms, threatening. I am very much alone. I did not manage to create any lasting relationships with people, didn't try either. My sons phone occasionally, the 'spiritual girlfriend' who pointed this place out to me … I don't hear from her. I have no friends, not one. Apart from the two here, Beato and Sophie. It's a pity that Beato already has a wife…

All things I thought were important are falling away, they just drop off. What meaning is there when there is only a short time left to live? The beauty of the world around becomes more perceptible, but its importance diminishes.

Greed becomes pointless, fear also. What is there to be afraid of? What have you got to lose? Only life - and that is already lost. The only thing that still matters is love, but that only hurts. And it will hurt her too – should I try to avoid that? Leave here? What nonsense! Then sadness would be here even quicker! Come on Gerrit! Remorse is the intention to do things better from now on!

We had arranged to meet at 10 am in front of the main building, to go for a walk together. I can't walk for very long but a round through the park I can manage. She hadn't arrived yet, I leaned against the railings. The sky was slightly milky with clouds, but the sun was shining through. I felt the resemblance between the Spring and the girl. Young, unspoiled and fresh... Where was she? I had already waited ten minutes. Imagine if she didn't feel like it anymore?... Insecurity crept in. What does such a Spring creature seek in Winter's chill? Bare, cold, on the verge of dying … Then suddenly I saw her, she didn't come out of the building but walked towards me from a distance, hurried. When she noticed me standing waiting she started to run towards me. I opened my arms to greet her without thinking, as you do when a child runs towards you. She literally threw herself into my arms and kissed my cold thin cheeks. Touched, I held her tight, just for a moment. Then we stood facing each other both with tears in our eyes.

"Excuse me for being so late, I misjudged the distance. This morning I was so sad that I started walking early."

"Why sad?" I asked, concerned.

"It must be your plight that I feel, Gérard. That happens to me with all the people I love. Come, let's go for a walk."

She put her arm through mine and I was again tested by the temptation of a Spring-like body next to mine, so close to me.

"How is it possible that you like the Winter, my dear child?"

"The Winter is beautiful. Full of spiritual forces and promise. Life begins in the sprouting seeds, though you see nothing yet. It all looks bare and cold, but the earth glows in reality with good will."

I wiped away the tears in my eyes with my sleeve.

"Where do you get all this wisdom from, my girl?"

She pressed my arm.

"Life is music. The music talks to me about the riddles of existence. That is why I don't feel at home in the world the way it is. The music does not resonate..."

"And you find that it does with this grumpy old man?"

"You aren't that old. You act as if you were ninety! Yes, with you I do find resonance. You aren't shallow, you have experienced a lot."

I stood still to catch my breath.

"I feel like ninety, you understand? I was always the boss over everyone, both physically and mentally. Now after a hundred meters I have to rest … ."

"Someone else in your position might very well be bed-ridden, on oxygen and a drip. It looks like you are healthy - maybe somewhat short of breath, that's all."

I could now go on.

"What do you have to do today, Sophie?"

"Nothing. Sunday is a rest day. What shall we do?"

I laughed at her eagerness.

"Enjoy this gorgeous day together. What do you find most interesting in this place, what is the theme?"

"Spirituality. But I am actually too young for everything. Professor Leven - Johannes – thinks I should first find my place in the world, so as not make spirituality an escape."

"That sounds sensible."

"We talk together for an hour every week. He advises me on what to read and he allows me to take part in several work groups. He is a darling man, Gérard."

"There is another man around here, also a doctor. Who is he?"

"Do you mean Dr Laurent? I don't really know him. He seems a very peaceful, unpretentious man more engaged with other things if you ask me."

"This place attracts amazing people. I know about people, I can see that they have mastered themselves. Beato the most, he has it by nature, without trying – and in complete balance."

We went to sit down on a bench.

"How do you see your future, Sophie?"

"That is just what I don't know, that is one of the reasons I am here. I was only twenty-one when I received the diploma from the conservatoire. I could go on to become a soloist, go and study with great violinists, I have the talent. Should I do that? Or should I teach at a music school and play in an orchestra? Will there be a man somewhere who would want to be married to an artist? Can I have children and bring them up? Is that what I want? Will I ever find anyone as interesting as you are? All questions without answers, Gérard."

"Life itself will answer many of those questions."

"But, I'm looking for freedom. I mean, I don't want to just blindly tumble into every situation and then say, 'Such is life'! It will make a real difference if I say now, I will take up that opportunity and study with a great violinist in Vienna or instead I will take on a little job at the music school."

"Don't you see that the answer lies there in your own words, child?"

"How so?!"

"Just listen to how you said all that. A great violinist in Vienna verses a little job. Well, what is it you really want?"

"To go to Vienna. But -"

"Well do that then!"

She searched out my hand and squeezed it.

"You are right, of course. But it is quite difficult to allow yourself to harbour such ambitions."

"Why?! You are very talented after all."

She was silent: her hand lay next to mine again. I said,

"I think I may have over-stepped the mark. But, if it means anything at all, life can be meaningless, too. I have seen you play once. I said 'seen', not heard. I know nothing about music. But I can see when someone is in complete control of something, when one can speak of mastery. You have that. As young as you are. I wouldn't worry about a husband or children. If there is such a person, then he is there for sure, waiting for you there at the top. Imagine if you didn't reach those heights – then you will never find him!"

She burst out laughing.

"You are just great, Gérard! Good, I will go to Vienna.

But I will only go once...when you..."

"After I have died?"

"That is what I meant, but we must not think of that at all. Let me say: 'I will stay with you as long as you live, Gérard. Even if that takes another twenty years."

"Then I will go with you to Vienna," I laughed and wiped my cheeks yet again.

Well, people will say things easily. They promise eternal faithfulness and then they leave the following day. Those were some of my thoughts when I went to lie down for a rest in the afternoon. The child doesn't know what she is saying... 'I will stay with you as long as you live, Gérard!' The memory of her words made me shiver. She was authentic, Sophie. Absolutely. She would honour such a promise. But, why? What do I have to offer her to make her love me? A wolf in sheep's clothing, that is me. Soon... I will discuss this with her shortly.

"Do you know the expression 'a wolf in sheep's clothing'?"

We were sitting opposite each other at a little table in a restaurant. I had only known her a few days and had sat like this, opposite her, many times already. She thought hard and then answered in her usual deep and straight-to-the-point manner.

"I don't know it, no. But I do, of course, understand it. I also realise that you see yourself like that – and you are probably right – in some ways. But I see something else, Gérard. That is the reason you have become as dear to me as ... my father, in such a short time. I see a lamb in wolf's clothing. Or rather a great amount of empty outward display – whatever may have caused it - from someone who, by nature, could love deeply and intensely. Who also yearns for that..."

She hesitated and blushed. I could feel the love she spoke about, but I also felt how that love was bound up with eroticism, with temper ... that throttled the love. I wanted to experience the love within my heart. But my 'other side' stirred violently. The brave girl gathered her courage together.

"I will stay with you, Gérard. I will repeat it again. I really mean it. Why wouldn't I, if it's what I really want? I don't have to account to anyone..."

Suddenly it was here. Remorse. It isn't a concept to be described, it is an emotion. It is the strongest emotion I have ever experienced. Maybe, like Beato, she has a secret capacity to plant something in me. But, most probably it was already there and was just woken by other emotions. Remorse. In a fraction of a second, I felt the enormous debt I had amassed throughout my life. The lamb could feel the heavy weight of wolf's clothing and suddenly I realised in full - even though only very briefly – how all that had to be atoned for. Evermore. The remorse welled up as an overwhelming emotion, like love, like broken-heartedness, like unrequited love. And that emotion led me to experience: the wolf I leave behind, for good. I'm sure he will rear his ugly head from time to time out of habit and attempt to catch some prey. But the lamb shall conquer him with the might of innocence. Love conquers all. I took my napkin and wiped my eyes. I looked her in the eye and with a trembling voice I mumbled,

"I – my child – Sophie – you have the most mighty and powerful weapons. You and Beato ... I love you, Sophie. And I think it should be allowed."

She laid her small soft Spring-like hand on the dead wood of mine and said,

"What do you want actually, Gérard!?"

"To be honest, noble and pure. Can a docker ever become a count? Can a count love a princess? Can a father who has no daughter find his daughter? What do you want? I don't understand who I am anymore, or what life still has in store for me. My heart is too big for my body, even though I have tried to reduce it to nothing. What do I actually want? I want to be with you and with Beato – but it must not do you harm."

She stroked my hand: comfort streamed from that. She said,

"It is all very remarkable. But harm? No, Gérard! You won't ever harm me!"

When I finally lay in bed, alone with my undeniably depraved self, things looked different again.

Sophie imagined a lamb in the wolf. She was so naive. Did she know what a wolf actually is? Absolutely unreliable apart from one thing: the prey, in any shape or form. That was my life. And aren't you what you have done? So that is me then, a wolf! And that feeling of remorse then, a while ago? I tried to relax, trying to recapture the mood of the evening? Purchased a bit of happiness for the price of overwhelming remorse! Who is Gerrit? Is he the wolf with no conscience, who knows no reason, no justice and no kindness? Or does he carry the lamb within his core after all? If I am a wolf I will eventually grab Sophie. So, first I will win over her confidence - and once I have that, I will destroy her. Just for the pleasure that destruction affords – the joy of absolute power. I can develop a plan, as I have done so often before. Step by step I can make her fall for Gerrit, and then destroy her. Then it'll be over, the diatribe about good Gérard. I could also just ignore her from now on, then that's not so bad. She just won't understand it, and cry a few tears. I sat up abruptly, pulled myself up out of bed and started to walk back and forth. I raised my voice and said,

"Gerrit, you must listen carefully! You will not allow yourself to be dragged along by that wolf in sheep's clothing that's in you. Think carefully! The way you were thinking then, that's how you have been thinking all your life. Throw that habit out the window. Sophie is a hero and an angel and you will start behaving accordingly, even just as practice. You know fine well that you will soon die and you also know for damned certain that God exists, that the devil exists and that you are situated on the wrong side. You have discovered an angel upon the road, two in fact!" That is how I addressed myself and I fought with all my might against the agonising thoughts that raged in from the past. Eventually I felt so awful that I pressed the bell for the nurse...

I regained consciousness in an ambulance.

"What the hell is going on!" I shouted angrily.

The nurse beside the stretcher said calmly,

"You've had a heart attack. The nurse and the doctor resuscitated you and you are on the way to the hospital in the city."

I was attached to an ECG machine, saw my heart beat on the monitor.

"What use is a hospital to me? I should be dead! Why can it not be now?"

"You will be examined there and stay a couple of days. They can't help you in the place you are living."

I remained silent; it made no difference anyway. A heart attack ... it was those revolting thoughts: my weakened body cannot take it anymore. I wanted to cry, that's how alone I felt. In the hospital I had quite a job convincing them of the fact that I was a terminal patient, almost terminal - and that they should keep their paws to themselves. It had, in fact, not been a heart attack, only a cardiac arrhythmia which had now been stabilised. I was put on a drip, was taken to the heart unit and had to stay there a few days. On Tuesday morning at ten o'clock I had a visit from Sophie ... She looked unwell, maybe she had been crying over that bastard Gerrit. She bent forward and kissed my cheeks. She took my chilly hand, sat down and said,

"I wanted to come right away but I wasn't allowed. How is it now, Gérard?"

"Fine, no different than before. Though lying down makes me feel even sicker. Tomorrow I can leave here. I haven't had any irregular heartbeats since, but I am swallowing lots of stuff."

"How did it happen, Gérard? Was the day too busy for

you, too many emotions? Or what?"

Ashamedly I answered,

"It was the most beautiful day yet, sweet girl. But the wolf is against it, he doesn't want to leave and threatens to strangle the lamb. I am sorry."

She kept still, she was certainly not that naive. Her presence relieved me of all those stupid thought-forms. Sophie is a wise one, an artist, a musician. Not just a dumb broad like the ones I always went around with before. Now one, then another - but always as stupid as possible. I pressed her hand and said,

"You are medicine to me, Sophieke. But when you aren't here, I forget and don't believe it."

She squeezed my hand and said,

"I don't have any idea of real evil, obviously. I only know that I am totally not afraid of you – and that is enough for me. But I can imagine that you have a fight on your hands and it won't be a trifling matter either."

I had nothing more to say and felt vulnerable in this high bed, in my pyjamas, on a monitor.

When she left I missed her so intensely that I could barely stop myself from crying, again…

The first person to visit me when I was home again was Beato. I had only just arrived and he was already there. He hugged me heartily and said,

"You almost lost it Gerrit! Aren't you afraid now?"

"I am not scared of death, especially not if he comes so unexpectedly. But I must admit that I would like to live just a little longer. I am scared of the 'post mortem' experience ... and I would like to better myself somewhat. Only

... I'm not all that sure how to go about it. That evil doesn't want me to leave the past behind and I have to fight hard against thoughts and feeling that burst in on me. I think that is the cause of the irregular heartbeat, to be honest. Look, when you are with me, or Sophie, then I can feel and be my new self, completely. As soon as I'm alone the old stuff stirs so strongly that it threatens to floor me."

"You need a priest, Gerrit. But a real priest. He doesn't need to be ordained but does have to be a priest through and through. We don't have an ordained one here but we do have a real one."

"Who? The professor?"

"No. Dr Laurent. I will ask if you can go to see him."

"Is he French?"

"He speaks Dutch."

With lead in my shoes I went on my way to see him. The umpteenth master on my endless path. What could he have that Beato didn't? His room was on the first floor. The door was closed and there was no waiting room. I knocked and then I was confronted, eye to eye, with Dr Laurent, who I had, of course, seen around. He offered me a hand, pointed out where I should go and came to sit by me.

As always when I am extremely nervous – and that happens a lot these days – I took everything in very precisely. The large, tidy desk, the shelves with books, the sun-filled balcony. But most of all the man himself ... completely normal, unremarkable.

"Would you like something to drink?" he asked in Dutch without any accent.

"A glass of water."

He got up, poured two glasses of water and sat down again. The man was peace itself. Not the balance of Beato, but a calm resignation. Well intentioned, all friendliness and with a certain fluidity. He held back till I began to speak and I said,

"Doctor, go ahead just say it. You have heard from Beato what the..." I began to feel an immense despair like desire that won't be fulfilled. I looked at him and noticed his searching gaze. He was the next miracle on death's border, my death. His calmness became so overwhelming, it transferred to me and I calmed down, too. He asked,

"What are you suffering from, sir?"

I couldn't keep my eyes fixed on him so I looked at the window frame and said,

"I have lived for power, sex and money. That's not that bad, really, doctor. But I have relished evil, destruction itself. Quite a number of people have died on my watch – because it was necessary. But, I enjoyed it, again and again. I have never yet admitted this to anyone, not even to my best friend Beato – well actually hardly even to myself. The compulsion for destruction keeps raising its head, I fight against it ... and I win every time. But I have become scared for myself, scared that I will fall back into it. What can I do to overcome these thoughts and feelings?"

I began to cry uncontrollably. I sensed the goodness of the man sitting beside me and a kind of faith came over me. I was so overcome that even my shield was penetrated. Beato embodies the balance; the professor, knowledge; Sophie, innocence. But this man is goodness through and through. He made no attempt to comfort me, but I could see that he was moved.

"You should learn to pray," he said softly. "I will teach you the 'Our Father', evil cannot penetrate that. With every attack, pray, out loud. Aside from those events, you must try to let the meaning of the words get through to you. You will see that it works."

He taught me the prayer the way a child would learn it. He said a line aloud then I had to repeat after him. Then the second, and then the first and the second. After half an hour I could say the prayer on my own. I felt like a child and the sentences were the father to whom I directed myself. Dr Laurent was imperturbable, it was not possible to object in any way. I had to undergo the purifying effects of repeating a religious text... Then he sent me away. He only said,

"Come back next week. And if there is a problem in the meantime you can always phone me. Here is my number." He proffered his hand and I was allowed to go. Overwhelmed, I walked down the stairs, through the hall and outside. I felt like I had been with an exorcist, a magician, in the twenty-first century!

It felt like I had been given a precious jewel, a hold-fast. Never again could these words ever be just words again, because I had learned to say them in a very special way. It was in the words themselves, it shone around them, rayed forth from them. As a child starts to play with a present, so I spoke the words aloud in my room, line by line and it made me feel cherished.

By now I had three friends: Beato, Sophie and the Lord's Prayer.

But it didn't last long, the feeling of purification. Once back alone in my room, the feeling of ridicule rose up again. Without wanting to, I ridiculed the session with Laurent, I ridiculed my docile obedience and I even ridiculed the text, line by line. But the ridicule was not really completely thorough, somewhere a tiny chink of light still shone, wanting something other than the devil. I still had no idea how to enhance that experience to make it more powerful... But, suddenly the memory came back to me: Speak the sentences of the prayer in a loud voice, so that you not only say the words but also hear them. My heart was becoming restless again; I stood up and began to recite.

After I had recited it three times it began to work. The devil knows God better than anyone and he knows when to let go. He let go; and I felt how I became Gérard again, Sophie's friend, friend of Beato... Laurent's penitent.

"My wife has invited you to spend the weekend with us."

I had thought I'd never leave this building again and was therefore a little ambivalent. Nothing would be nicer than three days with Beato – but nothing seemed more difficult for me than living without Sophie for three days. I replied, truthfully,

"I can't Beato. I only have a short time left and I do not want to spend a day without Sophie, never mind three days."

"She can come too! The children can sleep in one room,

and then we have two guest rooms."

"It sounds tremendous. If Sophie would like it ... you think that's a possibility, Beato? Don't you think I am too weak?"

He shook his head,

"It will do you good," he said with confidence.

So, on Friday morning the three of us drove up to Tessin.

The austere mountain landscape changed to a lusher and more romantic, almost subtropical, one on nearing Lake Maggiore.

Aah..., many times I had been here, my other I, the Gerrit from the past. The rich and mighty industrialist with his darkness just below the surface. Now a simple man, travelling to stay with his friends...

I looked at different things, now. Not at the villas with gardens for sale. Not at yachts on the water beside the hotels along the boulevard. I looked at the steel blue sky with white seagulls, at the huge fig trees beside the date palms, at the capable hands of my friend on the steering wheel… at the face of the girl on the back seat, filled with expectation.

"It is a miracle that I am getting the opportunity to see all this once more." I sighed, and the warmth of the late Spring sun warmed my sick bones to the marrow ... or was it from the love of these two with me?

He had rented a nice house right by the lake. He was certainly not poor. But nothing compared to what I had indulged in in the past … Sophie, on the other hand, knew only attic rooms - it was enough to silence her.

Chiara greeted us with strong Italian coffee. She had aged too but you could see that she was happy. I felt myself to be outside of myself. This did not fit well with my present situation, not feeling at home in my own being. I did not realise that people like this existed, that a life like this is possible. Not a life without difficulties - I don't mean that. Simply a life in acceptance of everything that it brings but without fatalism. That is how it I felt to me, to be here, in this house, with the view of the enchanted Lago.

Sophie was shy. She wore the clothes I'd given her, which made her appear somewhat less shabby. She does, however, have an unimpressive exterior, she is a grey mouse compared to Chiara, even though she is twenty years younger.

All in all, it was rather a tense affair. Chiara told us about the children when I asked, as they were at school. We then took our bags to the guest rooms. They had given us the best rooms, next to each other, with a view to the lake and a shared balcony, where Sophie and I, hand in hand, gazed at the lake.

"You feel embarrassed. That isn't necessary," I said softly.

"That is just how it is. I'm not very good with all this luxury; I feel I am a nothing, a nobody."

She was just a child, my child. I pulled her towards me and placed my arm across her bare shoulders.

The softness of her skin sharply penetrated my senses.

"Then you need to blow yourself up a bit, Sophie. How can luxury rob you of yourself?"

"Maybe it isn't the luxury but the beauty also of these two people – and of you. You do see the contrast, don't you? I also feel that!"

"You could be beautiful too, if you didn't hide yourself under a bush. You have a perfect young body - there are uglier women who fancy themselves enormously."

"That's disgusting, Gérard. I wouldn't want that. And these two here are beautiful without 'fancying themselves'."

"They are beautiful because they dare to be. You are a rabbit, a scaredy-cat – and then again, also totally not. You are a puzzle, Sophieke."

We stood close together for a while, the beauty of the surroundings made it feel so romantic. An unstoppable desire to stroke her, to touch, to kiss her overcame me. Before I could even start, she pulled away and stood at a metre's distance. That made the desire all the greater, as I now saw her through rose-tinted spectacles. Suddenly she was a great beauty, as she could be if she just took a bit of care. I swore, and went inside but left the balcony door open. The dice had been thrown in the air, who knows which way it would land?

She stood there in the open door with the sunlight shining on her. Everything about her was young and therefore beautiful...

I must think about her soul, her spirit, her talent, her wisdom – not the girl shape, the softness...

"Why do you swear so much?" she asked, irritated.

"I only concern myself with sex, remember? I am a guy, you are a broad. What do they do together?"

She didn't move. That is why my father beat my mother all the time, because women are so dammed stubborn. Go away, stupid girl! Go away or I will cause an accident! She stood stock still. She said, no, she shouted,

"I hate you, you know that? You are a complete bastard!" I was now sitting on the edge of the teenager's bed. She, Sophie, was the very first woman I had ever respected. But if she didn't keep her trap shut she would also be the first to receive a good hiding from me!

"If you want to avoid a beating you'd best clear off now!" She turned around and was gone.

Out loud I said the prayer again and again. *This way, I will have another arrhythmia attack!* Slowly the over-excitement dissipated and I began to feel shame and also regret. Maybe I had ruined everything now? I went out onto the balcony and found her there in a chair. She sat in the sun, totally relaxed, reading a book, damn it! She looked up and said,

"So, there you are again, then!"

Nothing mousy about her now, more like a lioness or something like that. Totally at a loss for words, I was.

"And?" she asked, cheekily. "What are you looking at?"

"What on earth has happened to you?"

"What has happened? I fancy myself because a guy like you wants to make love to me!"

Slightly offended, I still managed to see the humour of it and we found each other again, two friends that had weathered the first of passion's storms…

After the siesta we went to Ancona. Beato and Chiara, Gérard and Sophie...

We strolled along the boulevard back and forth, past the harbour, the narrow beach and back again. Sophie and I walked arm in arm behind the married couple and Sophie said softly,

"I still don't get why you were so angry this afternoon. What were you fighting against? Surely, we are allowed to touch each other - everyone does that, after all."

"Even if it's a girl who could be your granddaughter?"

"What has that got to do with it? We aren't actually going to get married!"

I stood still, gob-smacked. This innocent darling child had no qualms whatsoever about getting into bed with grandpa? My heartbeat went messy again and I asked,

"What in the name of God are you trying to say now?"

"That I think it's fine if you want to hold me, I don't mind that at all."

"Surely you are not that stupid, Sophie! I can't hold you and leave it at that. With me it's all or nothing. In this case then … nothing."

We walked on and I could feel her hand on my arm. She was silent and I had no idea what she was thinking.

"What are you thinking about?" I asked.

"That it is so beautiful here. Romantic. My life is so much richer now, because of you. It was rather boring before you came along."

I understood something about our relationship now. Without me, she would never have come across so many things – and I learned something new from her life too. For her, the problem was that she couldn't get real romance from me - for me, it was that I couldn't give it to her - just because of who she was. For passers-by we were grandfather with granddaughter, or maybe father and daughter.

What are we, really?

I freed my arm and placed it around her middle and I said,

"If I were twenty years younger and healthy ... I wouldn't think twice."

She also put her arm around me and said,

"I really love you very much Gerrit!"

We ate pizza on one of the terraces. Boats arrived from a day trip across the lake. Maybe I have never yet experienced true happiness because this feeling of evening coming, the busyness, lovely people around me, contentment ... nah, that I don't recognise. In a minute I will probably be abusing myself again with questions such as: Who is Gerrit really, does God exist, should I be Sophie's lover, do I have a future, what punishment awaits me over the threshold, coming closer by the day...?

In the evening Beato and I sat together in the living room, garden door wide open, women and children in bed...

"I feel a huge confusion; can you understand that?"

Beato nodded expectantly.

"You know how I have lived my life. Now my life is over and suddenly it is starting again. Two separate worlds, totally different. If it goes on like this, I will want to go on living. I was at peace with my illness and approaching death. What should I do about the girl? We are starting to fall in love. I have never ever met anyone like her before, she is quite unremarkable. At the same time, she is extraordinarily interesting once you get to know her. Something like a grey rock you break open and you find an amethyst inside. I don't want to have sex with her, I'm not even capable obviously ... but the beginnings of eroticism are developing between us and she wants that. I feel thrown off course. Who is Gerrit? Who is Sophie? What can we do together? What is life really?"

I just sighed and shook my head. The Gerrit from the past no longer exists, only in memory. Those memories are, by the way, rather unbearable for the present Gerrit. A sudden breeze from the terrace made me shiver.

"I understand you very well, Gerrit. Maybe you should not have come along, it has placed you outside of reality. On the other hand, this also is real. We are, really, sitting here. Sophie is inside lying in bed, maybe she is thinking about you, is waiting for you even..."

"How can you ever know if something is right? Am I doing the right thing if I bow to her wishes? It is of course my wish also, but it seems like the umpteenth immoral act in my life, doesn't it? I could say 'in the past I would just have done it,' but that is nonsense. In the past I would not even have noticed her."

"Doubt is a necessary factor in human development, Gerrit. In the past you just did what you wanted. Now you fear that you might be in error, you no longer know how to live."

"Thanks, that helps a lot." I grumbled. "And you? Where is your doubt then?"

"Behind the doubt lies the 'Saelde', the salvation. That is actually what the word 'Beatus' means. "

Most likely that's true ... personal development does,

most likely, exist. Beato is way ahead of me, but he also managed to take me quite a way with him. A beached Gerrit now aimlessly floats around in circles…

Purposefully I went upstairs, into my guest room then straight onto the terrace. Would she be there? The terrace was empty, her curtains closed. Disappointed and in great pain I lay awake for hours. When the cock crowed, I fell asleep … .

Harmony leads to progress

That weekend in Tessin has become like a great painting proudly displayed in an empty room. I woke up again after a short sleep and struggled to find the courage to start the day. But, once I was out of bed and had opened the curtains, I felt an intense happiness. Lake Maggiore is not only a feast for the eyes, because of its gorgeous situation and the abundance of nature, one also feels the European culture which has been such a magnet for great people. People from the world of art, science and spirituality. I had regarded myself a 'great man' of course, but that balloon had burst and what is left is a pathetic, worn out little sac, with nothing in it. It has being slightly filled – with something more than air – by those two giants in my life: Beato and Sophie.

She sat in the sun when I appeared on the balcony. She jumped up and with an unexpected spontaneity threw her arms around me and kissed me three times on the cheeks. The thickened, syrupy blood in my stiff vessels, was joyfully liquefied by it. I think I even blushed and to hide that, I held her close to me.

"I missed you last night!" I whispered in her ear. "You have kept yourself hidden behind your curtains!"

I felt all of her young softness in my arms. Quickly I

pushed her away a little, but still stroked her blushing cheeks.

"I also don't know what I should do about it, Gerrit. It is a ridiculous situation, you are so right. I forget that you are almost seventy and seriously ill. For me you are just Gérard and I want to be where you are, to feel your nearness. I feel your strength, your life experience – bad or good."

Now she was stroking my cheek, it did affect me a lot.

"I don't see anything bad in you, Gérard. Maybe sometimes ... when you say stupid things. To me you are a good person. Better than those guys who I went out with before. Boys who only focussed on one thing and who can hardly talk about anything else. They imagine they know what life is all about because they manage to pick up a girl, or because they know how to fix a flat tyre or something. Your personality, in comparison, is something like ... the opera The Flying Dutchman by Wagner, compared to a song by say eh ... Robbie Williams! Do you understand ... maybe your existence is a tragedy. Yes, I do believe that it is. But I'd rather have a tragedy than a soap. Then I forget that you won't be alive for much longer, that I am still so young and that it's altogether not sensible. I love our coexistence, Gérard!"

What else could I do now but take her in my arms again? Her warmth comforted me and her love healed my loneliness. Her faith in me stirred up the flickering light in my soul.

All we did was hold each other for a long time. It seemed that the morning sun gave us permission to forget all the circumstances and to live solely in that unique recognition of each other. In that moment I discovered that there is a whole world of intimacy that isn't sexual and that doesn't even need to go there.

Eros may well be the instigator in that world ... there was definitely a physical attraction between us. Later on, I was thinking about this. You can believe that sex is the ultimate realisation of love between a man and a woman. You can also believe that there is nothing else 'behind' that, that everything about the relationship between men and women depends on 'good sex'. You cannot convince Gerrit of that. I know everything there is to know about sex, also in the way that its force influences everything else in all kinds of ways, even in non-sexual areas of life; and how that force or power can raise its head in all kind of perversions. It is my power after all!

But, now I know that before the sex, come temptation and desire. Behind, outside of it lies love, the genuine intimate relationship with the peace of knowing each other in absolute trust.

Sex with Sophie is absurd. Thanks to that absurdity I can love her … We took a boat trip on the lake, we walked along the water in Brissago and Locarno. I experienced everything completely through her youthful perception of the surrounding beauty. Gerrit was forgotten, Gérard was resurrected. I bought clothes, shoes, perfume and make-up. Not because I wanted to glamorise her, but, because it was party time. She so much wants to be a woman of the world…

"You can achieve a lot with money, although they say

you can't," she said, sitting next to me on the balcony, well turned out, after the siesta. "I thought I didn't care about appearances, but that seems to be untrue. Being well dressed gives you a feeling of self-worth. Or is that a bad thing?"

"It seems to me evidence of high development if you can have a good opinion of yourself and a feeling of self-worth without the outward trappings. But if you don't have these, can you not meet yourself half way? You shouldn't have to strive for the unattainable, surely?"

She sighed and said pondering,

"It is also because of Beato. Something very special streams out from that man. Beato is harmony itself. What music can express so divinely – occasionally anyway – that feeling you get with Beato. He doesn't really do anything but something shines out from him."

"Tell me about it!" I grinned. And I talked about my memories of my first encounters with him. She held my hand, while I talked, occasionally she squeezed it. When I was silent she said,

"Strange that it is so difficult to believe in miracles. Life is a miracle, Gérard. Also, when we later have to part, I shall keep feeling that. I will never forget how the miracle of my meeting you, has shaped me, never!"

"I have to put my finances in order. I'll get onto it on Monday."

"Don't you have a will?" Beato asked. We sat together as we had the previous evening.

"No. The boys inherit it all. I have given them all of my

properties, and a good bit of capital. And some stocks and shares. The rest I will now give clear instructions for. I hope that I won't have to go back to Holland for that. If I have to, I will. Or I will give everything away right now."

"Do you have that much, Gerrit?"

"More than one human being can endure. The grandchildren will get a bit, you, Sophie and Johannes – his enterprise will get a legacy. Then they all won't have any more worries. You just decide what you want to do with it; you can refuse it, give it away or use it yourself. It is bad money. But officially it is as white as my shirt. Could a mindful soul like you accept bad money? Bank it? Enjoy it? How is that Beato?"

He did not answer straight away. Then, very seriously, he said to me,

"I shall never refuse it, even though it were harmful to me. That I would find cowardly, hypocritical. I will make sure that it is all turned to good, like yourself Gerrit. You change with every passing day."

"Don't think for one moment that it is easy. You enabled the turn-around in me, but the courage to keep going on that path comes from the love I have for Sophie. That is my repentance Beato. The love for another human being. A completely new experience for me: rather stressful – but authentic and absolute. I want to be the very best possible Gerrit for her. I have to make sure that something good exists. Besides that, the rest of my striving and my life fall into a deep regret. A deep remorse, an unbearable remorse."

"The people who, through your doing have lost their life too early – as if you were God himself – they resent you, their reproach torments you and will torment you more and more. The degree to which you turn towards the good, is evenly balanced out with the intensity of the torment that awaits you."

"Is that a warning?"

Beato shook his noble head.

"No, I am proud of you. I mean … like a father is proud of his son, you understand me. I admire your courage, I do not want to be warning you! I just want to alert you to be vigilant and be aware of what awaits you."

"Reproach from people affects me less than reproach from God."

"It is one and the same. God causes the people to reproach, it is his reproach."

"I have to go down on my knees, Beato. However difficult that may be for me. I want to come clean with myself before I die. I want to see who I really am so that I can defend Gerrit before God."

"Before Christ, only Gérard exists. Gerrit has to fall away." Later on, I stepped out onto the balcony for a few minutes before going to bed. Sophie's curtains were open. The balcony door also. I entered her room, she was still dressed.

"I waited for you," she said.

No, we did not go to bed together. I wouldn't even be able to any more. We talked till the rooster began to crow. About Gerrit and Gérard - about Sophie and ... Sophia. I was not old and ill. I was a healthy young man in search of his identity and I had the perfect partner, for conversation and for physical intimacy.

On Sunday morning Beato took me with him to church, after which we walked along the lake shore.

"To what do I owe all this benevolence?" I asked, pondering. "A girl crosses my path, who loves me like a father or a good old friend, who completely surrenders herself to me - old Gérard. I don't think for one minute that she is after my money – because she isn't. And she doesn't think for one minute that I desire her body – because I don't. I am completely honest, for the first time in my life, because of her sincerity. She cares for the flickering spark that is Gérard, she makes it flare up with her angel breath. She does that with her trust. I could misuse her, I know how to do that. But the gate to that dirty emotive world is shut tight and the key is lost. I also have to thank you for bringing us to this place. This is the right place to love each other and to find the courage to express that love in some way. Soon we will again be in serious mountain terrain and then this episode will seem like a dream. Three days in which I was not ill and not old, not a crook or a bastard... Here I was able to start again and know how to do it right."

"You could rent an apartment and come for a holiday here with Sophie."

I laughed.

"On holiday from my illness, my age, my life? No, I don't have the energy for that any more, Beato. You both seem to forget the state I'm in, just like I do. Every step I take is difficult, is really too much effort. I am finished, really. My body craves a bed to lie down on to die, to be released from that constant pain. It's only because of my love for you both that I am still living. I still have to sort out some

of my affairs and I have to figure out who I really am."
"And how do you intend to do that, Gerrit?"
"My technique was always: never stop, just do it and direct all your energy on the problem, never allow any backsliding. I am beginning to see my true self, Beato. Believe me, that hurts more than all of my symptoms. But it has to happen. What you said yesterday about the reproach by the people I have harmed, touched me deeply. I want to examine each of those events one by one. That is not easy, because my restless soul constantly wanders off to more pleasant themes and I have forgotten, half forgotten, many of the things I have done. Still, it has to be done."
"Your father?"
"He really was a bastard. Maybe I did something good by poisoning him. He would definitely have killed my mother one day. I cannot feel any remorse there. Although, that did awaken something in me that I do regret – so maybe it was wrong after all. Ach … you meet the wrong people, that is how it went. It makes no sense to want it to have been different than it was. I have to find the courage to remember, and then to realise what I have actually done. God will surely punish me accordingly."
Beato kept quiet for a while; he was deeply touched. Eventually he spoke,
"I think it's really awful, Gerrit. You are such a very special person. You will get there, but not without suffering. Absolutely not without suffering."

Sophie sat in the back seat on the way 'home'. The flowering of our love could only last a short time, we both realised that fervently. It was already dark when we arrived at the car park of the institute. I got out with difficulty: Sophie was already at the entrance.

"I will leave you two in peace," Beato said when he had taken the baggage out of the car. He kissed Sophie, shook my hand and walked away.

"He is sweet," said Sophie while she looked after him. She hugged me and said,

"I want to stay with you, why should we be apart?"

I could not stand very well but I held myself tight. I could hardly breathe but still kissed her cheeks.

"I have to rest dear child," I said. "We will continue tomorrow, and so to eternity..."

She started to cry and I felt very troubled.

I could not get up the next day, I was so broken that I just lay there. The nurse brought me breakfast; and at ten o'clock, there was Beato, my faithful doctor.

"Is this the beginning of the dying then, Beato?" I tried to make my voice sound steady.

He looked at me for a time and did some physical examinations, brought a chair nearer and said,

"I don't think so. Your vital functions are excellent. You did too much, didn't rest. Tomorrow you will be a lot better. Stay in bed, but do get up occasionally for the circulation. No visits today."

"You mean, no Sophie? I cannot do without her."

"Better a day off now and then many days together later. Listen to the doctor, Gerrit!"

He didn't stay long, because I needed to rest. So, plenty of time for self-reflection. I can see outside from my bed; the weather is bad today. Rain and wind. I wanted to sort out my financial affairs, that will now have to wait a day or two. It is quite good this, a day of doing nothing ... I can watch TV, but then I won't be reflecting on my life. Let me have a look at my twenties and thirties. It is the time of the Beatles and the Stones, flower power and hippies, the Maharishi and Krishnamurti. All that hate against America, 'make love not war'. I had been part of a completely different stream of consciousness then. One of the main principles had been to disallow your fellow man any and all freedoms, by stealing it from them. As I have said before, I had to learn to operate centrifugally, to direct everything within me outward, with as much aggression as possible. That is the art of intimidation. You can learn that by destroying every inhibition set in motion by conscience as it comes up. Step by step, every day a bit more. Later, I taught this method to others. The powers of destruction inherent in every one, are consciously brought to the surface and directed outwards. You can even see an unconscious release of these powers with many young people today. By observing violence from childhood in a completely passive uninvolved state of being, evil is initiated. Conscience isn't necessarily destroyed but is blinded to certain black magic beginnings. Coarse 'humour', endemic in society, is, in fact, the first overstepping of the threshold of conscience towards black magic. Certain music, particularly pop music, is composed out of inspirations very familiar to me. On TV you can see how the thresholds are deliberately crossed. When you are seriously ill, like I am, you become aware that overstepping this threshold even happens in the practice of medicine. That is the positive side of my 'development'; you can't pull the wool over Gerrit's eyes, he can distinguish between noble and human caring on the one side; and consciously wanting to destroy on the other. Having chosen the other side, I know it through and through and recognise, as it were, that face hidden behind noble principles! That is the self-same face that has also been concealed behind the quite handsome tall gentleman, Gerrit. Gerrit can live in two worlds, can behave like an educated wealthy gentleman, at the same time the devil himself rules the roost, because that is the way that Gerrit wants it to be – or, rather, wanted.

I did not get much further than that with my recollections, it made me dead tired and miserable. It took till Friday before I had revived. Then I went to visit the professor to discuss my financial affairs. I had stayed out of his way somewhat because his actual presence acted as a kind of living reproach to me. We do have some things in common, he and I. We look similar on the outside though he is a good fifteen years younger than I am. He too, is a paragon of self-confident power – but the difference is conscience. With him that is very well developed; with me it is pretty well completely removed... I am his negative, as it were... I thoroughly prepared myself on the subject matter at hand. I wanted to be his match in terms of power. I would bring forth my old self one last time. A meeting between Johannes the Living and Gerrit the Dead!

I will attempt to describe the meeting as precisely as possible, because Beato is but a boy in comparison to this giant, Johannes.

His office is on the ground floor of the main building, at the back, where the sun is. His desk is placed so that he gets the sun on his left side and visitors on their right. It isn't a doctor's consulting room. It isn't a director's room either. It is a library. All the walls are covered with books, books, books and more books as wall paper. The flower of the world literature displayed on the shelves, it seems to me.

The floor is wooden and has a simple rug on it. In one corner are two comfortable chairs with a small table. But the work-space is the desk, big, covered with piles of 'work', but still, organised. In the midst of all that reigns the 'flower of mankind', this noble figure, who, as forgotten professor has no standing in society and means nothing. As already mentioned: Gerrit, don't you worry! Gerrit looks straight through the façade, in the way that he sees through all the learnedness around here – if it wasn't for the fact that this man here does *really* genuinely impress me.

Something like this is an experience. Beato is real, through and through real, by nature. This man has something that stands even above that. He is aware of his talents but doesn't misuse them. He is friendly and easy going, but you feel that a whole world exists around him and he is totally aware of it all. I am like that. I act nice too, but with me that whole world I carry around with me is no good and I know that. I pretend to be better than I am, I have to, or I would not be able to communicate with anyone. He has to put himself out as being *less* than he actually is, to be able to interact with others. My actual 'soul mate' is the devil – and his own angels … or even higher beings.

He is quite big, but not too big. He has a good-looking head, with a high forehead and a mop of wavy hair, the blond hair still quite visible throughout. Just like me, he has clear blue eyes. These blue eyes take you in and then return his warmth to you. With me, that is somewhat different. My eyes are closed, even when they are open, I reject all impressions and only focus on myself. No one enters into me - well, yes, Beato a little and Sophie quite a bit more. That is why I am now no longer who I was.

I can see that this professor has achieved self-mastery. Thereby he does not need mastery over anyone else. I see this now, afterwards, when I remember how it was then. At that moment, though, I was very impressed with this man.

He invited me to come sit by him at his desk, sat down himself and waited patiently.

"Do you know who I am? Why I am here?" I asked.

He nodded and replied,

"I have seen your file. We have seen each other before. Beato is your doctor."

"I'm not here as patient this time. Beato is the best doctor I could wish for."

Again, he silently waited. On the one hand he is still a young man and does not display any signs of old age. On the other hand, he seems as old as the hills. You feel there is something special about this man, what a heavy load this must be. I don't know what it is, but he has a seriousness that is so distinctive of him.

"I have a financial problem," I said with a smile. "A little different from other people's … I have so much money that I want to share it. I will be spending my last days here – I want to give a donation. Not after my death, but now. So, I can experience it."

Surprised, he looked at me.

"Experience it?" he asked.

"Yes, the pain of renouncing all of my wealth."

"Surely that is not necessary!"

"Are you annoyed?" I asked carefully. But he burst out laughing heartily.

"Not at all. I'm trying to figure out what the intention is."

"Look here. I have made a great deal of money – I didn't say earned, mind you – and once you have that much, it just grows by itself. I am very attached to it, it is a part of me. I wanted to be rich, and I achieved it. You understand?"

He nodded and I felt like an idiot. He did, it is true, take me in, but he didn't give anything back. It was as if I bumped into something … I said,

"It is dirty money, there's nothing honest, no good manners behind it. I didn't steal it, I made it. I don't mean that it's counterfeited, but, received for all types of jobs. Perhaps I could ask you a question instead: what should I do with it?"

"Where it comes from is not irrelevant. It does have consequential effects."

"We can certainly use financial support here. We constantly struggle. Your money would burden us – but, on the other hand, we can't survive without money … every situation has to be judged on its own merits. I'll have to discuss it with the master and with the accountant. What amount did you have in mind?"

I named an amount, one that would cause anyone else to either go pale, or blush. This professor didn't even blink an eye lid. He said,

"I'll come by to see you next week, then we'll discuss a few things further, once I've spoken to the master."

I nodded and the conversation ended. I remained seated and wanted to say something more. But what?

"What awaits me after death, professor?" I finally asked.

He leaned back in his chair, and restarted the conversation. He said,

"You are strong. Very, very strong. With your strength you can still turn around. When the power of evil changes itself into the good, then something tremendous occurs. Something that rarely happens. You could accomplish that, you have already started. But it can be done faster, stronger, more radically."

"How?"

He looked me straight in the face and said with great consideration,

"When you were young, you made a choice, maybe not completely consciously; impulsively. You didn't choose 'small', you chose 'large'. That is to say, that you gave your 'will' a particular direction. In other words, you chose evil and you worked on that direction of will, to strengthen it and make it grow; straight through everything else.

"And now, just before you die, you became aware that

you made the wrong choice. You can reflect on every single deed you have carried out and feel remorse for them. That would be good and healing. But it is the long way around, and you don't have much time. Besides, your power is in your will, not in insights. You should come to 'insight' via the 'turning of the will'. Not the other way around."

"I don't understand any of this," I said, annoyed. "Just come out with it, say what you want to say."

"That it is in the *will* that you have to turn around, instead of in the thoughts or feelings. Your will does not really *will* it yet."

"I asked: What awaits me after my death?"

"That depends on what you do now. If, before you die, you choose for the good – but then completely – then you will have that will available to you after death also. Even when the judgment about all your deeds may be overwhelmingly crushing for you; your goodwill will help you through and you will be able to spend your next life in total service to the Lord of the Good. Insights and feelings are too weak, too flighty, to change anything substantially in your case."

I felt cold and warm at the same time, cold sweat broke out. Words of comfort were not to be expected from this man!

"And how, professor, does one turn one's will around, one hundred and eighty degrees, in one fell swoop?" I asked.

And, while I asked, I realised how it should be done. But, that is just what I, in my deepest self *don't* want!

"'No-one can do this," he said thoughtfully. "But you, you can. Really you could do this!"

I shivered. I felt Death, still a little way off. From here, to there … could I achieve this Herculean task in such a short time? Weeks, maybe months?

He, over there, read my mind, and said,

"This happens outside of time. Only a fraction of a second is needed. No time at all." He stood up and said,

"Next week I will come to see you, we will then discuss two issues, won't we?"

I stood up too, but couldn't quite say goodbye yet. I said,

"What I value so much about all of you, is that you aren't hypocrites. That you take in a man like me, the same as any other. That I find so fantastic."

I shook his hand and escaped…

A creaky old cart, that's me, one that survives much longer than is comfortable. I went up the stairs to Sophie's room, hoping to find her there. We had arranged to meet for lunch, but it was now only eleven o'clock.

She was in! I hugged her paternally. She was studying, music books were spread around, her violin and bow she had laid down on the bed. She cleared one of those dreadful kitchen stools for me and with a groan, I sat down. She stroked my head.

And that gesture touched me deeply.

"What is the matter?" she asked.

"I just received the greatest compliment of my life, and, from the greatest person I have ever met, as well. Only, it's dependent on a most gruelling task, I cannot imagine being able to accomplish it. I cannot comprehend the task and still I have to carry it out."

"You speak in riddles. Weren't you with Johannes?"

"I can't understand how you can address him with his first name, really not. He awarded me 10 out of 10 for something, but with strings attached. He told me that I was unbelievably strong – and that I'd better accomplish the impossible with that strength."

"I don't get it – do you want that then? The impossible?"

"It certainly is a challenge, that's for sure." With my head in my hands I said,

"Play something for me, lassie. Something melancholic, something that makes you cry … ?"

She picked up her violin and played tenderly…

I haven't spent much time thinking in my life. Reading was limited to the newspaper and the stock market reports. I have done much 'business', and there I learned to silence my conscience. Is my conscience now re-emerging? Not really, though there are moments of regret. Those moments pass by again and much has changed for me. I live bravely – but even with that I don't experience much, it is more a question of living by abstract rules – they work, it seems, very well for me. A small spark of love lives in me, for Beato and for Sophie. Hate is silent in me for hours on end, when it does emerge, I pray, I say the 'Our Father'. I think I can keep this up till I die, though the fear for Judgement – with a capital letter – is huge.

What now. I now am supposed to question myself about what my will *wills.* Did I really want evil and do I really now want the good? What does that involve?

Maybe it is a blessing that I know so little … no philosophy, theology and all that. The only thing I have at my disposal is Gerrit, and now and again Gérard. Gerrit would then be the baddy and Gérard the goody…

Ridiculing is also such borderline behaviour that can lead to evil; you make, what is serious, into something frivolous, or something like that. Well, good - Gerrit is what I have and I shall see what he actually *wills*.

I do believe that it is fear, that drove me on my path. Fear of my father and with that, fear of power, and of death. I have come to realise that you can shout it down when you have guts, brutalism and contempt for death. A soldier in the front line has to do that too, he has no choice. But that kind of behaviour doesn't belong outside of a warzone. You have to find another way to overcome your fear. I have learned to make the destructive urges, hidden within everyone, into my own power. You live like a bullet from a projectile weapon, and that doesn't allow itself to be turned around; unless Beato suddenly appears, who gently catches the bullet, and sends it in another direction in a most charming manner. I never returned from that particular direction, no matter how many times I have attempted to, over the past fifteen years. But can I 'will' that new direction? Willing and wanting have such different connotations. The professor asked if I have the 'will', I have to turn, in the 'will'. Can I do that? Radically?

"I went to visit your boss. And I have understood that the human being has a 'will', a will that chooses; or rather that you can decide yourself which direction that you want to go – bad or good."

Beato looked at me with surprise and said,

"That seems somewhat oversimplified to me. You aren't immediately aware of your own 'will'. You are conscious of your thinking, and a little of your feeling too. Your will does remain outside of your awareness. What does Johannes mean?"

"That is what I'm investigating now. He says that I'm so strong, that I can do what no one else can. Namely, turn one hundred and eighty degrees within what I consciously 'will' (want)."

He now nodded in agreement.

"That is a possibility. You have, it is true, worked on your will power, though destructively. You have now stopped that, but there hasn't been a real 'turn-around'. That's what I mean; when I ask about your lack of remorse … But, Johannes has a much deeper insight into these matters than I do."

"Remorse is something you have to *feel.* Sometimes I do feel something like that, it makes me rather desperate. What the professor suggests feels like a challenge, I like a challenge. But I don't know how to go about it."

"Neither do I," he answered with a grin. "You will have to ask the boss himself."

That's how it was that I went to see him again, before he came to me to talk about the money. The weather was spooky, as it can sometimes be in the mountains. You can feel the overarching power of nature: with one fell swoop of wind, it could all be over.

"The weather gives us a helping hand," Johannes said

with a smile, when he greeted me. "You can *feel* the willpower here outside, as if God was frowning..."

I shivered and sat down. I was intending to experience the willpower of the scholar sitting opposite me. Courage greater than that of my most dangerous enemy! With the best will in the world I may not taunt him. He is the professor and has to be respected.

I winced and sat down.

"Here in the mountains I feel my own insignificance. That's a good thing for Gerrit to feel."

"What do you want to discuss?" he asked straight out.

"You can imagine … I have thought about what you've said. I cannot see a way to do what you suggest. You do have to help me on my way."

He nodded his head, folded his hands and said,

"I understand. Your presence here, the last time you came to see me, made me say what I experienced with you. That is, your immense power – beside your presence of mind and your alertness. In Eastern wisdom that is called 'awareness'. You have stood before the blazing fire and have constantly won – your awareness must be optimal. Though you haven't used that power for anything -" he hesitated, "well, good, it is very well developed. That awareness, that presence of mind, that perceptivity could be united with your willpower. When someone else has the intention of dedicating his willpower to do good, then that decision is watered down within a few moments; life takes over and everything remains the same. If you, on the other hand, decide to turn yourself around – then your alertness could be put to good use: to monitor, every second, your progress, to make sure you keep that promise. No one can keep that up – only you could do it."

"I haven't been in training for many years now. My 'spirit' is dulled, too comfortable. Life is safe now and not that exciting anymore. You over-estimate my capabilities," I answered.

"Do you really mean that?"

"No. I can still, without too much effort, get myself into 'alert' mode, that's true."

"Just as if your life was in danger and everything depended on you being alert?"

"Yes. I don't have to live like that, but I can of course, still do it. It is second nature to me."

"Well, then, have I helped you on your way?"

I burst out laughing. He is so direct … I nodded.

"Yes, but I do find it difficult to leave you. You have something so congenial. I do so enjoy being near you."

He gestured with his head and stood up.

"That goes both ways. But I do have to honour my next appointment. I will come by to see you one of these days."

Thunder and lightning filled the skies. I could visit Sophie, but I went outside instead. The atmosphere was loaded. I walked slowly down the path, it was going to rain, but I wanted to feel that power outside. Would man be judged with that power, or with an even greater power? I wasn't afraid – more a question of gaining courage. A few moments before I had sat opposite: something to be admired for sure. I realised full well that a miracle was about to occur in my life. That I was going to do something that was 'impossible'. I felt myself taken up within the charged atmosphere of the thunderstorm. The power that can destroy, but can also purify. Alertness … I had forgotten that power. Nevertheless it was still present, I saw, heard, smelled, felt it all, to the minutest detail. I have never understood that people notice so little – but, I have developed that gift. With me it is a super-refined *suspicion.* Would I now have to focus that on my own will? But first I'd have to turn my own will around. If only he had told me how!

Soaking wet I arrived back in my room, took a bath, and went to sit down in one of the comfortable chairs, in my dressing gown.

Deny all the details of my life so far – that is what I have to do now. And then I have to ask myself if I want to 'will' the 'good'.

I didn't manage it, to search within myself so deeply. I could feel that I had great ambitions when I was just a boy. I wanted to get away from my neighbourhood, I wanted to be somebody. I was already strong then, always had to be the boss. But, my background was no help to me. I had to become a market stall holder or a minor civil servant, like a postman or something like that. That is what drove me to choose the path I then took. I wanted more. Not the easy path particularly, it certainly wasn't easy. I wanted riches and ostentation. Well, I'm finished with that now. If I hadn't gone 'my own way' I would have become just an ordinary little man. What does it mean to be the 'good Gerrit'? Falling back down into the bourgeoisie, the common decency? Yuck, how awful. Disgusting!

I said a prayer, the Our Father. At first my mind wasn't with it. Then, when I thought about my alertness it went better … and better. Outside it was still howling. Inside, deep within me, a certain feeling started to make itself felt…

It wasn't very pleasant, that feeling. I felt that there was a being standing behind me … surely no one could be here in the room now? I turned to look behind me. No one there. Outside the rain just kept on pouring down, it gave a feeling of safety that nothing could happen, of protection. For many years I have lived with two heightened levels of awareness: safety or danger. I have developed a sense organ for that, as the native Americans are said to have. Here, everything was safe … very safe. Might I have another heart attack now, was it going to be my time for dying? I felt safe but also uneasy. Again, I felt that presence behind me. Threatening? Not really. Quite disturbing though. It also felt as if there was someone next to me. Maybe there are beings behind everyone – and next to them too. Why did I experience this now? It isn't very pleasant to have company in what was thought to be an empty room! Still, I wasn't afraid.

What would a 'Good Gérard' be like? Not a numbskull, that's obvious. He has to remain just as strong as he was, his life experiences need to keep their value as do his achievements. Gérard would have to destroy any pockets of fear still remaining. Actual 'courage' would have to replace audacity, like with the professor. I could feel that courage as a possibility, there behind me. Audacity, guts, has a rudeness in it, courage is modest. With death so near you know things you would not otherwise realise. But what does Gérard need that courage for? He is safe after all … He needs that courage to turn, that's why he needs it.

That's as far as I got. Gerrit has only ever lived facing outwards. Now it is time to look at himself and he could only manage that for a very short while. "Help me," I asked the being standing behind me. I do want to have that courage…

"You are changing," Sophie said later at dinner. "You seem less severe, less distant."

"Severe?" I asked surprised.

"You are always aware, reserved and rather unapproachable."

"The things you have managed to achieve, Sophie! With you I am actually not so wary, but relaxed and open."

"Well!" she said somewhat bewildered. "Still, you have changed."

"That's what I want," I admitted. "Do you know anyone who has turned their life around in a blink of an eye? Not bit by bit, but all at once in one fell swoop?"

"Only Francis of Assisi … but he wasn't bad to begin with … "

"Like Gerrit was bad."

"You say that about yourself."

"Sure. Do tell me about Francis? How did he do that?"

"He renounced everything he previously had. He was the son of wealthy parents. I think he even took off his clothes and gave them to the poor."

"So, I would have to give away all my possessions, give up

my room, come live in the attic with you … Don an old pair of jeans and ask the master for a job?"

"That's nuts! Francis had a deep religious conviction. Otherwise it wouldn't mean anything. Gerrit remains Gerrit, with or without money."

"Gerrit will change when he has nothing left, you can count on that."

"Yes, a peevish git, that's for sure!"

I touched her cheek lightly and said,

"That's not very nice. So, I have to have a vocation?"

"I would think so. And then, not just any old vague idea, like: 'from now on I will be good'. That just won't do."

"How come Sophie doesn't want to be 'bad'? Why is she such a good girl then?"

She blushed, and looked adorable with it. There was eroticism between us which we both enjoyed. She said,

"Flirting with a man almost fifty years my senior is not exactly being a 'good girl'. Everyone has an opinion about us. Just about everyone."

"You know exactly what I mean."

"Yes." She grabbed me by the hand; other peoples' opinions were of no concern to her. "I care more about creativity, about beauty, about truth. That is just natural to me. I couldn't just destroy anything, I can't even want it or *will* it. I don't want anyone to have pain, or sadness – then I feel compassion."

I shuddered.

"Do you have sympathy for me then?" I asked.

"Maybe I do," she said, honestly. "But I do really care about you very, very much, Gérard. Precisely because you can be so *kind,* so full of understanding, so sweet … I want to comfort you, you are so lonely."

I again shuddered. Well, yes … if your motives are the other person's feelings … then everything changes.

"I also love creativity, my child. That is the beauty of youth, your beauty … "

"How could you ever want to destroy life, cause pain, torture?"

I felt shame rising up in me. From her mouth … the last judgement. She was innocent and wise.

"That's what hate does. Intense, deep-felt hate."

"Well then, that is where the turn-around needs to be then. Would you ever want to do me harm?"

I looked directly at her and said, truthfully,

"That is a possibility, yes. I know how to go about that." I thought: I could totally annihilate you, but I said nothing. She didn't get scared, the brave child. She looked straight ahead back at me and said,

"You are indeed a shit, Gerrit!"

"It would be a lot worse if I pulled the wool over your eyes."

She had let go of my hand and now grabbed it again. Slowly she replied,

"I'll take that risk. Have taken it already."

I squeezed her hand and said,

"I will turn, my dear."

Together we walked through the bright evening air. I placed my arm around her middle, felt her slim hips, and felt that I had to control myself. She pointed out a little bird, jubilating in the half light.

"You should feel the life within that little creature, Gerard. And the cheerfulness … "

"I can hardly stand it, sweetheart. I have tried to practise the opposite, the turn-around."

She stood still, and also put her arm around me, which made her even closer to me.

"Please, feel it, Gérard!" she begged.

She could not have imagined the effect she was having on me, how I had to control myself.

I forced myself to look at the little bird on the branch along the path, to hear it jubilate. There wasn't exactly that much difference … Sophie was also a singing little bird. The greatest joy of my life. I pressed her against me and said,

"I *have* to turn-around, Sophie. He says that I can do it. I will do it… "

She brings her gift, her offering. She gives her youth, her future, her life, for the healing of an old man…

Ach, well, it is just a few months, maybe a year … No, her life will never be the same. Her meeting with me will affect her whole life.

She gives herself to me, not physically – though she would have done that too – she offers her whole being. I have never experienced that before, the total surrender of one human being to another. She is my repentance. Not Beato, not the professor … but Sophie.

Beat is the *spark of good* in my will, Johannes is the example of the motive. But Sophie is the ground wherein both have to be sown to come to fruition…

The biggest obstacle is still the dissatisfaction. The problem of not being able to accept the situation as it actually is. To not want to begin with what you have, but to force what you don't have. Because you are so angry about your fate, about the fact that you have been given less than who knows who. It starts already in childhood. You look at the sons of rich parents – in so far that they enter your field of view. Everything that is more and better than what you possess, you want to have too. You will and you must have it, no matter what the price. It isn't even about that gorgeous shiny red pedal car, or the toy train set. Not even the new bike … it's all about position, image and honour. The honour of attending the best school, of learning about the tasting of good red wine … Being able to sail a boat and of going to university. None of that was available to Gerrit. And he was lazy to boot. His mother was a whore and his father a badass. Gerrit did not accept these conditions, he always felt cheated. Cheated by whom? By the injustice itself. I am of the opinion that all socialists suffer the same afflictions as Gerrit, deep down. They are dissatisfied, regard their meagre lot and demand sympathy from those others that have more. So, they have to remain poor and 'normal'. Maybe a socialist is even worse off than Gerrit. Gerrit is at least honest, he has realised his disdain, and just stole everything that he wanted for his own enjoyment. The socialist also does that, while hiding behind the mask of social morality, the solidarity of the weak. Well, maybe I exaggerate a little, I know that … There are also 'sincere' socialists. But I don't like them in any case. They are so unnatural and it makes no sense no matter how you look at it. For myself, I am as right-wing as they come, always have been. Had I been born in earlier times I could easily have become a fascist. But now I have met these fellows here. They have freedom. They are free men, but, they do experience a kind of love. Not mealy mouthed, sweet, but fierce and knight-like.

I tried to order my thoughts. Thoughts about myself, about the men – and the girl – around me. Gerrit is also a knight, a black one…

The professor came to visit. It was a festive occasion. The weather was radiant, the doors to the garden were open and we went to sit on the terrace. I had so much wanted to have a friend like this when I was younger! Here we were, a middle-aged man and one, soon to be elderly – if he ever makes it that far!

"Can I get you something to drink?" I asked.

"Perrier, please."

Here they don't say Spa water or Still or Sparkling water, they say Perrier or Pellegrino. I took two bottles from my fridge and opened them. I added two glasses to accompany them and we quenched our thirst.

"What is your answer?" I asked him.

He laughed happily and said,

"Just give it all away! We don't mind."

He lifted his glass and drank. More serious now he said,

"We don't want it for ourselves, obviously. A trust will have to be set up, a fund. Something like that. We have a friend, a lawyer, he will sort it all out. The best thing would be if you managed it yourself."

"Well, that won't be for long then, professor!"

"You don't know that, you never know. In any case you would be doing us a great service if you agreed to remain in charge."

"I just wanted to get rid of it all!" I grinned. "But it will be an interesting experience for me: to find an interest in something that isn't for myself."

"Are you sure you want to go ahead with it?"

"I'm sure, yes. It doesn't matter to you one way or the other, does it?"

"Oh yes. I feel grateful – the organisation here is more and more under pressure, the most effective way to deal with that would be to raise the prices up so high that it won't be viable for visitors anymore. Everything is getting so expensive that only the biggest companies can afford to stay in business. Independent people are a big threat to big business. Your gift makes our organisation - from a financial point of view – into a big company. Instead of having to shrink our activities, we can expand them. I warm to that! I just don't want to – you will understand that – start to enjoy those thoughts too much." I did enjoy myself. I enjoyed the sun, the man beside me, the sound of his voice, the thirst quenched by the Perrier. I enjoyed looking forward to having more days to live ... ten, twenty, a hundred? I would be involved with the direction of this institute as patron. It was my first 'good' deed. Small change for me, but, for the man beside me a deed with tremendous consequences...

He offered me his friendship in way of compensation.

Not that he 'paid' me with it, it just simply happened that way. At my request I was given a room in the main building, instead of my old room. My pills could be taken anywhere and I might have another heart attack which, as far as I was concerned, might as well be effective. The attic room next to Sophie's would have been fine with me, but they gave me a room on the ground floor, with a bit of South facing garden. Much too nice for a poor fellow like me – but to be really poor was probably an impossibility now, at my age. Johannes – that's what I can call him now – did not allow me to give it all away. I am to keep a good-sized bank balance and I also held money back for Sophie and Beato, my companions in the winter of my life. The remainder I gave away and I felt a great burden lift. I will make sure that it keeps on growing, but it isn't my business anymore.

I was invited to attend a meeting. I have, it is true, attended many a business get-together, in many different guises. A business meeting would be a cinch for the likes of me, you'd think. But I was not looking forward to this meeting at all, I worried that I might not be fit enough to manage it. Although I would be playing the role of Santa Claus here, I felt, of course, more like Black Pete … joking aside – I had to face two giants there.

The master received me in the conference room. Just as usual, I noticed every detail, I was in a state of total awareness. A beautiful old Indian table stood in the middle of the room surrounded by rattan chairs with white cushions.

The windows were dressed with red curtains giving the room a somewhat regal look, but still quite Eastern also... A bouquet of summer flowers, undoubtedly from the garden, stood on the table. Cups, tea, coffee and cakes were there too. A different kind of meeting than your usual one then.

The master stood at the window, dressed all in black, but with his radiance he somehow made that black look *coloured.* I was still afraid of him. Even though I had given a present – it would not affect his sternness obviously. You expected to see a sabre with which he could slice your head off – or a simple and elegant thrust into your proud face. But, nothing doing, the master was nice, he had a kindly smile despite all he could see in me. He shook my hand warmly and I was invited to sit down at the table. He sat down opposite me, with a peace-loving manner, and said softly,

"I am aware that you have undertaken this act for yourself, Gerrit. But by doing so, you save us too. The financial abyss beckons. These past fifteen years we have had to dip into our reserves, and we're now on the edge of the abyss, you know?"

"Let's not talk about that here, sir. Even if you had money to burn, I'd give you all I have. Things are good here and I have no one else. Do see it as a completely business-like transaction, not a bid for anything, or something like that."

He nodded his head.

"I understand, let's talk no more about it. Today we only want to introduce you to the directors. We have someone here who runs the business side of things, he always used to be my right-hand man. He will work with you, you will need to train him up -"

"- in order for him to carry it on after my death."

"Precisely." said the master, smiling kindly.

The professor entered the room accompanied by the man we had just been discussing. A Doctor Stern. A philosopher with a talent for finance, for accounting. He seemed dry but flexible, and devoted to the master. He is tall and thin, a bald head from all those sums, spectacles with, behind them, trusting brown eyes. Pale from hours behind a computer, but softened by the Eastern influences. A barrel of opposites and still harmonious. I thought him a bit of a wimp, to be honest. Rather common, maybe even a socialist. Most likely he was a bit scared of me, the evil Gerrit. But, he did look me in the eye, shook my hand with vigour, and took me on with genuinely charming laughter. He greeted me in beautiful Swiss-German. I almost wanted to spend time together with this man, to add and subtract and multiply and especially to divide…

Johannes watched us and began to laugh. I shivered. People can be really *great.*

You can feel how they are placed outside of the norm. The master and the professor. Sun up and sun down – the one light even bigger than the other. Narrow minded Gerrit, imprisoned in his safety harness to protect him from danger, receives through these two giants a glimpse of eternity and infinity. Time that has no beginning or end … space that extends ever further, further and further. A glimpse of holiness, in which I don't believe…

I bowed my proud head for a moment and experienced

my own poetic mood. Normally I would run a mile from that, start to ridicule. That did not work here. Neither the master, nor Johannes punched me in my self-satisfied face – but doctor Stern, the disciple, did. He was called Heinrich. Tame Henry and good Gérard, the two financial wizards. He has opinions about me and makes sure that I know it. He owns nothing, doesn't want to have anything, as he is an original Buddhist. He shouldn't have opinions either, of course, but he does. He doubts that I earned my money in an honest manner – how could he! I am a challenge for him, he isn't for me. Except when I get such a slap in the face, figuratively speaking of course. These Buddhists have something cruel about them.

"Can I call you Heinrich? Just call me Gérard, that's easier than Gerrit. A bit classier also … Do you know anything about the stock market, how it works and what you have to look out for?"

He shook his noble head doubtfully and said,

"Very little. I don't think it is a very sensible way of handling money. But it will have to be done, now. This is too much to put in the bank."

"You can make a full-time job out of it, you can also let it run a bit. You need to get a feeling for it. I will teach you how to do that."

We sat together at one desk in his room. In front of us lists of numbers, small and large sums, added together a nice amount of capital.

"You can use the interest produced freely. But you must never touch the actual 'stocks'. You can move them around, but never use them up."

"I do understand that," he said nippily.

I grinned, but went on unperturbed, with my lesson. After an hour he was exhausted and we called it a day.

"What do think of this?" I asked.

He looked at me with his kind brown eyes and said, slowly,

"I have to be positive. The continuation of this institute. It is great that you are doing this, Gerard."

Satisfied I shook his hand and went to see Sophie.

She helped me to move rooms. A suitcase with clothes and toiletries. That was all that was left of my possessions. The man who once sailed on the Mediterranean in his yacht, with this and then with that beauty at his side ... now had only one suitcase and a music student to help him carry it. He had gifted all his physical possessions to his progeny and his capital into the hand of the Buddhist philistine. He had kept a digital wallet, a few pennies to keep him going till he took his last breath.

"That is quite an achievement!" Sophie said. "You are no longer a patient now!"

"Beato will still visit me. And, my bones still let me know that I am a patient."

She pulled my suitcase on wheels along behind her and gave me her other arm.

"We can now sleep under one roof, in any case, and you will still live for a very long time."

When we arrived at my new room, she opened the terrace doors, put my clothes away and arranged my toiletries in the bathroom. It all was rather intimate ... I felt the eroticism in it all. Here there was a double bed, she could just stay here … I went outside onto the terrace to sit. A few moments later I felt her small hand on my neck, her lips on my forehead.

"So," she said, satisfied. "This is better than the hospital room. How will you now go on Gerard?"

"Go on?" I asked.

"With your 'turn around'? Your complete turnaround?"

"I have been rather too busy with all those meetings. If I'm not careful I will be the 'Big man' again – and that is just what I wanted to distance myself from."

"That's why I mention it."

"You are the guardian of my soul's well-being. Or rather: the initiator. There isn't yet that much well-being. It all depends on 'will'. A radical choice has to be made for the 'good will', then this good will has to be nurtured and guarded with the utmost awareness. That's easy to say. But it makes me want to ridicule the whole process – which I then do. There is, now, within me, something that does want to *'will'* the 'good', but my emotions do not go along with it. Hate remains, that's why I criticise and ridicule. That guy, for example, that Heinrich. I hate guys like that. I try to overcome it, but he is a first-class bastard, that chap – while he pretends, with his Buddhism, to have overcome all egoism. He hates me too. To him I embody everything that should *not* be."

"Do you never have feelings of love, of wanting to do good, of generosity, sacrifice … you name it?"

I looked at her, she moved me. The girl Sophie. She lives her life questioning, full of wonderment, filled with worship, even for me. Particularly for me. She is in harmony with me by her sacrifice, she resonates with me. She is music. My soul is her violin, she is the bow. She plays on me, and under her capable hands I become music … I nodded and felt a huge wave of Humility coming over me; I let it flow, and nodded to her.

"Oh yes child. I want to be your instrument … to learn from you, how you are. To be in harmony with you … I love you Sophie. Only, the eroticism mustn't get the upper hand, for therein lies all selfishness."

"So, what is so bad about that? It's fine with me if you look at me with such pleasure. Then I get the feeling that I am a pretty girl, desirable for a man like you."

"That's why I let it happen, just a little. Only a little. You do understand that it has to remain only a little … "

Devotion leads to atonement

It is not necessarily unpleasant to do some things in life totally differently. It is obvious that I have lived completely for myself, always. That is why I know for a fact that things have become very different now. My life is done and I must give it up, so it is a simple thing to take my leave of it. What I still have is meant for others. First of all, there are my days, which are numbered. They are pretty much all intended for Sophie. For some still inexplicable reason she has developed a deep love for me. My own feelings towards that are twofold: on the one hand it makes me feel very grateful and I feel a certain pride; on the other I feel shame. I have, after all, nothing to give her apart from a fat wallet – which she isn't after, I know that for sure. I've a finely tuned sense of suspicion, I would know if she was after my money. What does a girl want from life with a man ready for palliative care? The psychologists would have a field day with her unconscious motives. But for me, the wary one, I know her motive, it is love – and I feel deeply ashamed. Devotion leads to atonement. You can, of course, devote all your days to a loved one - and I do love her very much – that alone is insufficient evidence that you are not just living wholly and completely for yourself. I can honestly say 'not wholly and completely'. A little, but by and large I am devoted to her. That is a wonderfully strange feeling.

"Dear Sophie, we are getting closer to September, when you will be leaving. What will you do?"

"Leave? Not on your Nellie! I am staying with you as long as you live. "Till death do us part." That is an unbreakable promise, Gerard."

"You have to think about your future."

"That is not possible. I am living now, not then. Imagine if I were to leave – my whole heart would remain here. Just let me, Gérard."

"Maybe I will still live for another ten years. These past few months I certainly haven't deteriorated."

"That would make me very happy. Then I will stay with you for another ten years."

"Can you stay? Does Johannes approve?"

"Of course, I have already arranged it."

"Good," I admitted and I felt strongly that I too could devote myself to her. I will dedicate myself to her well-being. If she offers up her young life, I also must offer up mine...

The second thing I set in motion 'for others' is my financial expertise. I have quite a lot of work to do to make sure that transferring this is a success, and to train Heinrich. There is friction between us and I am trying to turn that into something positive by showing interest in him personally.

"How did you end up here, Heinrich?"

"I studied philosophy, graduated and didn't feel satisfied. I came in contact with the Master at a lecture he held in

Zurich. It was the era of the Maharishi, of Krishnamurti, of all kinds of Eastern influences blowing into the West. The Master taught more or less classical Buddhism and I was on fire – more for him than for his teachings initially. When this old hotel was taken over for conversion to a meditation centre, I was the first to sign up as a student – and also the last, apparently. The Master is a hero - a real holy man. I followed his lessons and achieved as much as a rational Western person can. I placed my ego into his service and do what he asks or demands."

"And the professor? Don't you disapprove of him?"

He shook his head slowly.

"The Master loves him. That is enough."

"And you, what is your relationship with Johannes?"

"He is the leader here – and that is how I see him too. I know that I don't have qualities like that. One has to be realistic."

I didn't get a very clear impression of him. This Westerner had managed to achieve the Eastern art of impenetrability.

In the third place I wanted to make Johannes into a friend. He had given me his friendship but how do you respond to that? I was completely out of his league. I had nothing. His scholarship, his inner nobility, his love. Nothing. What then can you give someone in return? I had given my wealth, but that is nothing. That is a signature on a piece of paper from an accountant. I wanted to give something of myself and I discovered there was only one thing, to try to implement his call to 'repentance', to turning myself around.

Finally, there was Beato, the founding father of all this.

Faithfully he came to see me four days a week in my new room. He prescribed all kinds of drops and powders, but it was his healing presence that worked in particular.

"Beato, I have to tell you something. We have known each other now for more than fourteen years. This morning I realised how much I have changed – and that is because of you. I have cursed you, many times, have accused you of doing this to me ... but today, I want to thank you. You have demonstrated by your life, that a good man, an honest man, a handsome man, can also be strong. That the very qualities I so prized in myself can also be natural and then naturally aimed at the good. You were the most beautiful, the most aware and perceptive boy that I ever encountered. Even though I am one hundred percent 'hetero' – I could easily have fallen for you – I did fall for you! You are the only one who has ever conquered me. There must have been a knight like that in history, who won every duel, a good knight. You were such a knight, and still are. Everything you touch turns to gold, even Gerrit. The lead bullet he had instead of a heart ... is starting to shine, has turned a little into gold. I am so happy, my boy. I want to thank you for that. I have had a terrible time, but now a new era has begun. I even think it sad that I am dying. I can't imagine that it will be quick. Maybe I should have some tests done – I don't need to know the results, though. Forget it, I will see what happens. I still have pain, so it is still there, but it seems less penetrating. I thank you, son. Here I have friends, and a girl-friend – and, most important, I am beginning to understand that I must be a friend to them myself!"

I had touched him. He sat, as always, relaxed, facing me, a bit shy from all the praise I'd heaped on him. He didn't recognise me like this.

"I haven't done anything intentionally Gerrit, it just happened to work that way."

"That is why it was so radical, because it was natural. I couldn't have handled a 'technique'. But now, fourteen years on, you have more work to do with that blessed nature. You have outgrown it, haven't you? What are you still doing here anyway? Are you learning anything?" He nodded his head.

"My healthy balanced nature enables a healthy balanced thinking. This drew me to Johannes. In this place I have learned to look into myself at my own conscience, with that healthy well-balanced thinking. That thinking can see itself – and there is no obstacle at all."

"What kind of obstacles could there be?"

"If the thinking is unhealthy and unbalanced, it sees itself, with the help of itself, as a kind of cripple. That would then need to be cured first of all – that is a long and difficult process of self-education. I don't need to do that, which makes it all much easier."

I paid close attention and asked,

"What is the point of looking inwards?"

"That essence within us, which is constantly busy looking for meaning, is made conscious, its own meaning becomes understood. You then begin to see that nature is the consequence of the search for meaning – not the cause of it."

I can't say that I understood much of this. To write this down I had to ask him to repeat it, and repeat it again. But, even though I didn't understand it, I did feel something. I felt the presence of Johannes. What he described with this is the quality that Johannes has, what he is through and through. I had thought he was a scholar, he had been professor, after all. But I now realise that it was this, what Beato described. That is why Johannes is a king. His crown is what Beato has learned from him. It is precisely what I had wanted to possess myself, the reason I entered onto the opposite path: to use unhealthy, unbalanced thinking to destroy good natural instincts so that they didn't bother me anymore. Then, to let nature speak … and she speaks with great might ... but there is no crown, only physical power, emboldened with magic if need be. I trembled and quickly pushed those thoughts away from me. I continued this conversation the next day. I asked,

"What are the consequences of finding meaning? I mean ... why do you make all this effort?"

"Can you remember how it all went Gerrit?" I smiled and replied,

"I have read the lesson several times over."

"Healthy, well-balanced thinking – is the thinking which is truth, it is the 'real idea in reality'. It is perceived by itself. Therefore, something streams through it, like a river through the landscape. It is the good self that reveals itself there, the Idea of the good. But as a reality. They are real impulses that you can feel, experience, and, which you could translate into love."

"Well, yes, you were already like that though."

"But not consciously. Now I am developing the awareness of that - that means a lot."

"Never mind, it is all a bit too much for me! Let me go away and think about it – after the weekend you can test me. This is all foreign to me – my nature is far from healthy and my thinking is undeveloped. But I want to know it, even though I cannot do it on my own."

He looked at me sharply and said,

"Gerrit, if you did *know* what this means, you would realise that you have just developed the first bit of healthy and well-balanced thinking – even though you *can't*!"

Happiness is very vulnerable. You have only just realised that you are happy – and the feeling is gone again. I received an enormous slap in the face from a direction I had thought completely safe before. And it shouldn't have been a slap either! It was Saturday morning, the first one in my new room. Sophie and I always dine together after which we spend part of the evening together. We are always apart during the night. I sat, reading the newspaper, on the terrace when Sophie came, much earlier than usual. She came to sit next to me and I could sense her insecurity.

"Just come out with it," I said, concerned.

"How do you know that something is up?" she asked.

"Well, I may be a godless person, but I'm also a psychologist – I've had to be. I feel things and what I feel at this moment doesn't feel good to me. So, do please loosen the tension."

"Tomorrow there is a coffee concert as you know. I will be playing together with a boy who has been here for a week. He has asked me to go out to dinner with him tonight. I didn't want to just say 'yes', without asking you first."

I kept shtum. How could I have expected that something like that would affect me like this? I didn't want her to give up her life, did I? That she might find a good man? Make a beautiful career? Apparently, I didn't want to face that. Only after my death, not now. Now it affects me so very deeply. Not to a young musician!

"You don't approve," she sighed.

"I'll cancel."

I sat up straight.

"Of course, it's all right. Fine. Perfect. You mustn't feel tied down, but free. You really don't need my permission."

I stood up and moved in front of her, stroked her cheek and took her well beloved face in my hand. "But Sophie ... I do not want it, you understand! I never expected you to do something like this. I assumed you were there completely for me, exclusively. You have turned to me with so much love. Well, I am in shock. I know I shouldn't be, but I am, shocked!"

"I really don't feel like going, but -"

"Why are you, then? Because you thought it might be fun to do something different for a change and to talk to someone your own age? You are so right, child. Just go! Only I do think it terrible."

I sat down again and turned away from her.

"I just couldn't say 'no'."

"You are ashamed that everyone always sees us together."

"No."

"Well, what?"

"I have to play together with him, he is nice – and I couldn't say no." she replied.

"You shouldn't feel you have to."

"What do I do with you Gérard? You want me to live a normal life but when it comes to it you'd rather I didn't!"

"I think you should lead a normal life – but I do not want it!"

I could feel an abyss developing between us for the first time. Suddenly she was just a young girl with desires.

"Just go, get out of my sight, go to Vienna – at least then I won't know all the things you get up to!"

She sighed again and groaned,

"You don't understand. I want to stay with you, but you yourself won't allow it. 'Because it isn't proper'. And then, when I want to do something else – you won't allow that either. So, actually, I'm not allowed to do anything! Not choose you – nor go my own way."

That did hit the mark, obviously. There is an ordinary little man within Gérard, who, through unselfishness rejects the claim on Sophie. Meanwhile he demands all of her, too.

"Good. You go out for dinner with that chap. I will wait till you come home; come by to say goodnight, OK?"

She stood up and kissed me on the cheek and went away. Away!!!!

Time dragged on. Every moment I was aware of her sitting at a table with that guy. Her laugh, her lovely gaze, her voice, her gestures – all for that juvenile, that baboon! Maybe he will try to kiss her soon. What will she do then?

It was taking far too long. She left at seven and at half past ten she still hadn't returned. I had grabbed my mobile three times already to phone her and put it away again each time.

"I have no hold on her and wouldn't want that either!" I said to myself. "She is young and beautiful – thanks to the self-awareness and the clothes she now has, courtesy of me – and she must get on with her life!"

But my feelings were saying something very different. I was angry at her, that she made me wait so long. A girl, making Gerrit wait! I picked up my mobile phone for the fourth time and dialled through – voice mail! I jumped up and began walking back and forth. Finally, at five to twelve, there was a knock on the door.

On the doorstep stood a lovely young girl. Sophie. I really wanted to lay her over my knee, even though I had never yet hurt a woman – not one that was my girlfriend, anyway. But I have also never ever yet loved a woman. Maybe my father did love my mother? In any case, I love this girl, standing on the threshold, to a ridiculously degree. I pulled her into the room and pushed her in the direction of her chair.

"Where have you been?!" I shouted.

"Shhhhh! You have neighbours!"

"Answer me!"

"We went to see a film. I couldn't easily call you, could I?"

"Did he kiss you?"

"He tried, yes. Listen Gérard. You are going to have to make a choice. I made my choice long ago - but you haven't. Because you do not want to tie me down."

My anger disappeared like air from a balloon.

"It cannot be, Sophie, dearest child..."

She came and sat on my lap and I was even more confused.

"Let it go Gérard. Isn't it good the way it is? We aren't doing anything wrong are we? We want this, don't we? We don't live like husband and wife but we do adore each other. What is wrong with that?"

I pulled her toward me and kept quiet. What is wrong with it?

I sat in the first row, waiting for the concert to begin. I was always there, whenever she played and I always sat in the front row. This was at least the tenth time that I had prepared myself for a concert of classical music. I was getting slightly used to it, sometimes I even enjoyed a passage. But I was particularly in awe of the first violinist, who directed and was so completely master of her art. In the meantime, I had learned all the gestures that musicians make when they play without a conductor. The looks of understanding between them, the bow held a little higher ... but today she would be making music with that bloke, and I would see him in action. He was the cellist in the string quartet... He turned out to be quite a handsome guy, well into his twenties, with dark brown curls and light blue eyes. He, too, was master of his instrument. He, too, let us see and hear incredible ability. They had practised together, you could see what they'd agreed previously with the slight nods of the head and little hand movements. I felt totally excluded from that musical world. I didn't recognise the – serious - music, thought it more beautiful to hear than to watch. And I felt a piercing jealousy. Sophie looked gorgeous, in her long – new – black skirt with the minuscule summer top. She had had her hair lightened a little by the hairdresser which gave her more radiance, as did the make-up she had started to wear on my recommendation. That guy wouldn't even have noticed her had she not become so beautiful under my influence … After it was over I went to see the four musicians in the room behind the stage … I kissed Sophie on the cheek and shook the other three by the hand. The fellow looked at me insolently with his light blue eyes and said in affected Dutch,

"How do you do ... my name is Floris. Are you Sophie's father? Grandfather?" I looked at him sharply and said with a grin,

"No, I'm her grandson! Can I offer you children an ice cream? Step into to Grandpa's automobile, we'll go into town and eat pizza and ice cream."

I noticed how he recoiled. I opened the buttons on my jacket to show my chest and said truthfully, and with sarcasm,

"My revolver is in my bed side table. Unloaded. So, there is no need to be afraid."

They burst out laughing and Sophie blushed.

"Grandpa will pay," I added, after which the two others greedily said "yes"; and so, Sophie and Floris had to come too.

Once outside I lit a cigarette and stepped forth, confident in my image as a hard, successful businessman. The young people climbed into my still rather new Jaguar; I slid behind my sporty steering wheel and tore out backwards, and drove competently around hairpin bends down the hill. Sophie sat – now somewhat pale – beside me, the other three were in the back.

They knew us in the Pizzeria, we were given a good table straight away on the terrace under a big umbrella. I lit my second cigarette and said, holding the menu in one hand and blowing smoke,

"You all played well. What was it, actually?"

Floris answered,

"A string quartet by Schubert and one by Beethoven. It did indeed go well yes, especially Sophie, she really plays fantastically well. She just carries us along!"

We ordered. They wanted to drink some wine after all that concentration, even though it was only one o'clock in the afternoon. I really did feel like an old man now, listening to the musicians' stories, reminiscing about their performance.

I also realised that my jealousy was unfounded. Floris was a handsome fellow, a little simple perhaps, a bit 'wet', a nerd I think it's called. A Harry Potter, very gifted but a bit of a simpleton.

Sophie was much further developed than this boy, she deserved a man of the world – like me, I said to myself with a bit of a smirk, but then a bit younger and a bit more accommodating. I am not clairvoyant, I am only trained to be aware. But with that I did experience the significance, the exalted status that Sophie possessed and the narrow-mindedness of the boy Floris.

I was utterly in pieces, on returning to my room. That was how I experienced my illness; the exhaustion really was abnormal. I shut the curtains and lay down on the bed. Sleep didn't happen just like that, so I started deliberating.

The pains in my limbs gradually abated, which always gave a me a feeling of light, of bliss … Within that bliss I felt myself, as I now am. Slowly but surely there isn't much left of the old Gerrit.

During the lunch, this afternoon, I was acting like him, but it isn't 'me' anymore. I still remember what he was like but it is another person, the old Gerrit. I am very grateful to destiny, for bringing people my way who have changed me this much. Long ago I had a friend who lived in Argentina, he was about twenty years older than me. He's probably dead by now, though some of these guys can be ninety or a hundred. As a German he did his very best during the war, to be a 'good' German, you know what I mean. With a glass of Champagne in his hand he loved to tell me about his greatest passion, which he still had. He hadn't a grain of remorse or doubt in his mind, nothing. I found it very instructive to spend time with him ... but when I think back on it, I don't get it, I don't understand that guy at all. Had he never met anyone like Beato or Sophie? How would things have turned out for me without them? Perhaps I would have spent my years in jail? Or maybe I would also have had to escape to another part of the world? By now I have lived quite innocently for fifteen years or so and feel that I can meet death in safety. The strange thing is he doesn't seem all that close any more. For months I felt death so very near; could, as it were, look him in the eye. I had the feeling that every day was a gift, a miracle. I do still have that, but a vista of a future has arisen all by itself... Weeks, months … Gerrit was given a little time to do what he had to do: to turn himself around.

Gently she knocked on the door and came in hesitatingly. I sat up, smoothed my hair down and said in surprise,

"You are early my girl?" She sat down on the edge of the bed and I think I noticed traces of tears. She took my hand and said,

"I found this afternoon horrible."

I laid my arm around her,

"Why?"

"They don't understand any of it, can't really expect them to, either. Floris feels incredibly superior, because he is young and talented. You, you behaved like a criminal in a Mafia film – which was also very tedious. It has destroyed me completely, Gérard."

"I was so, so tired. We should just live normally like we both want to. The rest can look – or look away … But why are you so unhappy?"

"It is all so difficult, Gérard. I thought that you were angry with me and that was why you were behaving so strangely. I so much want to be completely at one with you, our thoughts and feelings in complete harmony … ."

I was deeply moved and said softly,

"But Sophie … I am only scared I will lose you, that's all. I am never angry with you, that isn't even a possibility! Through you I can still learn what life is really about. For me, it was just a whirl of one thing after another, total ruthlessness; now, I enjoy the simplest details, find peace therein..."

"I would like to return to the conversation about the complete turn-around of the 'will', Johannes."

I had made another appointment with him to discuss

things further. We sat together in his room in the main building. If you can get past the bracing nature of his presence – somewhat like going through freezing cold seawater on the 1st of January – you come to an extraordinarily kind, intimate human being who empathises with your lot, as if it were his own. You can almost feel how he aligns himself with you and, with amazement, experiences your foibles – but only when you ask it of him. Neither he, nor the master would observe you in all your nakedness, without your permission.

And, even if there were only one very small point of light within you, that is precisely what he would focus on and would try to foster. In me, he praised the quality of awareness and, with that, my developing recognition of my own willpower.

"The road to holiness is long and hard," he said. "A schooling of the art of thinking is necessary to achieve it, preferably scholastic thinking, which would then also need to be 'forgotten' again. It wouldn't occur to me to suggest a path like that for you. Your life has not been like that, you cannot connect to something that isn't there."

"I wasn't exactly searching for holiness … ." I muttered.

"Oh yes you are. For you there is no middle way between good and evil. Evil has after all already prevailed?"

I cast my eyes down and nodded.

"The road of letting things happen gradually is not realistic. Of course, you do change gradually without doing anything. In the months that you have been here you have become a different person. But you have been living an outward life only. If you really want to take a step forward, it will have to be done in an extreme manner."

"I do get it, you know. You had already convinced me, it's just the 'holiness' … you know."

"Let's use the word 'goodness' then; the development of true virtue, that encompasses all human integrity and morality."

I felt very small – and it was a good feeling. With this man you could feel small without any fear at all. He would offer you his hand and help you to become as large he was.

"You should try, for a week, to focus your awareness on your own behaviour and on your ... impulses. On what comes up in you in the way of wishes and desires … Not on your feelings but on what you want."

With my wakefulness, I noticed straight away that I wanted to protest, and I let it be. I nodded and said,

"I get it. I will do what you have said and next week I will report back. I will pay close attention to my impulses, in the same way that I always paid close attention to my enemies' behaviour. I will be my own enemy, Johannes. That is what you mean don't you?"

He smiled and said,

"That is exactly what I mean."

It was as if he'd turned on the light. It ruthlessly lit up my inner drives and impulses. I knew the instincts and impulses of my enemies so well! Now I was seeing them in myself, every movement, every impulse was experienced so intensively that it hurt. The pain in my bones was nothing compared to this encounter with my own life of desires and impulses. In every movement, and every impulse that triggers a movement I saw something ugly. This enemy is the biggest egoist I have ever come across. Every breath he takes he takes only and exclusively for himself. And everything is speeded up, I must have to be always in a hurry I guess, in case I miss something…

I kept this up for an hour, maybe two with constant intermissions, within which it seemed that the will activity sucked up my self-awareness. Then it didn't work anymore, with all the good intentions in the world I couldn't make it happen again. When I met Johannes again I said,

"I do believe you have underestimated something."

I noticed that the look in his eyes became sharp for a moment, but he listened submissively and with resignation to what I had to say.

"Look, I may well have great awareness but, the problem is that it is intertwined with my will, and my instinctive life. There is no room in between. My will reacts like a reflex to my consciousness – when necessary. For the rest, my awareness floats on top of my instincts, is one with it. I never look back, that is not a possibility. The training was precisely focused to prevent awareness functioning as conscience, to only ever direct it outwards. For a short time after our discussion the last time, it worked, probably because of your influence and presence."

Johannes did not only listen with complete devotion, he really participated, he tried to copy within himself what I told him, that's how he revealed this to me.

"When I attempt to realise with you what you say, then I feel the impossibility, the powerlessness, yes. It is difficult for me to imagine it, I have indeed underestimated that. Would you mind if I look with you a bit deeper?"

I nodded, with some trepidation. He asked for permission to look into my soul... He seemed lost in it for a few minutes, then raised his eyes to mine and said,

"There is still a source of light within you, a very careful conscience ... ."

"That has been there since my first meeting with Beato."

"From that point onwards, you have wanted something different from the rest of your will..."

"It is complicated; but yes, that is how it is."

"See if you can unite your wakeful awareness with that aspect? Only that?"

"Aren't you overestimating me, Johannes?"

Pensively he shook his head.

"You have enormous strength, Gerrit. If it can be turned to the good ... then that will be something like a nuclear explosion, except it will be a creative one. You have an inexhaustible supply of energy."

"I am on the point of dying – so they tell me."

"Every man is dying."

"I will try it again. For the first few hours it will probably work, but after that..."

The words 'nuclear explosion' had triggered something in me. An awareness of something minuscule with gigantic potential – if the natural bonds can be broken. Something like that. I was familiar with that power, but only as destructive. After all, I have worked with it all my life... Now I was being asked to make the same thing happen in that little point of light within me. I know about magic, I know the impossible can be achieved. I experienced a foretaste of the energy concentrated in that point of light and how it was possible for that energy to, not totally destroy, but (perhaps a better description) disarm, the evil.

I walked for a while up the mountain path. I'm not really fit enough for that... I won't get further than the master's chalet. But I forgot the pain, the exhaustion, because I was fascinated by the image of the explosion of my core... It was as if I was immersing myself in a world of extreme temperature differences. Everywhere I looked, the world seemed frozen, except there ... there was warmth, well-meaning warmth ... exactly the right temperature. If you could just surrender yourself to that, Gerrit, not half-heartedly but wholly with all that you are, and have and could become...if you could resign and immerse yourself, melt into it … There is also another kind of warmth, scorching heat that sets everything alight. Not that, Gerrit, that's not the one…

I walked on and on, fascinated by that other world, that seemed to lie compressed within my core. Johannes inhabited that world. Beato also ... Gerrit had intentionally left it behind and locked the gate. Now he stood there at the edge, the gate was open. Scorching heat and a frozen world... I must choose the new world... I heard something, but the language was not understandable, I saw something but my eyes were not adjusted properly to see it. I experienced something, but I did not recognise it … only the warmth, the mercy, I could recognise. It is my own warmth, it is me. As I could have been ... as I am now, for just a very short moment. Maybe this is me dying, I thought. But I continued to live, with every step. What is it that I hear? Is it my name that resounds? Not 'Gerrit', but my actual name? I saw light, I felt it. Was I that also? It rayed forth, soft and intimate, without force ... that is where I wanted to be, in that warmth, that light, that name ... the way I was pushed to walk onwards on that mountain path, straight through my exhaustion - that was how I wanted to unite myself with that world behind the gate, barging right through all my destructive powers! On I sped, but the portal, the gate, seemed to rush along too, but away from me. I held back, I needed to turn around. The moment I turned, the portal surrounded me. I stood there on the threshold for a moment - the next moment I was touched by its core.

Around my own core, leading it, stood Beato. In another totally different guise with another name – still unmistakably Beato. In between some unintelligible words he spoke clear understandable language.

"We have known each other for all time. We have fought each other again and again. You wanted to be like me but did not want to make the effort like I did. You have tried again and again to rob me of everything, to bind me to you, to seduce me – till you eventually realised that your envy is the result of your love. You loved me, you have always loved me. Your love for me was my greatest danger. In your life before your previous life you realised that, and that is why it is now possible for you to be led by me. You had to develop the reverence worthy of my higher being – only partially able to live within Beato.

"The evil in you has tasted the good in me and has learned to love it, to love it eternally ... to love it so that it has bound itself to you like a husband and wife are bound - spiritually speaking. Surprisingly, the evil within you took me on and became powerless, rendered helpless by the reverence and the desire. Leave the evil behind on the threshold and step inside! You will die even before you taste death. The little that you are, shall grow – bear fruit. You will be poor and powerless. But rich and strong as never before!"

I had fallen to the ground, rendered powerless by the insight. The fight had been fought, I gave up all resistance....

I lay there, full length, face down on the ground, in the evening sun, in the half-light ... totally pervaded with humility, in awe of what was happening to me. I could feel my old personality floating away, this must be what it is like to die. You realise that it must be so, you have, after all, died many times before ... It was indescribably painful, worse that the pain in my bones. It felt like I was being torn asunder, one piece of me stayed fast, while another was being torn off. I wanted to run away, but I stayed ... it had to be done. Only the sun, going down, was witness, along with the buzzing insects, the crickets... a bird.

"He is going away now, but he will still be connected to you. You will have to do much work to release him to the extent that you can be together again. Only then, will you be who you really are. Till then, you will have to suffer, intensely suffer..."

Once the evening air had cooled down and the moon shone on me, I could finally get up. I brushed the dust from my clothes, moved my limbs till they functioned again and felt my way down to the road. In my room sat

Sophie. I had missed our dinner date. Her anger changed to consternation when she saw me.

"Gérard! What has happened?"

Silently I took her in my arms and stroked her hair. I could not speak, couldn't cry, couldn't laugh.

"Come, you are having a bath!" she said and undressed me carefully. When I was half undressed, she took me to the bathroom, where the bath was filling up; she shut the door and I had to make some effort. I felt a bit better when I returned to the room, washed and fresh. Sophie was waiting on the terrace. I felt somehow void without Gerrit's power, in Sophie's light and the majesty of the starry night.

"You don't have to say anything Gérard," she said, picking up my hand and bringing me to my chair. I sat down, looked at her for a long time, felt my own deference for her and asked, hesitatingly,

"Child ... tell me, what do you live for?"

Her eyes grew big, while she asked,

"Why?"

"I would so much like to know what drives you ... what moves you to love an old man like me?" I saw tears in her eyes.

"I can't help it, Gérard. That first meeting, at that little table in the cafeteria was decisive. You just realise, at a moment like that, that you know each other very very well. Age is of absolutely no consequence at all. Everything external falls away, the only thing that stays is the relationship, the connection between us. That I felt so strongly, Gérard."

I shivered and asked softly,

"But ... more generally ... why are you on earth? What possesses you, little Sophie?"

"I want more than just the obvious. Since I met Johannes, I know that I am searching for the spirit; for that which lies behind all creation. The essence, especially of my fellow human being. Just ordinary friendships disappoint me. You are the first real friend I have ever had, someone who can give so much, from whom I have learned so much…"

I said nothing and felt shame. I may not speak about my experience with anyone. It is not allowed...but, writing I can do, and so I try to hold on to what happened to me. When Sophie returned to her room I remained sitting outside. It was as if I had never yet seen the starry skies. The gigantic immense height, black...with shining heavenly lights that seem to have some kind of essential reality. I shivered with reverence, it was as if the universe spoke a Word to me. As if admonishing and at the same time encouraging me … My body felt so heavy, like lead. Maybe I was dying after all? I have heard that evil sails away out of you before you actually die...Had there been a nuclear explosion? In that case the core had burst forth in full bloom – even though I felt very weak. Weaker than ever. Small, obliterated even. But still…

Beato came the next day; I felt very tense and very nervous to be near him. Did he know who he was? Did he know about my experience, about our attachment in all eternity? Or was it only his higher self who knew about it?

"You look well," he said, satisfied, while he shook my hand.

"It's all good, yes."

We sat down. He was as always, in balance, handsome, radiant. I asked,

"Tell me ... do you know anything about your true being? About previous lives and such?"

His surprise was the answer. He said, rather dismissively,

"I'm not that far yet, you know. Actually, I only began serious meditation when I came to work here. Spontaneous insight therein is uncommon."

"But you would make quick progress, no?"

He nodded, but said nothing. It was an odd situation. My relationship to him had totally changed, but the way he looked at me hadn't changed at all. He did see a change, but he didn't know what he saw. After a while he asked,

"Do you still need a doctor? I cannot now imagine that you'll die soon - which I did a while ago."

"Maybe I don't need a doctor. But a friend, yes, an adviser. I need you, Beato."

"Good, good. I'm not trying to avoid it, you know." I could almost touch the longing, precisely because of the fluttering style of our conversation. I would have to find a new relationship to myself, and to my environment. My awareness had lost the element of suspicion, and was changing to an almost painful awareness. But the people around me weren't used to me being aware of them with their interest at heart... And I wasn't used to experiencing all these details filled with love. I sighed and said,

"I feel like a child, Beato. A groping, fumbling, searching being, amazed by all that there is – and what I still don't know about yet."

He looked at me thoughtfully and he did now seem to

get a glimpse of what had changed in me.

"You have forfeited your 'I', your real self, your organising principle, Gerrit. Partly anyway. You will need the support of the all-encompassing 'I', it will replenish you and help you grow."

"And how do I find that?"

"Experience your powerlessness!"

Never had I seen the sun like this, felt its warmth, its goodness. The grass in the garden, the well-tended rose beds, the flowers in the park... The birch trees with their white trunks and rustling leaves; Johannes' and Dr Laurent's students walking around in small groups. The children playing. I had never known that I loved my parents, my wife, my sons, all of my girlfriends … I hadn't loved them before now, the love was just now coming into blossom. The pain associated with that was excruciating. Nothing could, after all, be done about it now, it could not be made good. All I could do was to do it better with all people I met from now on. I went to see Johannes.

He sat in the sun on the terrace of his office, for a well-earned break from his work. Still, he asked me over, to sit by him.

"You have to help me, Johannes. No one here can understand what has been happening to me, only you. You can see it, can't you?"

"I know what has happened," he said simply. "Impossible to express it."

"My awareness is huge, while the power to carry that

seems to have gone completely. What can I do about it? I cannot make any judgements - everything comes into me as it is."

"Don't 'carry', but try to endure. Try not to offer any resistance, let everything come as it will, experience as much as possible."

"That is unbearable..."

"It is the Lord himself who wants to reveal himself to you. You have an unimaginable strength that hasn't disappeared."

"Everything touches me so deeply and brings me to tears..."

"You have experienced a total turn-around – everything is new now."

The old Gerrit hasn't disappeared, he stands some distance away and now reveals his true nature to me. You only really see something when it is some distance away from you. Not too close and not too far. Exactly there, in the balance point between close-by and far away, stands Gerrit as he reveals himself. It is in fact all my memories that have removed themselves and are now being experienced in a very different way. A different Gerrit - maybe he is called Gérard – observes them with a moral compass. A stricter judge you cannot imagine. He scrutinises the minutest detail and righteously he judges, not all in one go, but detail by detail... Gérard needs to weigh up how every detail reflects righteousness, how the universe rejects it – and how he himself turns away from it. And because every detail, after all, is interwoven with Gerrit himself, it is an operation as painful as surgery without anaesthetic. The memories are like so many sharp knives, scalpels... they operate on me, while it is particularly that, the resistance, that stands outside of me – it no longer functions.

What else can I do but let it all just happen? Everything that belongs to my life and all the rest flows straight into me, I haven't any ability to resist it. I really must consult the Master…

"I discussed it with Johannes," the Master said straight away, when I went to sit by him. "What is your question?"

"I have the feeling that your … spiritual configuration is, by nature, like mine is now. I shall have to come study with you, to survive this."

"You are strong," he said calmly, while gauging me with his piercing gaze. "Very strong!"

"You all keep saying that, so it's probably true. Still, I feel I won't manage to survive."

He shook his head confidently.

"Oh yes, you certainly will manage to overcome it, you are already doing that, aren't you?"

I sighed, and said,

"I need your help, Master!"

"Of course. You will have it." He kept looking at me for a while, while he was silent. I was no longer afraid of that gaze. It can, after all, never be more destructive than my own gaze!

"Look Gerrit ... you are no longer capable of making any judgements - that is why you are vulnerable. The only one who can judge you is Gerrit. Apart from that, nothing and no one. That judging strengthens your personality. In the past you were stronger than anyone, in your negativity. You will have to find a new form for your power. I will help you. Come, we are going up into the mountains."

Two men, both about seventy, one, the picture of harmony and health, the other ... morally a baby – and sick right into his bones.

He paced his tempo to match mine, and was filled with compassion for my condition and lack of physical strength. Did I ever find him creepy? He was a friend now, the best kind one could wish to have. Gentle and compassionate; but, with clear boundaries. The whole of the animal kingdom, in all its beauty, splendour and wisdom, seemed to be united within this man; with on top of that, a truly *human*, gentle, pervasive compassion. What I felt now put me in a lyrical mood. It didn't hurt, it softened the ache and I felt how my whole soul was brought into movement, moved to tears. But, I walked on beside him as vigorously as possible, along the path uphill. The same path where I had tasted death...

"A human being is not only skin, muscles, bones and organs, Gérard. There is something that makes it all grow, blossom; that's why there is life. The same 'something' also contains memory and in a higher sense, all-pervading wisdom. Because of all that has happened to you in the past days, weeks, and your firm will to repent, a loosening of that 'something' has come about in you. Making you stand outside yourself - well, actually, only some of yourself - facing your memories; in the way one normally experiences this after death. Your essential inner being is less connected with your body, with the physical, than it was before; that's the reason you feel different than you are used to. Your task now is to attend to that 'feeling', to be mindful of it. You can't any longer be distracted by physical impressions, you *must* experience inwardly. That feeling means pain and suffering. Try not to escape it, Gerrit, but give it your full attention. The increase in your pain will be manifold, but the soul will be refined and purified. That was after all your wish, your supplication: Purification before death? If you had been given a prison sentence you would also have to have undergone tests and ordeals of a more outward nature. The physical imprisonment would have forced you to confront yourself and reflect on your situation. Even then though, you could have been distracted. This is the same. You have to undergo a complete confrontation with yourself, you might also try to escape it. But don't do that, concentrate all your attention on the matter!"

I experienced the reality of punishment, of penance: of being tied to something so painful, for the purpose of self-development.

"Why are we walking here?" I asked, exhausted.

The Master stood still.

"To admire the majesty of God in all his splendour. To learn how to be with what is greater than Gerrit!"

I felt enormous tension flow out of my soul, out of my body. The tension of pride.

"But, Master, how does Gerrit prevent himself from falling into the depths of worthlessness?"

"By devotion, my friend."

All my deeds were now outside myself, like a horrible accusation … there was nothing I could do about them anymore, it just was so. But within me there was still something I could touch, namely, the one who had wanted this to happen, who had consciously striven to make this happen – but who at the same time, now had to put it all behind him. To not want that any more, to want something totally different... A terrible struggle ensued. A giant presence, filled with evil, is fighting with a point of light made up of good will … But, in the same way that the flame from a single candle can bring light to a whole dark space, this point of goodness is infinitely stronger than that giant evil creature.

We had walked back to the master's chalet, where we shook hands like good friends.

"Be aware!" he said when we parted.

I walked back to the main building. It was peaceful in the grounds, I only saw a couple of children playing. I waved at them, they waved back. Their trust affected me deeply. The tears welled up in my eyes. I cried bitterly. Instead of entering the main building, I walked on a bit, downhill along the path. I felt love, like a desire that can't be fulfilled. A softness, like women have ... but then pure, without seduction. Deeply moving, intense desire, yearning love ... remorse. Yes, now I felt remorse, like a straight forward rejection of my past behaviour. Wasn't there anything good to see, anywhere in my life? Well, yes, in the last few years – honest love for Beato, and now for Sophie and for these mighty men here. That was something good, that

I recognised the qualities of these people and so, obviously, had something to do with them. But I felt the love that I had never known before, in particular. The unconscious love for my father, my mother, my wife, my children ... the girlfriends ... even the victims. Squashed love, turned into hate. Conscious hate. But the one who had done the turning was now powerless; the consciousness of it still remained but the activity was absent; he had died ... and he, too, stood outside of me, though a bit less far away than my memories. There was still some connection, and a certain familiarity also. Except that everything that had been his strength, was now my weakness.

I heard footsteps behind me. Normally there was no one on this path, because everyone knew that the path suddenly broke up. Only a walker like me, who simply wanted to walk a short way goes on such a path – or someone who is not familiar with the area.

The footsteps were light, but still not those of a child. I noticed the springing pace of my heart, where everything manifests itself, it seems. I wasn't afraid, fear also seemed to have been cut out of me … I did feel a trembling, reverence, fear of God without dread. I couldn't stay upright with these mighty footsteps around me. Just like before on the path up hill, I fell onto my knees. I do realise that for most people this may sound like ridiculous nonsense. But I cannot do nonsense anymore, that also has been taken away from me. Everything that occurs is staggeringly real. I was on my knees, my back curved, the head bent, as if awaiting a terrific beating – meanwhile the sound and the effect of the footsteps became ever stronger, louder, deafening! It thundered all around me, a storm appeared, so, now, surely, I would die!

I came to, while I was still bent double and on my knees. The storm was over, a clear late-afternoon sun shone through the leafy tree tops onto my path. I did remember the footsteps. No one had come, I hadn't had a beating, hadn't died... But what was it that I was feeling? What kind of wonderful feeling was that? Why did I suddenly feel so intensely loved? By whom? Why did I see myself as another? Small and of no consequence, it is true … but intensely loved and with a capacity for development that put me in a happy mood. I wanted to stay in the kneeling position, fully aware of my lowliness. I was someone who had just started something new, and was in the happy position of being fully confident of having been given the talent to reach the goal he desires … On the one hand it demands a great big sacrifice from him – on the other hand he knows he is a genius. And the ingeniousness has been given to him by God!

The stones on the path were painfully cutting into my knees, my back felt as if it were broken. But my heart was whole, large and shining, warm and light … Where is Gerrit? Oh, well he is still there, he will have to bow to this healed heart. He is the sacrifice that has to be made. He has to be delivered to the power of those footsteps.

I knew no church, no religion, no faith, no holy mass, no sacrifice, no communion ... but within me a choir of angels sang:

"Agnus Dei, qui tollis peccata mundi."

Generosity becomes love

This is where Gerrit's history ends. Gerrit does still exist, it's true, but he cannot write about Gerrit any more, he hasn't the power. And Gérard ... about him it is possible to write, but he is keen to keep his heart pure. A pure heart stays silent about itself ... Still, the story must go on, it is important that people can read this. Gérard deliberated about asking Sophie to write down her experiences with him. In the end he decided to put pen to paper again himself. Who better to describe Gérard's state of mind than Gérard himself? Therefore, he writes about himself, but not out of a desire for self-expression, which previously moved his hand to write.

When I left the path behind and re-entered the park, I saw Sophie. She was sitting on one of the terrace steps, waiting for me. I had lost all concept of time, likely I had missed another dinner date with her. When she saw me, she jumped up and came towards me. I noticed her movements, her moving, more than her shape. I saw Sophie in all her purity, in the love she had for me. I received her in my arms and felt how my big heart embraced her.

"My girl!" I said softly. "How long have I kept you waiting?"

"Don't you have a watch anymore?" she whispered, with

her head against my peaceful beating heart, my warm glow.

"I had forgotten that you can look at it." I looked. Half past six, not that bad. "Come let's go and eat."

She took me by both arms, held me at a certain distance and looked at me.

"What have you been doing on that path? You are covered in sand and leaves. You change every day, Gérard, what is happening with you?"

I couldn't answer, absolutely mustn't.

"I fell. Not badly. So much is going on with your friend, inwardly, my little Sophie. Tell me if you don't like it."

Her searching gaze pushed its way into my eyes, which filled with tears. She stroked my cheek softly and said,

"It's good, all good. Very good." She pulled me along with her and said,

"First you have to wash, I'll come with you."

Here I was put into a bath again – the bathroom door shut, while she waited for me in the room. The warm water had a relationship to my heart. The light of the sun seemed coloured, divided into soft supernatural lustres. But Gerrit always keeps his distance and looks on with cynicism. He is trying to infect me with his trusty old thoughts and feelings. He is a criminal, led by the devil himself, in his many guises. He is proud and handsome, intelligent and witty. He is careless, in the worst sense of the word, he doesn't care about anything, which has led to the deepest melancholy. He had no right to the status he acquired – he got it by extortion. Not through hard work, but by transforming dissatisfaction into coercion. He has ossified into an imposing piece of rock, but with such hardness that you could smash in someone's skull with it.

Laziness is the spring whence all that is evil bubbles up, Gerrit is the personification of that, there he stands as he relates to my own life, my own personality. And, in unbearable contrast stands Gérard, in his soul being. He is empty, humble, but filled with effervescent will. Even though this will has not achieved anything yet and has no content yet, there is a huge desire to start to use it to good purpose.

One should not just wallow in the beneficial warmth of the bath. So, I quickly stepped out, dried myself and put on clean clothes. I felt a broken man but also still fit...

The food in the dining hall of the main building is simple, but good. Sometimes I have experienced desire for a gourmet meal, as I had been used to. Snails, goose liver, truffles, duck...

I can now experience the lust that is associated with that, maybe even worse... 'gluttony'. I sat opposite Sophie, at our little table and ate a quiche with salad, and pudding with raspberries for dessert. It was as if my sense of taste had become more refined. More refined, but also.....with an awakening thankfulness for the grace of nourishing substance. I drank mineral water instead of wine – wine tasted too bitter to me... Sophie stared at me and suddenly asked,

"Where has Gerrit gone?"

Sometimes she said a few words in Dutch, like just now. I felt a shiver and said,

"Gerrit has to be transformed into Gérard, Sophie. A man like Johannes is at one with himself. Gerrit isn't, you know that. A man like me allowed cruelty, which lives in everyone, to grow within himself. I don't support that all that much anymore, but there are milder versions of these such as wrath and cruelty. Ridicule is such an expression, or negative emotion – condemnation. This needs to be transformed. The soul needs to be expanded, it must become big – but who can achieve that on their own? To want something is one thing - to actually make it happen is magic."

"You have changed so much."

I took her hand and said nothing. I experienced her delicate frame with the soft girl's skin – and for the first time I did not feel an urge to subjugate her. It had, it is true, been an urge I had overcome, repeatedly, that I had never actually acted on. But now the actual urge had gone. The effect her hand had in mine now called forth a feeling of love for the being that used that hand, for Sophie. It had become like an image of radiant purity of that girl opposite me. Light footsteps, a small tender hand, the evening sun through the window, the scent of raspberries and vanilla…

I couldn't sleep. I stood up and opened the curtains. It was one of those rare bright dark nights, the heavens filled with stars, a sharply carved sliver of moon. My fear lived outside of me. Fear for the immeasurable grandeur of the night ... which should encourage everyone to surmise the existence of God, that the Spirit exists. You suppress your trembling reverence, look away quickly at a street-light or a lit window – so as not to experience those feelings. All those diversions were no longer possible to me. Unprotected, I had to experience everything, again and again, in order to experience my own powerlessness, helplessness, emptiness. According to the master this was the beginning of the punishment I had to undergo. A *total* immersion experience, one where there was no possibility of resistance. Was it only the *feminine* side of my being that was left? That of sacrifice? If only I had been more developed, then I would now have something to help me understand all this overwhelming magnificence. I cannot grasp all this; I can only *experience* it.

A car stopped outside in the car park of the main building, where I was walking at half past five in the morning, I couldn't sleep anyway. The door opened and ... Doctor Laurent stepped out, the man who taught me how to pray. I felt myself noticed and walked towards him. We shook each other by the hand. Once, I had been afraid of him, of his simplicity, his love, his silence. Now I saw him without fear. I looked into his eyes, surprised by the wonderful depth thereof. I saw a twinkling, something humorous, but mostly I felt the diverse glory, as it is expressed in nature, mirrored in those eyes.

Ach - I experience so much, and I do not have the concepts to understand it. He experiences much more and he has the understanding - and so much more!

"You are on the road early," I said, not knowing what to say.

"You too," he said, unapologetic.

"I couldn't sleep. Are you going to work already, Doctor?"

"You can call me Philippe... Yes, I prefer to start very early in the morning - in winter a bit later. You then get the freshness of the dawn."

"You don't work in the clinic, do you?"

"Only with exceptional cases, very occasionally."

We just stood there, I could not walk on. He also stood still, apparently something else should happen.

"How are you? You look well," said he.

"Then do please call me Gerrit. It's going well, lots happening."

He nodded like he understood.

"I would like to invite you for a coffee, but they don't open till six o'clock. Do you fancy that? Then I will drop my briefcase off in my office and I'll see you in the dining hall."

Surprised, I said 'Yes' and we went our separate ways. I found communicating with him difficult, stiff. His silence was full of expectation, like the proverb 'silent waters run deep', the depth was unfathomable. In the same way that I saw the starry heavens last night, I now perceived a well-developed human soul. You felt that your words were of no consequence, your attitude inappropriate, that your whole right to existence was in question. I was already living in a state of great disadvantage, and then being seen by Philippe Laurent was for me a serious trial. With Johannes I did still have something in common – with Laurent absolutely nothing...

I continued my walk for a while and made sure I arrived at the breakfast hall precisely at six. Laurent was waiting for me in the doorway. Maybe twenty years younger than me, unremarkable at first glance, but very powerful. He smiled and let me go first. We sat down opposite each other. To the waitress, we were just two ordinary, perfectly turned-out gentlemen, well known here. But I had the feeling that a trial awaited me, maybe not the last trial but still … Why was there such a strong religious aura about this man? Such a totally normal, unremarkable presence…

"As colleagues we sometimes discuss our patients. I have discussed you with both Johannes and Beato, Gerrit. For us it is an unusual experience, to be allowed to take part in what is happening with you."

"It's all to do with you, not me."

"You have given yourself over to what goes on here, you haven't denied it - not too much, anyway. What happens to you concerns us, too. I feel a heavy responsibility." I looked him straight in the eye, I do still possess some *courage*.

"I so much wanted to talk with you properly, not just generally and vaguely. I wouldn't have made contact though, we hardly know each other. But since we just met like this by chance I want to take the opportunity to ask your opinion, Philippe. Straight and to the point and in detail."

The coffee arrived and a basket with rolls, butter, cheese and jam. He waited till the girl had gone again and nodded his head.

"I am not by nature judgemental, Gerrit."

"That is just it. I can see the things but I cannot make judgements, my thinking won't function properly. I am only allowed to experience. Johannes gives me courage, the master compassion – you can help me to judge myself. I am not a developed person, haven't learned anything, never read anything either. I only ever just did things and now that isn't working anymore. I view my deeds. I experience my life as it was and also as it is. But I don't understand any of it. I do know that I have to overcome myself – and pretty well completely!"

I looked into his eyes and they looked very deep. My sensitivity made me aware how this human soul was filled with a quiet humour, an overwhelming wisdom and, at the same time, a rare willpower - you don't expect that with such a silent type. I am not clairvoyant, it's just that I have no defences...

He leaned forward a little, looked at me and said,

"You are a Faust of our time, Gerrit. Have you ever heard of Faust?"

"Of the name, yes, for the rest I don't know much about it. Didn't he make a deal with the devil?"

He nodded.

"He had a great 'desire for absolute truth' and could not achieve that in a regular way."

"Knowledge has never been of much interest to me."

"With you it is also desire, desire for more than what everyday life can bring. You went further than Faust – but that is also typical of this materialistic age. You have run out of spiritual resources to take from - you did that, in the past. Life is flat, without depth."

"I have never had a noble aim. Absolutely never. Even my meetings with Beato didn't bring me to that. Since those meetings I have only felt something that was in total opposition to my own being. Or, the other way around, my being was in opposition with that strange insertion. That continued to grow in me, became a roaring fire and eventually turned my evil will to ashes. Something like that. Now I am unable to want anything bad - I can't even think it now. It is a paralysis: you realise that you still have a body, but you cannot enter into it, it is beyond your control. The only thing left over is the realisation of all that you did with that body. Now I know that I wanted this, I wanted to transform. But I don't understand what has occurred. I also know that there is a total ban on my speaking about the event."

"We won't go there. Instead, I will give you a short lesson on human knowledge." His eyes twinkled and I felt a great happiness about my sudden friendship with this man. He began to speak slowly and thoughtfully.

"When you look at a human being with your senses, you get an overall impression, which depends on very complicated and numerous signs. A human is much richer in content than a thing, a plant, or even an animal, isn't he? It all rests on an interweaving of several different worlds."

"I don't understand."

"When you look at water, you see a fluid, it looks unambiguously like a simple substance. However, we know, thanks to chemistry, that it is made up of two elements, Hydrogen and Oxygen. Those elements are, in their own way, also made up of a complex world. But when you look with the naked eye, you see 'just' water. In the same way you also see 'just' a human being when you look at me -"

"You aren't really 'just' a kind of person!" I protested.

"That is to do with those different worlds, the ones you cannot see with your eyes, but which can, with the help of 'extra sensory chemistry' definitely be distinguished. Various elements, which by themselves, constitute different worlds, and also possess their own history."

"I still don't understand any of this."

"Are you understanding the words I am saying?"

"You are speaking clearly enough, but I cannot imagine anything from what you say."

"You do understand the comparisons?"

"Yes."

"Good. The mistake made, these days, in the understanding of the human being is that only one of the four - well, even seven worlds is recognised. Every human being does, it is true, experience all these worlds, but the capacity to recognise them isn't present, isn't there. The only capacity to know, lies in the knowledge of the physical world.

"That world is seen, touched, heard etc. But this physical world is intertwined with higher worlds that express themselves therein. For example: your eyes are as blue as they were a few weeks ago, still, their quality has completely changed; due to a different configuration of your soul, of the higher worlds within you." I was beginning to get the message and had an idea,

"Are there any other worlds lower than the physical?" Feeling somewhat more comfortable because I was beginning to understand it a little, he said:

"There are. Everything is *balance*! If you see the physical as the middle point, visible middle point, then the three higher worlds are held in balance by three 'lower' ones. If you call physical manifestation, 'the natural world', then above that you have the supernatural world and below that, the sub-natural world, which provides the necessary balance." He was silent, as if to spiritually breathe in. I understood a little of it by watching him. Those eyes of infinite space showed me a higher world, but not only 'higher', also 'more beautiful' and 'better'. I asked if I might write it down, knowing that my memory would lose it all straight away. He agreed...When I was done we spoke further.

"The idea that you see only the physical body, is an illusion. You see the results of the other worlds appear in the physical. You cannot differentiate between them unless you have developed an organ for that. Then you see with 'super-sensible organs' that the body lives, you can 'see', the life-giving processes such as growth, nourishment, breathing – not eating, moving of the chest, but the road taken by food material within the body, the actual uptake of oxygen - that is life – and the expelling of carbon dioxide - which is death. These life processes are the second world. By acquiring awareness of this second world within the physical, distinction can be made between a living body and a corpse."

His words struck me so deeply, that I had to hold on tight to my chair. Scared of losing consciousness or fainting. I saw Gerrit, causer of corpses, intervening in those two, mighty worlds of body and life! Whip lashes are less painful than these perceptions. An invisible hand deals the lashes and they cut in deep somewhere, in an equally invisible skin. The whole invisible self-created unity of the individual personality falls apart... Philippe, the courageous, could see what was happening and said in a friendly manner,

"I think we need to leave it there. If you want, we can talk again another time."

Gerrit is strong, primitively strong. He has an immense primal power which needs to unfold now through great endurance and suffering. I looked him straight in the face and asked,

"When?"

"This afternoon."

I was thankful for that and said yes. Philippe Laurent understands exactly what is going on with me. Even though it may sound like the self-flagellation of a medieval monk - it needs to happen, I have to achieve insight – before I die.

I went to the library in the main building. I have never read anything, except the newspaper, the news and the stock market reports. Now I wanted to read Faust, but I had forgotten who the author was. There was a lady sitting at a small table where you could get information. I asked for 'Faust'. She nodded and led me to a row of high bookcases and took two thick volumes off a shelf and placed them in my hands. Faust l and Faust ll. I gave her the second one back and took the first one with me to my room. Goethe. Faust. Pretty high-minded for Gerrit. I can speak German quite well, with my friend Beato for one. But reading it is something else entirely. I didn't understand a word of it.

Zueignung, Vorspiel auf dem Theater … My mind was captured by a few sentences:

DRAMATIST
So, give me back that time again,
When I was still 'becoming',
When words gushed like a fountain

In new, and endless flowing,
Then for me mists veiled the world,
In every bud the wonder glowed,
A thousand flowers I unfurled,
That every valley, richly, showed.
I had nothing, yet enough:
Joy in illusion, thirst for truth.
Give every passion, free to move,
The deepest bliss, filled with pain,
The force of hate, the power of love,
Oh, give me back my youth again!

COMEDIAN:
Youth is what you need, dear friend,
When enemies jostle you, of course,
And girls, filled with desire, bend
Their arms around your neck, with force,
When the swift-run race's garland
Beckons from the hard-won goal,
When from the swirling dance, a man
Drinks until the night is old.
But to play that well-known lyre
With courage and with grace,
Moved by self-imposed desire,
At a sweet wandering pace,
That is your function, Age,
And our respect won't lessen.
Age doesn't make us childish, as they say,
It finds that we're still children.

Even though I could not understand everything in all clarity, I did experience the 'music' of the words and their meaning, an encouraging achievement for an old gentleman like me. I couldn't help but be deeply moved by the words and by what I thought they meant. The Germans say 'Ahnung' for understanding. I only had a little 'Ahnung' and lived with the words, seconds, minutes... till my mind could pick up something of it.

"My mind has been full of rubbish, my little Sophie. Can you blame a boy, who takes in nothing but rubbish that he only wants to relate to evil things? Beato told me about his childhood. How his upbringing was full of beauty, love and wise lessons. I, on the contrary, saw nothing but grey paving stones, and the left-over rubbish of a market day..."

"Still, there are people with a background like yours, who -"

"Who don't go wrong. You are right. But that is how it was for me. It is an interplay between who I actually am and what I have met along the way. I have had a great desire for magnificence – and pulled it towards me with violence and foul play. On the other hand, there wasn't any other way to achieve my desired goals."

"What good does it do to keep harping on about the past?"

"Understanding, I want to understand. I have never made the least effort to try to understand anything – I just did things. Now I want to try to comprehend something, my dear. When I see you playing the violin; heard what you can do - I also find that magnificent. With me everything remained flat, with you there is tremendous development. I perceive that, it touches me deeply, it helps me understand. Can you see that?"

Sophie nodded and stroked my hand. She has become a real beauty and I have taught her that. She knows how to dress; her hair is lovely, she is well made up, which makes her somewhat ordinary face become very special. Most of all though, she has learned to shine, due to the self-awareness she has gained from the attention I have afforded her. She will do well in life, of that I'm sure. For the time being she remains with me…

I visited Philippe in his room, where he had taught me the prayer. I felt intimidated by the radiance of this man in his room and by the shining of the sun outside, the blossoming French geraniums on his balcony. But especially by the piles of wisdom lining the walls, a poor reflection of his own wisdom. It all affects me so deeply, I am so vulnerable, so open. The pain in my skeleton pales into insignificance with the immense pain in my most inner being … my soul?

"Would you rather drink tea downstairs?" he asked me, understanding me so well, which also touched me so intensely. I shook my head 'no'.

"I should be able to take it. It is an overwhelming indication of your learnedness compared to my emptiness." We sat down in the comfortable chairs, not at the desk. Philippe folded his hands, lovely slim hands, flexible and love-filled. He said,

"You once possessed such learnedness, Gerrit. But the truth is that you want it without making any effort. You will not make any sacrifices, you want to possess the full glory of wisdom without doing the corresponding work, inner or outer."

"I am not aware of that. Outwardly, I am of course. I don't owe my success to honest effort. But learnedness was never an option for me. I have honestly never made a choice between becoming or not becoming a scholar. It was pre-ordained, no?"

"That's how it is. But that pre-destination has a deeper cause, namely the rejection of inner activity in a previous incarnation, just as you rejected making an honest effort to gain success in this one."

"That'll be right." I accepted his assessment, and said,

"Tell me more about the different worlds within the human being."

"We talked about two. In the world of life processes you also find wisdom, which is the fount of knowledge. It is also the element of time."

"Is the time not a human invention, a system of agreements?" I asked.

"Plants sprout, grow, flower and die back, in real time. They wouldn't hold to our 'agreements', could they? They themselves live in time. As do the planets in their orbits. We direct our arrangements to the flow of time, not the other way around."

"And what about space then?"

"Space is the realm of the physical body; it does, after all, take up space … that category falls away in the world of wisdom. There you find the concept of 'time' as an essential active element. When death appears, the life body departs completely from the physical body. The latter remains behind as a corpse. It is also possible for a partial separation to occur. The body stays alive, but there is still an experience within the life body similar to that experienced during the first few days after death. It is as if you stand outside of your memories, you are no longer one with them. But, that does give you a different moral compass in relation to your life."

I realised that he was talking about my situation; I also knew that he was doing that on purpose, though he left me free to understand him or not. The way he taught me, made me feel a great love for him and also an unshakeable trust. Although he looked like a boy, he was a good father to me, one who shows his son what life is all about. Isn't everyone deeply lonely and filled with an insatiable need for nurturing and protection? In the same way that a baby has to cry itself to sleep, I had been lonely up to this moment. With this man I found the concepts, the only thing that can comfort … because they place you within yourself, who you missed so much. *How is it that Gerrit can feel so deeply?*

"It is in the world of life processes that we find life itself, Gerrit. Wisdom is alive there. Nothing is ever still or not in motion. Beings move within the stream of time that never become physically visible. Just as your finger is part of your body and cannot exist without a connection to the whole, so those beings are a part of an all-encompassing being, which is the being of understanding, because it forms the source of all that is. Even though that being comes from a world far, far above the world of the life processes, it is present in the ether world – which is what we call that world. It comforts, heals, it reconciles. It gives understanding, it is self- knowledge."

The memory of the footsteps came back to me. Footsteps without observable feet, an enormous effect without a visible being. And this man Philippe, he brings comfort and reconciliation. Maybe even healing…

"One says that 'time is a human invention'. That we invented time to organise day and night, summer and winter, orbits and so forth. But, if you think it through, then you realise that day and night, summer and winter are themselves expressions of time. We ourselves also live within time, we have an age. We didn't make that up, we have of course learned to orient ourselves towards time, and have divided time so that we can measure it. It is not the watch that determines the time, but time that determines the watch."

"Obviously."

"Your whole life, your biography is present in that time-being – the ether body - everything is present there, your thoughts, experiences and deeds, as are the life processes of your body up to the present moment. Only a doctor who can perceive that, can understand the true state of health of a patient. You can 'see' in the stream of time how development is going. That is more complicated than the whole of the study of medicine ... but it is possible. Johannes and I work together to develop the skills and hone the 'knowledge' gained thereby. One is then in the realm of the Creator - and that can only be done by those who truly know their own place. When you sit down at the computer, you know that just one image on the internet is conveyed by an innumerable number of signs, programmed by the person who created the image. Push through to the secrets of the ether body and you will see an unending number of beings and processes that make up the basis of the factual presence of the living body. It is obviously stupid to believe that that complicated, self-generating living being – the body doesn't acknowledge a creator..."

I listened as intently as possible, knowing that here I was being given a unique opportunity. That I, Gerrit, could find out at first hand, what was going on here in these mountains, what was being 'done' by these learned men. I felt timid, but knew this was an honest experience of modesty, and not of being intimidated. "Once upon a time, Gerrit, you also had that knowledge ... when the stars still gave their wisdom to the human soul. Later on, when the stars were silenced, and people listened to the words of Man instead, you lost the old star wisdom, you stopped your development. What was once the right way, became a lost wandering later on. Now you cannot find that old star wisdom anymore and you haven't prepared yourself for the new - in fact, the opposite is true. Out of your unconscious desires you have turned towards evil, and have worked with the old powers."

I don't remember anything of that, though it does all ring true. What else could I do but hang my head and ask,

"What should I do, master – to make amends?"

He looked at me seriously and said,

"First develop insight, Gerrit. You are an exceptionally intelligent man, I will instruct you further about the manifold being of man. Then we can work together to figure out your path. I am no master, Gerrit. You have to learn to become your own master..."

After the evening meal I took a walk with Sophie. We walked in the direction of the clinic and of Johannes' house. I held her hand in mine and was deeply moved by what that felt like within my ... soul. I could feel her youth, and her love in the quality of the pressure of her hand. It was not erotic at all, it was an intimate experience of 'she and I', of our relationship. She awoke something in me, something more than just Gerrit, something that went beyond Gerrit and made him conscious of the fact that there are other people in the world who also matter. My last days seem to be ruled by a delicately organised plan, each day has a purpose, and every day is part of the process of remorse. With a gentle - and sometimes not so gentle - hand I am led from event to event and every event can only happen because of the one that has gone before. That is development – and that occurs over time, in time…

"It does seem like a different life. The life I had when I was living in the clinic," I said, when we neared the building I spent several months in. "It was the end of the life of Gerrit. Now he is no longer here, and still, here he walks! It really is the same man, he says 'I' to the same person – and still... It is rather confusing, Sophie."

"Is this then freedom - or is this your destiny? That's what I'm thinking about."

I thought about it.

"I really wanted this, I begged for it – that was certainly

my own free will. But to have made that happen – no, that I haven't done. So far … Gerrit is still within reach, I could wear him like a coat, then my suffering would temporarily be over. The fact that I don't do that, that I leave him where he is, outside of me ... that is my freedom. I have asked freely for something and I have accepted it. And, even though the gift is so painful – I accept it, in freedom. It's something like that."

"You were a man with a strong outward-focused decisiveness. Hard and experienced. Now a softness is appearing, a mildness – an unexpected wisdom. The question then is: Who, then, is this person? Is it like this with everyone? Are you the 'hard' Gerrit or are you the 'wise' Gérard?"

I squeezed her hand and asked, with a smile,

"Which one do you care about the most, my Sophie?"

"This one. The other has left its traces behind in you, but in a positive way. I was sometimes scared of you, naturally, of your cruelty – though never directed at me. Now it seems that all that life experience – and it is huge – has been transformed into wisdom. Maybe it is like that with everyone, only you don't notice it during their lifetime – maybe after death, you do."

"Who am I, Sophie?"

She stood still and threw her arms around my neck.

"It seems that you were a crook. I am glad that I know nothing about that, that you have spared me that. You haven't been one since I've known you. At first you were a desirable gentleman, a 'chevalier avec grandeur', rich … charming. Now you are more of a Buddhist, who is aware of enlightenment. You radiate empathy, suffer for the abuse of creation – to which your own being also belongs."

I pulled her towards me and hugged her like a father. A girl in the arms of a man, I experienced her presence without desire, only with the memory of what desire once was.

"Are you never scared that you will be found out? It could happen, that someone discovers something, or that someone betrays you?"

She imagined me as having been a little conman, or a normal thief or even a murderer. I went to sit down on a bench beside the path and she sat down next to me. I put an arm around her shoulder and said,

"It's not like that, my girl. Gerrit is a cornerstone of society. You pull him out, and the whole godforsaken caboodle collapses."

For a minute there I experienced the old Gerrit, who wanted to creep into my words to gain entry, into my new life. I reiterated,

"There is too much that is tied up with me, Sophie. I made sure of that. I am untouchable, I am a respected industrialist – or something like that. I have made it perfectly clear that I am very ill and that I won't be 'rejoining the fray'. I severed all relations – believe me, I am safer than you are."

She shivered.

"He is like steel, that Gerrit. Rock hard, sharp as a steel blade. Still, I love him so much – and Gérard also!" she said.

"It is just unbelievable how careless we are. You just live it up, you allow everything, more and more and more –

without the slightest awareness that everything, into the minutest detail, the most fleeting of feelings, the most insignificant action, is recorded. Enduring. People make such a fuss if a glass bottle is or isn't recycled – while at the same time they allow one disgusting thing after another to enter in to their life, they even seek them out! And it all ends up in that book, like a ledger belonging to the accountant … credit and debit. It is also the book of transgressions, Sophie. Everything is in there, permanently. It cannot be erased. That book is slightly outside of me, I am not now completely within it any more. That is why I can see it ... and it is so shocking. There has to be a divine being to whom you can pray, 'Forgive us our trespasses!'"

"Don't you have to make it all good in your next life?" asked Sophie.

"Probably. But what is written there, is written!"

"There is something more to add to that Gérard... that you forgive others their trespasses."

"And that is exactly what we never did. No mistakes were allowed, I never made any either. Mistakes were ruthlessly repaid! No, not a lot of joy in a life like that. I did have fun, but it always tasted sour, like precious antique wine that has been badly stored. Relaxing was not possible, you had to remain vigilant at all times. And I couldn't stand someone else's good fortune. That had to be ruined – do you understand that?"

She shook her head: No.

"How could a sweet soul like you understand such a thing? I myself don't even understand it now – but I do remember it well, I can even see it clearly before me." Silently we walked back. She accompanied me to my room, we drank a glass of wine together. She is not afraid of me, nor does she blame me for anything. It is her trust in me that has brought about the change in me. When someone absolutely rejects all possibility of there being badness in another person, then that badness cannot prosper.

"All that money is a burden to me. I have to get rid of it. It was always a great feeling, but now every cent feels like a heavy weight on my shoulders."

Beato grinned and said,

"But you have given everything away."

"Oh no, the bank accounts are still full. I'll put half away for your children, the other half for Sophie."

"What are you planning to live on, then?"

"I'll ask Stern if I can work for my rent and food. I don't need any more than that. I am too arrogant to even wash a coffee cup. It would be good for me to help in the kitchen."

"But you are going too far, Gerrit. That is nonsense?!"

"Maybe. There isn't much point going around having insights all the time – and then leaving it at that. That is also nonsense."

"You are not that young anymore, and you are ill. Ask Johannes about it."

I left it at that and said,

"You know, Beato … there is such a thing as 'sympathy', well 'sym-happy' also exists. Both, I have ripped out of myself – or maybe never had. Sympathy I certainly have 'achieved'. To be happy about someone else's good fortune is evidence of a pure soul. I have never been able to do that.

I hated the happiness of my fellow man, even of my own children! I have always done my best to destroy happiness – because I am never happy myself. I do not know joy. Contentment maybe, satisfaction of desire, probably – but, not happiness – that is something else. That 'ailment' has now been taken away from me, Beaat. I now do experience happiness, joy, and also that of others – the same with sadness. When I look at you, I taste a kind of bitterness. Is something wrong?"

He lowered his eyes and sighed.

"Chiara is ill, Gerrit. Seriously ill. Johannes and Philippe will examine her – maybe treat her also. I'm landed with the children and will have to stay at home."

"What's wrong with her?"

He looked up, his eyes were moist.

"She suddenly went completely yellow. She has been tired for a while – I haven't been paying enough attention to her … ."

"How is that possible? You are such a perfect human being, Beato! It must be something acute, something that will get better again."

He looked doubtful.

"I don't have a good feeling about this, Gerritt."

"You need to stay with her, in any case. When you come here, just bring the children with you."

"They have to go back to school."

"Then they can go to school here, in the village, for the time being. I am your friend, Beato. You can count on me, whatever you need."

He nodded his head and seemed somewhat encouraged.

"First, she will be examined. Who better to be her medical doctor than Johannes – with his many years of experience as a consultant."

Compassion … I experienced intense compassion. My perfect, completely well-balanced friend – was being tested, while I had been pardoned. How to make sense of life?

I let things ride before speaking to Johannes. I would get enough opportunities to make myself useful, and more would be asked of me than just washing the odd tea cup – the thought of fulfilling such a lowly task did fill me with dread. Beaat would need help – I wanted to give him all I could.

A few days later, very early in the morning, I had breakfast with Philippe. No one else was in the dining room and he continued with my 'education'.

"The real origin of the … let's call it 'sin'... does not lie within the living physical body, Gerrit, but in a higher member of the human being. It is your actual soul, something so much closer to you than your body, which is eternal and cannot die.. The soul is the bearer of the purest innocence, but it can also be filled with a gross egoism. Every human being has to work on his soul, to transform it to innocent purity and unselfishness. Conversely, you can also work on a reversal of the pure human."

"I don't understand much of this – maybe because I have been such a damned atheist all of my life. Do try again, if you want."

"You know by now that you have been on earth several times, in a physical body. What you brought with you from a previous life as a kind of moral 'result', but then specified to the tiniest detail, that has been worked on, transformed after death. It has formed a new earthly life, under the auspices of heredity. Ensouled by that which was present in you before your birth, that moral result becomes a new physical body and, within that, the life-body. A part of it remains free, isn't transformed. That part takes in everything from life again and carries it through death to become 'moral result' again."

I let his words penetrate me - it made me very sad.

"This is really too terrible for me to contemplate Philippe! So now I have to think that my deeds are carved in my soul, and with that I have to build a new life?"

"It is the truth, Gerrit. After death you are taken up into a spiritual community. You are born into it as you are born here. Higher powers transform your moral results, you cannot do other than be part of that, you don't want to not be transformed either. It is also possible that you will be rejected for a long time, that you will be locked out, because there is hardly any relationship between your soul and the spiritual world."

"So there isn't anything more that I can do about it? Nothing to improve the situation?"

He was silent for a long time. I could see that he was moved, and I felt it too. Finally he said softly, while he looked me in the eye,

"Of course you can. You have, after all, committed yourself completely to the power of the good? This has been growing in you for fifteen years – and has resulted almost in 'mastery' since you arrived here."

"No matter how much good I do – the overall 'moral

result' would remain in debt, Philippe!"

"It isn't about money. This is not just a simple arithmetic sum. In the turn-around, that you yourself have instigated, lies an enormous power. You will need to atone for every detail in your history before your turn-around, but the way forward has been permanently made smoother. You can count on that, Gerrit."

I recognised what he told me and could feel the truth of it. My personality, my anger, my ruthlessness … they had after all been taken away, by my own will to cause a nuclear explosion within myself. Philippe's emotion touched me too and I said with all honesty,

"I am very, very, sorry, Philippe. Regret, remorse. For real..."

Whatever was my soul - my experiences, my life of feeling - filled with deep sadness for Beato. I looked for him after breakfast and finally found him in his room.

"Where is Chiara?" was my first question.

"Johannes has gone to her. He will decide what should be done - admission to hospital or to stay here."
"Why didn't you go with him?"

"I will go later. I need a little time to gather my thoughts. I might be gone a while..."

"How has this happened, Beato? Or would you rather I left you in peace?"

"No, no, you are my friend, Gerrit. I like talking to you. I have already spent half a year on my own at weekends, Chiara has always been very strong, she didn't mind at all

– she said. I blame myself that I maybe did neglect her?"

"My dear Beato!" I exclaimed. "Listen to the advice of a friend. You are the only man I have ever met, who is absolutely well balanced. More so than Johannes, more than Philippe, more so than the master, even. They do undeniably have other talents which exceed yours, but you are perfect harmony and balance. That's how you will be in marriage, as a father, as a husband. The problem is with the girl herself, in Chiara herself."

He looked at me with his beautiful brown eyes and nodded.

"All I can do is to think about her, stand by her, support her. Thank you, Gerrit."

I stood up and hugged him. Outside I took my handkerchief and blew my nose…

Silence becomes meditative strength

Four people of giant stature work together here. Alongside them there is also Evil, though without the power to attack. All I know about these four is what they themselves have told me. The first one is thinking personified. He is all of it, through and through, in all its greatness. It's not the thinking that we mortals call 'thinking'. It isn't even what we call 'scholarship', though it does come across like that. He is thinking, but thinking with the power to act. It is actual thinking itself but also the very best thing that exists. Many thinkers aren't that good at doing, they are rather paralysed by their head. This one, on the other hand is all will, and yet, he is still the thinker. The second is per se the best, he is what we call 'goodness'. But then raised up to knowledge. I, Gerrit, never knew that any of this really existed. That I can actually write it down comes from observing, listening and, in particular, from feeling for half a year. Since my turnaround, the experience of feeling has become so intense, that I understand things that are not understandable – and such a thing would have been totally irrelevant for the previous Gerrit... The second, the best one, has the ability to explain the un-understandable in a razor-sharp manner. He can explain, what cannot be touched, in such a simple way that even I can understand it – though I still can't remember it if I don't write it down straight away. The third one is a giant in feeling. He is no thinker, doesn't really achieve that much, but he is open and acquiescent, which has the effect of making his feelings behave clairvoyantly. I used to hate him, now I love him. He mirrors his visitors, you see the 'I' in him, what you really are, yourself … There is no one more honest than he is, he is righteousness itself … The fourth is the youngest. He tells me that his development has only just begun. On the other hand, he has confided in me that his memory reaches back to before he was born, and even before that, to a previous life. But when I ask him who he and I were and what our relationship was, then he remains silent. What the other three have accomplished with their development he, the youngest, has intrinsically. He is the absolute balance, he stands apart from the three, but encompasses all three also. In his presence, evil cannot rule – believe me, I know! You have to love him, you can't help yourself. His harmony throws every other person off balance and jealousy cannot prevail, he is too nice to hate... How is it possible that the person who lives with him, day in day out, beside him, becomes seriously ill? His harmony is like healing power itself, and still... I would like to talk to her myself, I really don't know her.

The two men, Johannes and Beato, brought her and the children back with them as I had hoped they would. The high season was over, houses and apartments were readily available to rent and accommodation was arranged for them. But Chiara was admitted to the clinic, she was very ill. I was afraid to ask what she was actually suffering from; it was after all, none of my business. For several days I only saw Beato as he passed by. Then, one day he did come to visit me again. Surprised, I stood up and accepted his warm hug.

"How are things?" I asked clumsily. He looked tired, but his balance was not upset. He sat down and said,

"It's good. It isn't what I feared, being a surgeon. As a specialist you see only part of all the ailments people can have. What she has is an internist's speciality, no one better than Johannes then."

"Will she recover?" I asked carefully, reluctantly.

"Everything is possible," he said, and he meant it.

"Is she allowed visitors?"

"Certainly. Gladly even. She asked for you..."

They'd put her in 'my' room! The only room available, as it happened. It seemed a vindication of my suspicion that there was some kind of relationship between my conversion and her illness ... I had a fright. She was skinny and indeed completely yellow, which made her look like death. It wasn't cancer, apparently ... but it must be serious. The yellow was repellent and I had to pull myself together to hug her generously. I haven't overcome many of those kind of hurdles in my life, nor have I aspired to do so. I took her in my arms and kissed her hair. I had nothing to say, took a stool from beside the desk and sat down at the edge of the bed. Her liveliness had disappeared, she seemed flat and tired, sweaty and pathetic.

"Thank you for coming, Gerrit," she said in German.

I kept silent and only smiled at her. What could I say, I am so clumsy when it comes to commiserating... It was actually my silence which made her speak. Her head was propped up on a pile of pillows so she could look at me. Her eyes are beautiful, brown, Italian and translucent.

"You ask yourself, how it is possible to fall ill with such a blessed man as Beato by my side?"

She posed the question and then gave me the answer. She spoke softly, her voice just as flat as her whole being.

"I do think about that a lot. I don't know for sure why I am so ill – who could know that? But Beato is like the sun itself ... if you come too close without protection – you get burned."

I never thought that I would get burned even if lived with him twenty-four hours a day, seven days a week. So, I said,

"Without protection? What do you mean, my dear Chiara?"

Her eyes welled up with tears, was it because I didn't understand her correctly? I must understand what she means! How do you understand someone who is so differently put together than you are?

"You know very well, Gerrit, that Beato is a balanced person. In marriage this is also the case. And with the children. I don't think he has ever been unjustifiably upset, or too angry, or too nice."

"He is kind of perfect, that's true."

"In his presence you yourself cannot be inharmonious." She was quiet for a while, exhausted by speaking. What is it that is wrong with this lass?! Then in a flash I understood.

She enjoyed living in the warmth of the sun without actually doing any work on herself. She has remained the same as she already was fifteen years ago. If you live beside Beato, you have to change, or you go under.

"I have also been envious," she said softly, while she stared straight ahead. "Jealous of his abilities. He really can do everything, Gerrit... Do you know how irritating that is?"

"So, the envy was your protection against the sun?"

She nodded, but apparently, she had chosen a dreadful defence. She should never have been allowed to be so passive! I felt the human drama, the tragedy. We have the highest calling, but then just don't feel up for it. Too much effort. Then when we meet someone who does want to reach the heights, and wants to work on his development, work towards it ... then we also don't like that. This example is unbearable. It really should not be, it should go away! And if that isn't going to happen ... well, then self-destruction is the only answer. That was the state I had been in, in all seriousness. For Chiara it was the same. It really was rather careless of her – but she could do nothing else.

"That will have to radically change!" I said convincingly. I saw her hesitate. She still hesitated! I shook my head and kept looking at her silently. There is something stubborn about this woman, repellent even, like that yellow … Oh, well, you should have compassion for the sick, maybe she will even die. If she doesn't transform, she will die. Or is that nonsense? It is her destiny that she is so ill. But illness has a purpose, you shouldn't be fatalistic about it. You have to get to work! I hadn't known that, but it had been revealed as I went along. I was in the process of dying, and still am, but I am transforming myself while I do so. She should be able to do that too!

"I am an expert in 'experience', Chiara. I have been approaching death for over six months. Here, in this room, it was supposed to happen. In the meantime, I have moved out and I am still alive. Everything that was good in my life comes from your Beato."

"You recognise him completely, Gerrit. That's why I wanted to see you. I am resistant. Because I cannot be like him."

"Neither can I. I have also been very envious of him."

"But you place him above yourself. I don't."

I was astonished by her, Beato's woman, the mother of his children. She was quite repellent... I took her hand in mine, a second overcoming of myself, and looked into her yellowed eyes.

"Turn around, Chiara! You cannot win this fight. Take the place that belongs to you. Look at the sun and realise that it casts a shadow. Stand in his shadow and be humble!" She relaxed, I noticed. I loved Beato so much, my impassioned words were filled with that love. Beato loved her, but she ... she didn't know love. Really, Gerrit knows more about it than her!

"Have you talked about all this with Beato?" I later asked. We had been sitting together in silence for a while. Not that unusual in itself. Usually you get the urge to move on quite quickly when that happens, the silence becomes too uncomfortable. But now I sat there peacefully; with my soul open and I could feel enormous activity. She regarded me with a little more attention than before, it seemed to me.

"Ach, Gerrit, that isn't possible! It would make him so unhappy. I do really love him. There is also another side, a positive side, to our relationship. I do want to live ... This illness leads to death within a couple of years, unless you take heavy drugs. I have passed the care of my body to Johannes - he will have to decide what needs to happen, he is after all a talented internist."

"Have you taken him into your confidence?"

"No, I can't do that. They are so high-powered, these men, so much above this kind of thing ... ."

She trusted me; I was, after all, many times more ruined than she was with her little sins.

"You will have to get over that. They will know already anyway – they are leaving you free to tell them in your own time."

She grabbed my hand and said,

"You have so much good-will, Gerrit, I am such a chicken."

"Do you doctors ever work with psychic problems, Johannes?"

I could, of course, not give advice to a professor of medicine, but I was interested in his methods. He smiled and said,

"Illness does have its source in the psyche, but it isn't so that every abnormality causes an illness. Then no-one would be healthy – and a criminal couldn't become seventy!"

I chuckled and picked that one up adroitly.

"What then, professor, is the cause of illness? Is it possible to heal oneself with self-development?"

"In some ways, yes. But also no. Illness is caused by disharmony in the interplay between body and life on the one hand and soul and spirit on the other. A real doctor knows the healthy harmony and recognises disharmony. It is quite a lot more difficult than the suggestion of a diagnosis and the setting up of a therapeutic regime the way an internist does. Still, all the details are expressions of a disturbed inner balance."

"But ... don't you need to find out about a patient's innermost feelings?"

"I know that by looking, listening, experiencing. What people say is after that, not really all that important."

"How, then, do you intervene in the illness process?"

"We use everything that we have, Gerrit. Everything. If you are working with someone who can and wants to meditate, that helps a lot. Praying is also a possibility, but often there isn't enough power in that to break through to re-establishing harmony."

"What a wonderful profession, Johannes."

He nodded, was silent for a while and unexpectedly said,

"You are talking about Chiara, aren't you?"

I nodded.

"Has she told you something relevant?"

"Yes. I have the impression that you should discuss what is occupying her mind with her. I know absolutely nothing about it, but I do feel many things. I don't think she can ever get better. She doesn't live with a normal guy. Beato is too much of a challenge, because of the way he is. What is it like to live beside that? How does your wife manage it?"

"Eva? By using all her inner strength to develop herself."

"Do you support her in that? Does she let you?"

"Naturally."

"It isn't all that natural, actually."

Now I had to keep my mouth shut or I would reveal too much. Johannes said,

"I will speak with Chiara again."

I felt the heaviness of taking on someone else's destiny. My whole back was aching with the weight. Doctors must be strong as iron - if they want to be good doctors anyway!

Sophie caught me up in her arms, when I went to her room.

"You change every day, Gérard! You look completely different again!"

"Every moment hides a new secret, Sophie. I never used to notice, to just walk past, walk over. Now I dive in and under - I can't help it. I cry about everything ... life is just such a great tragedy!"

Silently she held me. She is my angel: who appeared, suddenly, when I was at my end; she has stayed with me and will be with me till my very last day.

I was not looking forward to my next meeting with Beato. I had the feeling that I'd become privy to one of his secrets ... but his presence dispelled all of my worries. He hugged me and said,

"She is much happier after your visit. What did you do?

Give her a kiss?"

I smiled, quite relieved by his joy.

"She is the wife of my best friend. It was a very special encounter, Beato."

He sat down and became serious and said,

"I do know what is wrong with her, Gerrit. She doesn't tell me anything, but I'm not stupid."

"Certainly not."

"It isn't easy living with Beato. I did tell you that before, but you didn't believe me."

"You talked about neglecting her, that is just nonsense!"

"I should have encouraged her to express herself. I respected her independence, I had to."

"I keep thinking that it is something within the girl herself. Just as I can't be blaming others for my illness, now can I? How do you interpret that, Beato? Have you spoken to her?"

He laughed again.

"You really are an extraordinary man, Gerrit. You do know that I've always loved you very much."

"Loved who?"

"Gerrit! Your ability to take control, your conviction, your power. Your strong body, your awareness, and so on."

"And the evil?"

"I ignore that, Gerrit, I don't pay any attention to that. I can see that that immense power of yours is now beginning to work within you. Who would have thought that a conversation with you would invoke healing powers? Chiara really has improved."

"I understand that she has a serious condition. I'm sure

more is needed than just a conversation with Gerrit ... Have you spoken to her yet?"

I repeated my question.

"She is proud, my beloved Chiara. Very proud."

"That does seem to me to be the problem," I said.

"Superbia. One of the seven sins from Dante's Divine Comedy. How do you deal with 'Superbia', Gerritt?"

I consulted with myself, and then burst out laughing and replied,

"A small dose of Beato seems to me to be the cure. The illness itself should cure her. I believe that we should approach the problem from a completely different angle. It is impossible to become ill in your company, unless the illness is part of the healing process."

"What would you do if you were married to her?"

I shook my head fiercely and replied,

"Impossible! That would be a disaster."

"Why? She is an extraordinary woman, Chiara."

I sighed. My open-heartedness wished for an obvious solution, for the untangling of this dreadful knot. Why on earth should this blessed man darken his golden heart with Chiara's schemes? I used to be jealous of her, of her place next to the blessed one. Now I was angry because she didn't even make use of her position! I sat up straight and said,

"Never mind freedom! Come on Beato! Tell her the truth, take charge of her, demand honesty from her. She has to stop her whining!"

"She is ill, Gerrit!"

"So am I! You didn't have any sympathy for me and I am completely at your mercy. Some people just don't deserve softness. Superbia? Acedia is at the base of all sin, remember? I haven't forgotten. Laziness, passivity, that is the source of all evil. Just 'I don't feel like it'! And then, in your company! Shameful, it is shameful!"

My antipathy towards her was audible in the venom of the outburst. I thought I had become so nice? So soft, big-hearted even? Beato answered my unasked question,

"Love is not always gentle, Gerrit. I will think about it, you may well be right… "

When he had gone, repentance set in. The old Gerrit had come nearer again. I had been confronted with an ordeal... Chiara was a peaceful, friendly, very hospitable girl, and now a caring young woman. She had always welcomed me most heartily. She was a good 'child'; compared to her, I was the devil himself. What was I thinking! Setting her husband up against her! To betray her, in fact! Is she not allowed one small weakness, one that could surely be overcome! Remorse drove me outside, I had to visit her, to ask her for forgiveness. I was filled with remorse. Who had I become? In the past I never looked at my own behaviour at all, only at others'. Now I had to ensure the other person remained wholly untouched and the full force of blame was directed at myself. If only I had a God to whom I could pray for forgiveness! Was there anyone 'above me' who I could entrust myself to? Like a child can trust its parents – something I had hardly experienced. I wanted to entrust myself to His protection. But I did not know 'Him', doubted His existence. Was His existence not just wishful thinking? While reality was ruthlessly hard – like Gerrit? I stood still. That was impossible. If reality really was as hard as Gerrit, then Gerrit could not now be going soft. I knew very well, after all, that I had begged for that softening and that it had been granted... By whom? By Him. That thought gave me strength. Maybe it wasn't that bad after all, what I had done. Chiara had, after all, improved... I turned back. Beato should really visit her first.

That afternoon I received a message on my phone: Chiara would really appreciate seeing me again. Cheerfully I set out to see her.

She was just as yellow, but she was somewhat less dull. Her sweet eyes had a little more light in them, she was even sitting straight up in bed. She stretched both her arms out to me, like a child with its father. I hugged her sincerely, with warmth, this time with no reluctance. She actually pressed herself against me and I held on to her as long as she wanted, with all the strength I could muster. My soul became over full and I was moved to tears. When she let go of me and noticed my tears, she passed me a tissue.

"Gerrit, you're an angel," she whispered.

I shook my head and blew my nose.

"Yes, it's true. Beato came and I was able to say it all to him."

"How did that happen then?"

"I don't know. Because of you. I saw him and he is so kind. Then I told him everything."

"Was he angry?"

"He is never angry, you know that."

"No, he never gets angry. Can he endure anything then?"

"He attaches no value to the negative side of things."
"Why have you waited so long, then?"
"I want to be just as perfect as he is – and I'm not. I feel so much better now, Gerrit. I hope that I can stay alive, that I will get better..."

I was living in a different world than before. This was a world where people recognise and understand each other. I had an active role in that. I was no longer an outsider, I had become a participant. I experienced the love that bound Chiara and Beato together, even that I could be part of. Chiara had hugged me like a father, this was the first time in my life I had done something positive for a fellow human being, just because I wanted to, with all the passion Gerrit could still bring forth!

"What people call 'the I', is the most problematic in the human being."
Philippe continued with our private lessons, speaking with great emphasis to make sure that I understood the importance of what a human being actually is...
"The 'I' is the fourth part of the human being, it is the crown, it is what makes a human being 'human', it is the carrier of self-awareness – but also the source of egoism, and consequently the point of choice: between good and evil."
I remained quiet. So, my sins had their origin in my 'I'. I had more or less chosen for the bad – but conversely, for this past half year, I had chosen, even more consciously, for the good.

"As long as there is a soul only and no 'I', one cannot speak of 'evil' really. Just think about a predatory animal. It carries out 'bad' deeds, but you would never regard them as 'evil'. It cannot do anything else, it is as it is. It acts out of instinct, it is un-free.

Thanks to the 'I' you can decide for yourself, you can oppose your instinct or you can indulge it. Self-awareness makes its presence felt as body awareness. Your body is the outer form of the 'I', you regard it as 'yourself'. If self-awareness and body awareness became one and the same, it would no longer be possible to have a concept of the spirit, that aspect that leaves the body behind like a coat and passes on, with death. It would be impossible to accept the existence of an eternal spiritual world, when you are your body, and that is what you are! In the world of the imagination it is also like that. The senses carry the outside world in, and imaginations are formed. The 'I' appears and blossoms within the imaginations, like peach blossom sprout forth... The body belongs, in that sense, to the world of imagination, an imagination of the 'I' that is physical body and that flowers into death. But a germ grows in the heart of the blossoming. Namely, that which has been accomplished in relation to the will. There lies the source of spirit awareness; so, not in the imaginations themselves. You, Gerrit, have by your turn-around given yourself a hefty push so that that germ has been given enormous power. By what you are doing for Chiara, the germ will grow on and bear fruit. You will have more opportunities to help make that fruit grow and develop – so that a new balance will be established with the powers of death that have ruled your life till now."

There was nothing more to say, so I said nothing. He looked at me with his beautiful eyes with their deep effect, and continued,

"It is easy to see in your life, Gerrit, how the 'I' has to do something for itself if it isn't to go under. Freedom exists in self-awareness. The self has forgotten where it comes from, but by the fruit of its labour it knows fine well that it is connected with God."

I sighed.

"It is so complicated Philippe. Maybe you can tell me more in a while? I hear what you say, I understand, can even repeat some of it ... but what it all means?"

"You can think about it later on, mull it over, no?"

This made me laugh.

"My thinking has the power of a wet rag! Not very useful, without a purpose, and weak … "

"I don't know, Gerrit. Your physical condition will deteriorate further if you don't train your mind more. You have enough intelligence."

There is much to think about here. Which is perhaps a bit strange for someone who has been orientated towards the outside world all his life. My motto was always: Direct your destructive power totally towards the enemy. Use your common sense and intuition to figure out who your enemy is...But now, my mind is filled with unknown activity and I have to reorient myself. My physical condition is slowly deteriorating. I am in a lot of pain and I feel like I can't breathe. I don't complain about it, the diagnosis is clear and it is a wonder that I am still alive. The only drawback is that I now want to stay alive. When I first arrived here that had certainly not been the case. Over the past few months, my will to live has blossomed again due to my relationships with such fascinating people. Here I have friends, I wonder what it will be like after my death? My father, mother, my wife... but particularly my victims, are all there. They won't be my friends. I am casting back into my memory for friends who have died – I haven't found any. Not a single one. And what about those higher beings that are there, apparently? I can't expect any support from them. Waiting for death is becoming a heavy burden – only relieved by the company of others.

"I would so much like to go to Lago Maggiore with you again, Sophie. It is September now, it will still be possible... next Spring will be too late. I am really too tired to travel, but I would so much like to go..."

I had made her sad, her eyes were full of tears, she nodded.

"I will go anywhere with you, Gerrit ... but please don't speak about death, please! You could still live for a such long time!"

I sighed.

"Sometimes it is so hard, Sophie. My body lets me know that it doesn't want to get better..."

"But it did to begin with, didn't it?"

"Maybe somehow, it has something to do with Chiara? She is getting better and I am dying."

She held my hand and didn't speak.

We could use Beato's house on Lake Maggiore but I didn't want that. Johannes spends many holidays in Ascona and he recommended some good places to stay there. I booked a hotel on the promenade with a view of the lake. Sophie did not, under any circumstances, want a room of her own, so, for the first time ever, we spent a whole week actually living together - as father and daughter you understand. The drive there was really too much for me. The previous Spring, travelling from the Netherlands had been relatively easy; now, to drive a couple of hours was really too much. But I didn't let on; drove directly to the front of the hotel, dragged the suitcases inside, got the keys and we took possession of a simple room with breath-taking views of the lake and the buildings on the surrounding hills. It was busy, many people promenading, many boats on the water, much traffic noise. It tired me out, but on the other hand it revived me and gave me back my lust for life. I lowered myself to Sophie's standards – she viewed all this as extreme luxury. She went outside to sit on the terrace, but I had to go and lie down to recoup my energy for the evening. I wasn't really sure how it would all pan out - looking forward to spending the days together but worried about the nights.

I woke up when Sophie softly laid her hand on my head. I must have slept well!

"If we don't go and eat now, there won't be anything left!" She laughed.

"You're out and about with an old guy," I said, while I hoisted myself up and smoothed down my sparse hair. My age did not bother Sophie. She is all generosity and sacrifice and I never knew that a woman could be so loving. A girl, a child...

"Isn't it great that no one here knows us!" she said as she clutched my arm once we were outside. "Come on Gérard! Let's act like lovers. I want you with me for all time!"

Her voice dropped; our future was surely only the next few days, weeks... But the tragic circumstances gave our relationship a special sheen, like the red in the evening sky. Strange how something impossible lurks even in my only ever real loving relationship: a difference in age of almost fifty years!

We found a small table in a garden on the lake. High season had finished but still all the terraces were packed with all kinds of people. Humble old age pensioners sat next to extremely rich people. Swiss, Italian, German and one or two Dutch... I looked at the boats and was reminded of my own, which I had sold a few years earlier. The things that went on, on that boat! It would be the same here now...

"What are you thinking of, Gérard?"

"I hope you stay as pure as you are now, Sophie. Financially you don't have, and won't have, any worries. But do stay as uncomplicated as you are now. Find a normal but loving man, one on your own level."

"I don't want a man, I have you."

"I mean, later on."

"Stay another ten years, Gérard!"

"It is not up to me – and I feel rather weak. Brittle, fragile bones you could break me in two just like that!"

This made her very sad and I felt a little guilty. The one who stays behind suffers most. On the other hand, the memory of a real love is the most beautiful memory a person can have. And if I hadn't been dying, we would never have found each other.

"Don't cry, sweet Sophie. We have a whole week ahead of us, it will feel like an eternity if we live every second to the full."

We stayed together all night, for the very first time ever. I felt too old to be kissing her, but we slept hand in hand and I slept through in a oner till six in the morning, after which I just watched her sleep. For her, our being together like this day and night was the greatest happiness there could be. As for me, I have never really felt very much, I have avoided feeling. It is as if the emptiness is filling up with an intensity that overwhelms me. I felt so much love for the young Sophie, as if it were something physical, it permeated my whole body, my heart, my limbs, without becoming sexual. For sure, I still knew how it all worked, but, I could leave it too – and I did. Sophie's whole being was poured into me. I could feel how she was, how she thought and felt. I experienced her musicality and her desire for harmony. Whenever I said something extreme, she would bring the opposite point of view just to bring harmony. Living with her was like music. She also enjoyed detail. I had challenged her to experience every second of our time together – she challenged me to enjoy everything. Just a normal sandwich became a special treat, the everyday sun became cosmic light.

“How do you do that?” I asked her, amazed.

“I’m not that experienced, that makes a difference. But it’s the romance, Gérard. You should play with everything you see, smell, taste. Don’t just carelessly ignore things as if you have all the time in the world. Every impression is a gift – because I get to receive it together with you!”

After breakfast we sat on the terrace of our room, under a ceiling of wisteria, which unfortunately was not in bloom at this time of year. Sophie took a book out of her bag and said,

“May I read something to you, Gérard?”

“You may do whatever you want. Reading to yourself isn’t an option but reading aloud is. What is it you want to teach Gerrit?”

“Something about life after death,” she replied.

“Has anyone ever returned from there? Someone who can write a travelogue?”

“Dante’s ‘Divina Commedia’ is such a travel log. But there are also people who can investigate that kingdom during their life-time and come back to share what they have learned.”

“Someone like Philippe? Like Johannes?”

“Yes. But their communications are nowhere near as numerous as those from the Master of the Occident, which form the foundation of their work...”

“I do know who that is, my Sophie. Go ahead, read to me.” She read out a piece about the nature of the human being. I could easily follow it because of my lessons with

Philippe. When she stopped, I asked her,

"Why are you reading this to me?"

It was crowded on the promenade below. Many people were walking along by the water; boats arrived and departed; and lorries loaded with provisions did their delivery to hotels and restaurants. Rubbish lorries were making a terrific racket. She stopped talking till she could be heard again and said,

"We live there, high up in the mountains and gather strength from the spiritual life there. I believe we should also be aware of the source where all that is good comes from. You have been given such a different end-of-life-care experience than most other seriously ill patients haven't you, Gérard? I regard it as a kind of gratitude that we also deepen our knowledge a little of what's behind it all."

"I can't read something like that. The newspaper is my limit, I'm afraid. My powers of concentration are not accessible to me," I replied.

"It's a question of interest and practice. That is why I read out loud. That works doesn't it?"

I nodded. I certainly did find it interesting. Now that my ridicule and doubt had been driven away from me, I could absorb the highest ideas without prejudice. Once you can do that, the truth reveals itself.

"Would it be OK then to do some of that every day?" she asked carefully.

I slowly pulled myself up straight and bent over forward to give her a kiss on the forehead.

"Everything that comes from you is fine with me, little woman. Everything," I said.

"The last time we were here, with Beato and Chiara, you didn't want to stay in a hotel, you said you could no longer do that. But now you can..." she said.

"I feel worse on the one hand - and better on the other. Back then I had just survived a heart attack. I don't know where this is going, I am fitter, clearer, but have more pain and tightness of the chest. Then I needed to be by myself for hours at a time to come to myself. Now, indeed, things are good, I am also sleeping much better."

We walked down to the promenade, had a rest on a terrace, and walked on again. Even here, the people looked at us. An old man and a young girl walking arm in arm. But here you see so many strange people and things! An extremely rich guy stepping from the most expensive Mercedes, dressed in an old overall, grey hair in a ponytail accompanied by a glamorous woman, but so skinny that there is no fun to be had. A villa here will set you back at least six million, if you are even a little bit fussy. I am so glad I have nothing more to do with that world. I am happy in a friendly little hotel in the thick of things.

In the middle of that busy mundane world in the little town by Lake Maggiore, I felt a great desire to develop self-awareness. When I went for a rest in the afternoon, before falling asleep I tried very hard to organise my thoughts and feelings. Perhaps that is the start of learning the art of meditation. It was very difficult, but I had to take a good look at myself. There was Gerrit, who had lived my entire life. A man who had made something of himself, with the help of some totally wrong methods. Gerrit was a self-serving, idle, hard, yes, even cruel, man, who lived exclusively for power and pleasure. He was handsome, had overcome his oafishnesses and behaved like a great gentleman. He had learned to know the world, down to depths not many people can reach. In that aspect there had been something of value in Gerrit's life. That Gerrit had now left me, and what was left over was Gérard ... a sick man, weak, but calm and kind. He had very little education, not much experience when it comes to feeling or to altruistic behaviour. An underdeveloped weakling was Gérard, somewhat simple, even. Because he had let Gerrit into himself he had been able to make something of his life. As for Gérard, the most appropriate life for him would be the life of a monk in a religious order. A simple life in the outer reaches of a monastery somewhere. Much useful labour, much prayer and a life of sacrifice. That is how Gérard should spend his last days. Not here in the mundanity of Ascona ... but there, in the sombre institute in the mountains, amongst people much, much greater than himself. I permeated myself with one very powerful thought: Never again will I let anything enter into me besides my own being – or the source thereof. I mean: I will never let my being be occupied by 'Gerrit' ever again, or whatever that false power may be called. I wanted to be who I was, albeit simple and uneducated – and try to start to grow and to blossom from there. Even if it meant I had to place people like Johannes way above me.

It was as if Sophie always knew exactly what was going on with me. During the evening meal she said,

"Gérard... you are even larger than 'Gerrit' now. I know

you don't rate yourself - but I do! I see the old 'Gerrit', but now purified, as he was actually meant to be. Gerrit was a caricature, Gérard is the actual being. I do love Gérard so very much! The stiff sternness, the ridiculing irony, the flaccid spirituality, they have all been driven away, are altogether disappearing from view. You may think nothing will be left over. But it is only an outsider who can see how it really is. You have gained something youthful, Gérard, but not ignorant. Honestly!"

"Go on... I do so enjoy listening to your interpretation of 'Gérard'."

"I am so grateful that I don't know anything of your past. But, all that evil that you may have done has also left its traces behind in you, in the way of skills and capabilities. If only you could use these for doing good! Even now you are still a man with much experience of life, you are clearly quite at home in this culture. Not in the arts or sciences, but business-wise and in the ways of political life. It is obvious that meekness has replaced irritability when reading the morning papers or smoking a cigarette... but Gerrit has left some positive traces behind too!"

Her words gave me new material for self-reflection. Could I perhaps do something positive with these 'traces of Gerrit's'? Maybe I needed to spend some time reflecting on what I had learned as 'Gerrit'? I was, after all, very knowledgeable about how the big world out there worked. Maybe I could do some good, if I very conscientiously thought about what the fundamental principles are in today's society...

"Still, Sophie, you have to consider the situation from the other point of view also. You only met me after something 'good' had been developing in me for fourteen years. Something I thought I had rooted out completely! You can't possibly understand what that all means – just as well. At first, I thought I would work it all out with Beato, like a confession. But I mustn't talk about it all, for your sake. Speaking about it just calls it all up again. It might help me, but it would harm you. Still, it is of importance to realise that 'Gerrit' was no petty thief, but was totally immersed in crime and evil. Completely, through and through. That may have brought forth some of the skills you mentioned. But the evil is still much bigger than that, I have no illusions about that."

"I do realise some of that, Gérard. In the beginning, I did feel some of it, that scared me. It was only by focussing on the positive that I could endure it."

"Why did you want to endure it?"

"Because you are such a fantastic guy."

I trembled. A fantastic guy! She meant it too, and she was honest and didn't fantasize. She is an artist, capable of listening for the reality, behind it all. I sighed and felt deep shame.

In the evening, before we went to bed we hugged each other, intimately and for a long time – without sex. I kissed her on her forehead, never on her mouth. Her breasts against my chest only brought a feeling of tenderness, not lust. The excitement, driven out with 'Gerrit', belonged to a previous life. Now there was only tenderness and Sophie seemed satisfied with that, too. There was no sense of separation, we lived together, intensely in the belief that the days were numbered.

"There is something that concerns me, Sophie. Up there, in the mountains where our home now is, with Johannes and a number of great men living together for an 'ideal' … where are the great women? Has emancipation not yet reached the spiritual life? That whole palaver around Mary Magdalene, being the wife of Jesus ... women love that. But where are the female initiates, of the stature of Johannes and Philippe?" I winked at her. "It looks to me like a worthwhile task for Sophie!"

"You should ask Johannes to explain it to you. He has an amazing wife, Eva – but she is no Johannes. There are also a number of women who work closely together with Johannes – but none of them are as far developed as he is – or as doctor Laurent. Do ask him about it!"

That was how I went 'home', with two intentions. I would explore my experiences in the world of politics and maybe discuss them with Johannes. And, I would ask about female initiates.

Courage becomes the power to redeem

One day after we returned to the mountains I had a long conversation with Johannes. That he had the patience to talk to me at all, amazed me every time. At first, I still believed that he did this to be able to milk me for my money … later I let go of this idea completely. Johannes does not trade in middle class conventions; his word is never just an empty phrase... I had always used lies and untruths every day – he had done the opposite. "Both roads lead to the same place, Gerrit. But as soon as the desired place has been reached the roads bend away in opposite directions. The road there is opposite, the longed-for place is the same, the results, are again, the opposite."

"You speak in riddles. Truly."

"You, Gerrit, followed your training. You managed, by paralysing your conscience, to gain access somehow, to the place that is beneath the wellspring of our memories. Whenever someone remembers something, a process is mirrored within his consciousness of the change undergone in his organism as a consequence of an event. Within memory you have mirroring, not the real event. Underneath the mirror of memory lies the subconscious. Therein lie two worlds: the world of the drive to absolute destruction and the world of cosmic creation, sometimes called the microcosm. These worlds reside behind a closed portal, inaccessible to everyday consciousness. The portal can be opened in two ways. When you cultivate a relationship with the destructive powers you force it open. A thief, a robber or a murderer enters into the world of destruction. You will, however, not find the world of cosmic creation, only its power."

"What is the other way to open the door?"

Johannes was silent and looked at me for a long time. He was hesitating, not sure if he could talk to me like this ... that was what I thought anyway. He sighed and said,

"Our spoken words are full of - and paralysed by - everything we have done with them, from swearing, to proclamations of love, business deals and shopping lists. How can you possibly use those same words to express the most intimate, the most spiritual of holies, without polluting it and bringing it down? I don't know if you have ever read the Gospels? The New Testament? The Bible?"

I shook my head,

"No." then I said,

"But I'm not a total idiot, obviously. I do know about Jesus and such. I regarded him as the opposition, I had to ... you know fine well, Johannes, that he has protected me." Johannes beautiful blue eyes were very soft and expressed deep emotion and tenderness.

"He is the Door, the Portal. He does not open it, he is it. Whoever takes him into himself, gets to know both worlds, the one of the cosmic creation and the other, which He restrains, of destruction." I was silent. Its words had an effect - which needed courage to allow them in. Don't say or think anything too quickly, but just let the words enter. You need courage for that, great courage. I had cultivated the courage for evil, now that was proving useful. I can keep silent, and endure for a very long time...

But Johannes was in no hurry, he had no intention of sending me on my way. From which I must conclude that he genuinely enjoys our conversations. I wanted to include him in my thoughts regarding politics, so I said,

"I'm sure you are already familiar with what I'm going to tell you, but I did so want to share this, and hear your opinion. As you know, my 'work' placed me right in the centre of the field of world politics. Because of the necessary suspicions, for security, I was always vigilant and aware. You experience and see more under those conditions than normally.

"It is sometimes said that we live in a 'constructed society'. Well now, isn't that the truth! Coincidence doesn't exist. Everything, but then really everything is 'organised'. Everyone is allotted their little bit of space by the 'powers that be' – and you'd better pay heed. Your work here is permitted because it is better to allow it to operate in a small way – but it can never grow big. When you were still a professor and operated in a manner permitted – then you could become 'big'. Wars break out 'to order'. Only they don't always run the way they were intended, because the 'powers that be' are made up of various interests. But there isn't an individual person with hunger for power – like in James Bond films – who sits somewhere with a pussy cat on his lap making all the plans. It works very differently.

There are councils of 'men' who operate from behind the scenes. They make use of good and bad powers, as needed. I received as many privileges as ... well, you name him, anyone who is seen as important in world politics, I am not famous, I also worked from behind the scenes, after all. As acting manager, not as deciding power; carrying out the plan on a large scale, mind."

I could see that I hadn't told him anything he didn't already know, but he was very interested to hear about my experiences anyway.

"That's why I have nothing to fear, I was a cornerstone in the foundations. I had a great time. I enjoyed the honour, the power, the invulnerability – of the lust for evil. If you look at it like that, then I have had a brilliant life. I never doubted, ever, doubt is the first thing that is banned. I felt a part of a huge power-system of people who know how the world should be governed, how to keep the masses ignorant. The media play the starring role. Whenever an important event needs to be kept quiet, you divert the media by feeding them one or other sensational bit of news to distract attention from what is really going on. If you really want to know what is going on, pay close attention, not to the main subject at a demonstration or other excitement but, look for the 'unimportant' items in the side-lines. Well, I know that I would be regarded as a paranoid nutter by everyone, not by you! As someone with a persecution complex. Such people also believe that 'everything is manipulated', but they only relate it to themselves. I have blissfully joined in with all that and all those brave souls that "don't believe in such things"; well I had good laugh at their expense.

"Now all that has been taken away from me – and I feel how small I actually am. How great is the contrast between power on earth and power in eternity's light. My power here has turned my real self to stone. I don't want to talk about that now. For me, it was about taking control of the course of events on earth – as they really happened."

Johannes nodded and asked me,

"But now, here, something unexpected occurs, Gerrit. For example: You give your fortune to an institute, one that is not earmarked for becoming big. Your deed is not anticipated and, naturally, not desired … I would be able, for example, once the children have grown up, to give lectures in many places – there was no money for this before now. What do you think will happen then?"

I shrugged my shoulders.

"As long as only a handful of people are interested – they will just laugh at you. No interest in what you do!"

"That's very reassuring," Johannes laughed. "And you, Gerrit? Don't you ever think that maybe you are also just a pawn on their chessboard? That your thoughts and deeds are guided by a hand you don't see?"

"If you are talking about the giving away of my complete fortune … no, that is absolutely my very own initiative. But my so called 'power'... is in all likelihood based on nothing. You are probably right. The strange thing is, that you can see how others are manipulated – and you still believe yourself to be 'free'… "

"That man, the one you met when you were young, the one who taught you the techniques of evil... he will have been led to cross your path. Just like on my path, a teacher, a Master, came along to help me find a way forward."

"All the same, I feel I am guilty. I can't find any excuse for the path I trod in life. I was completely involved and knew what I was doing."

"The one doesn't exclude the other. I only want to point out to you the nature of your feelings of power. You have been swindled just as much as everyone else, Gerrit."

I understand that there are people who just hate Johannes, from the bottom of their heart. They say 'oh him, you cannot teach him anything, he always knows everything better than the best professional'. But I didn't feel any hate, only admiration for his freedom of spirit. He, who initiated me onto the road to the Good.

"Do you still have time?" I asked, after a period of silence.

He nodded. I have come to love the patience, the sacrifice of Johannes, very much. You might think that he would have better things to do than have conversations with all those little people...

"Then I want to ask you something else. There are a number of quite exceptional people gathered here: Beato, Philippe, the master and ... Johannes. Why are there only men? Where is the female master?"

Johannes nodded slowly.

"That is an important question, Gerrit. Actually, women are much better suited to achieve initiation. Their body isn't as much of a hindrance as ours is, really. It is less earthy, has fewer materialistic qualities to hamper the individuality that inhabits the body. But initiation cannot be achieved on the grounds of one-sidedness – no matter how unique. A great equilibrium is required to get ahead in the spiritual domain. If you knew my biography you would see that there has been a constant searching – and still is – for equilibrium, for balance. I have suffered under the one-sidedness of my maleness, have longed for the counterbalance of the feminine, not only outside myself, in the longing for a partner, but especially within myself. A man who becomes an initiate must have enough affinity with the feminine. Real affinity, connection, ability. So, you will recognise what I mean in the other men here. A woman who becomes an initiate, will also have to have a generous relationship with the masculine, if the initiation is to be balanced and stable. There are a number of women, who have taken on the path to initiation and who are making good progress. They can only become Master when their thinking has acquired a male quality, just as with the men, thinking has to take on a female quality. An especially strong schooling in logical thinking is required – which has to be let go of again later on – to achieve a modern initiation. I still have to meet the woman who has that by nature. Yes, you protest! There are female scholars, presidents of countries, ministers etc … But it isn't about that. A man has to be able to consciously handle the feminine in his logical intelligence. A woman has to integrate the masculine – the strictly logical as second nature – within her and be aware of it. The will is present in a number of women, but the natural disposition also has to be there."

"Why, then, are there no less than four men with the apparently natural gift for the feminine – and till now not one woman?"

"Of course, they exist, but maybe they don't have the masculine need for self-assertion – well, that isn't exactly the correct term either. Regardless of all the emancipation, men and women have different qualities, which rest on their different physical bodies and a different etheric, or life body, to go along with that. Should you want to become initiated you have to learn to view the life body. A man does that by developing his 'feminine' super-sensible thinking – and the woman a 'masculine' thinking. That way balance is established. It is very difficult to describe the specifically female initiation, because her starting point has to be in the masculine. Once she has acquired that, she is initiated immediately. With her the starting point is already an initiation. The starting point for a man is his natural inclination, which is a hindrance as well as a great advantage. Well now, it remains vague, I understand that very well."

"For an uneducated person like me, it is all very difficult to take in. But ... just tell me ... is there a woman who can compare to you all here?"

"Yes. There is a woman, who because of her ability of thinking with her ether body has a masculine intelligence. By developing that thinking, she will achieve initiation, much more directly from out of the spirit than we can."

"Who is that? Do I know her?"

He shook his head.

"What a shame," I said and gave him my notes. I would never have been able to write up all he had said from memory...

I thought about it all some more while walking through the park. Women are less rational but more sensitive. Johannes is rational but also very sensitive. His nature is no hindrance to some miraculous thinking and acting. When you compare him to a girl like Sophie ... there is, though, a big difference. Sophie is a very good thinker, not irrational. Still, she thinks in quite a different way than Johannes, but that may also be because she is no professor. Well, let's leave it at that. I wouldn't mind meeting that female master one day!

I went to visit Chiara. She was still as yellow as a canary and very subdued, but again I felt no antipathy towards her this time. On the contrary. I hugged her warmly.

"You look terrible, my dear," I said.

"It is awful, yes. But, there is something positive. They redid the investigation and from the bloods it looks like it's something different from what they first thought. Not as serious, apparently. I don't really understand it all, don't really want to, to be honest. But Beato is very happy with the result and I can get better, so they tell me."

Then, as for me, I will have to die! That thought shot through my being. Emotional pain permeated me. But it had happened, as it should happen…

Alone I walked along the path up the hill. My body felt heavy in the autumn sun. By now an old man, seriously ill ... and with an awakening conscience. It seems like it grows a little every day, my conscience. Which made the gift of an extended life simultaneously into a protracted *hell.* With a soul as cold as ice I have lived and done things that a healthy person would never do. It made me stronger and stronger, but the ice became so cold and so hard. Now it is beginning to melt and it runs in warm tears down my face. I suffer from who I am, just like my victims have suffered on my account. Here walks Gérard, the guilty, bald head exposed to the sun. The sun that shines for everyone. With revulsion I realise that this is and was, me, Gerrit, and that such things can exist. Everyone knows, of course, that cruelty exists in shapes and forms you would be better not to imagine. A healthy person sees this as revolting. With even a slightly sick mind, it is already possible to experience some pleasure when meeting cruelty – even without ever doing anything like that yourself. But to actually carry out such deeds – and to then experience that it is you, yourself doing it, or have done it ... that is just horrible. That one-time Beato made me see the light, for just a fraction of a second. And now, that kindled light illuminates all of Gerrit. Images appeared, concrete memory images, like a film outside of me – but unmistakeably from my own life. I didn't feel like myself, not the active Gerrit... I experienced what had been done to the other, so real and so completely authentic! But, I kept on walking as though I had the urge to self-destruction. My heart and my lungs were no longer capable of such an effort. Climbing, on and on... Suddenly I felt an enormous power outside me, that held me back and forced me to stand still. Nothing on earth can compare with the inexorable severity of that power. And yet ... it made me feel comforted, saved.

I stood still and looked around me. No one. I attempted to take a step forward. Impossible. Not forward, not back, not sideways. Imprisoned in a cylinder of power ... or maybe I had lost control of my body? No, I was breathing; I felt my heart pounding, the sweat on my head, the tears on my cheeks. I felt no fear, there was nothing worse than hell - and I was in hell already. I knelt down, it was the only thing I could do. This was the third time that I had fallen down on my knees, the hard stones and tree roots hurt. Within the power around me I again saw my life, my memories, but now with my awakening conscience. Gérard is judging Gerrit – no stricter judge can be found - because Gérard is totally involved – and, at the same time, remains objective. Imprisonment in a jail is but a poor reflection of what I experienced. Locked up in the power of my own crimes. The walls of my prison were inescapably me and only me; the me and what I have done to others. When I thought I could endure it no longer, the power dissipated like a gust of wind ... and was gone. I could stand up and walk, downhill this time, and back home.

But I had walked up a long way and the descent was hard; I now missed the forward push of that power. The memories flashed up brighter than before all around me, flashed up and disappeared again and again - and again. The tiny content of mildness and compassion in me was too small and made the images into an unbearable torment. I needed help, from one of the men here below. The fear of hell ceases when hell pours itself out over you. My compassion with those I'd tormented began to grow and grow... I had to have help! There ... a few hundred meters below, a man appeared, coming up the hill. The man. Beato. He didn't notice me, he looked straight ahead. I hurried on, forgetting my age, I was like a child on the way to his father. There he was coming around the bend, he saw me. He spread his arms wide, in the Italian style, and I let myself be embraced.

"I noticed you going up the path, Gerrit, and you didn't return. I came out to look for you."

We stood opposite each other, the healthy harmonious Beato and the sick guilty Gerrit. I looked into his warm brown eyes, he into my thawing blue ones. I could feel eternity springing up between us, the strength of our relationship and the difficulties also. Suddenly the presence didn't matter, it wasn't the only thing anyway. It was as if Beato now had full consciousness of our connectedness, as if he had true knowledge of who we had once been and who we are now in true reality. There he stood, my superior, always and in all things better than me, further, healthier, stronger ... you name it. And I, small from the jealousy of his greatness, not realising that it is precisely that jealousy that keeps me small. I saw the reality, concealed no longer. Beato as a large individuality, with more harmony than anyone else possesses... Gerrit as a figure of not much merit, when he abandons all his tricks – but very rich because of his friendship with the 'Balanced one'. The connectedness living within our friendship is what totally transforms me. In the prosaic surroundings of the twenty-first century, without knights and young maidens, without castles, without tournaments, without mysticism or magic, even – although these do come up in both our lives - our relationship has become what it truly is: The relationship between a chosen one and a damned man. But then not predestined, but self-willed and sought for. The chosen one is a friend of the damned man and is his exorcist, his healer, his joy and his truth…

I now understand what the Eastern mystic means with the ego. Maybe it is easy for me to understand because my own ego has such a huge circumference. Once Beato and I had come down from the mountain, we said our goodbyes and resumed our individual prosaic twenty-first century lives. I could sense that very insubstantial Gérard, the only part of me that can survive, that is actually worth anything. The rest, condensed in that little word 'ego', had been placed outside me, just like my memories. It still exists as a kind of hanging together of something, that must be overcome. But it has been completely severed from my real self. Just like my memories, I could put this ego on again – like a suit of clothes. The temptation to do so is great, because that part of me that is left over, Gérard, is a very unattractive man – most likely greatly reduced compared to what he was previously. On the other hand, his simplicity and humility may do my resting soul much good. I feel comforted, peaceful. And I feel great courage - reformed it is true - but still, a great strength, which will hold me together and will manage the deliverance of my ego. I turned in the direction of the Eastern master. As an old patron I am welcome everywhere. This position gives me the courage to just knock on the great man's door, and expect him not to mind. He opened the door of his chalet himself, and I do think he was genuinely surprised and pleased to see me.

"Ah, Gerrit! What a pleasant surprise. Come on in!"

"Am I not disturbing you?"

"Please don't be so formal, my dear friend! No, I was just about to make a pot of tea. Would you like a cup?"

He let me go before him into the living room, where indeed a tea cup was already on the table. He placed another cup beside it and we sat down at the table. He spoke again,

"Here, with us, a veritable wonder occurs. There are two roads that lead to fulfilment with the Lamb of God, Gerrit: to have an encounter with Him, the way He is, invisible to the human eye, amongst us. The one way is the one of constant inner work, of unrelenting striving. The other is the way of grace. The Lord of Karma himself will bend down towards someone, comforts him and has mercy. People in great trouble, or in danger of their life, in hellish pain or great anxiety, can by His grace be chosen to see Him and thereby be completely changed. But, also, an intense desire for change and the release of powers for the soul associated with that, can be a cry for His grace."

The water boiled, an old-fashioned whistling kettle called out from the kitchen. The master stood up and left me alone with my stirred-up emotions and thoughts. The power that had captured me high up there in the mountains, was that the Lord of Karma? Did the comfort I felt after that oppressing event come from Him? Had He taken my ego and placed it outside of myself to liberate me? I am now a simple man, without much knowledge, with a slender world of feeling, but with an enormous amount of courage to go on. His courage, had it emerged from my temerity to offer up everything?

The master returned with a teapot and small bowl of cakes on a silver tray. My ego had despised this man, what was left of me now loved him dearly. His tiny stature, his sober and perfectly tailored clothes ... his large head with its splendid mop of greying hair. We were about the same age, but some black hair still showed amongst the grey. And, when he came closer, you could see his black-brown eyes, which could be filled with infinite love, but also hard as iron, derisive and dismissive. They looked, as it were, behind you and reflected what they saw... He was all softness when his visitor was in a good way. Were his visitor in a state of untruth and falsehood, he became ruthlessly unforgiving. That had been my first experience of him. This time I experienced his gentleness. He poured the tea in a manner that made me think of the Far East ... you could sense the tropics, maybe the rice paddies or the tops of the Himalayas. A monk's discipline coloured all his actions but blended with spirituality like Johannes', which I only knew by its effect upon me. An intense shivering came over me and tears welled up in my eyes … So, the ever-so-tiny Gérard is capable of loving, with an overwhelming, immense intensity. I felt unmeasurable affection for the master, for his presence, for his actions, for the life he had led.

"The greatness of a man comes to expression in his courage to see his own shortcomings," he said gently. "With such insight you can be a great person, even if the shortcomings are numerous."

"It isn't that difficult to be insignificant here. With no money worries and protected by a couple of giants in place of parents, just like a child that can grow up in safety. That isn't difficult, no. But before that was the pregnancy and the birth, they were exceptionally difficult, well, almost impossible even."

I shivered again. What will happen with me now? I have no power any more, no money, no physical strength. Lies cannot pass my lips anymore, untruthfulness in my behaviour is no longer a possibility for me. With that powerless soul I look at who I once was, what I have given up. Whoever sees me, sees the same figure, the same head, hears the same voice. But, that which lives within ... is something ... holy. Something I don't yet dare to say 'I' to. And yet, I experience it as my primordial self.

Mastering thinking leads to truth

The summer has long gone, it is November now, but it remains warm and sunny, on and off. I feel at one with the autumn … within me also, nature is dying, the summer sun penetrates me to my bones, and death's approach is unmistakable. Spring, summer and autumn in the mountains ... they have been the most beautiful days of my life. I am at peace with the approach of death. I am almost looking forward to the life hereafter. Like a boy who has just done his final exams looks forward to getting into university, that's how I see it: the examination of death and the 'higher education' thereafter.

There is nothing I can change now about my present life. But, here, I have learned that the processing and transformation of life begins after death. It will be a *hell* also, of course, but my positive good will has grown in strength. That, I can take with me over the threshold, I'm sure... I have the feeling that I have reached the limit of all that I could have achieved in this life, having attained both the heights and the deepest point. More is not possible; my reserves are all gone. Just as you go to bed at night to be renewed through sleep, so I will find death to make me a better person.

I see things around me now that have been hidden from

me all my life. Every day I take a short walk with Sophie. I cannot walk very far anymore; climbing I cannot do at all. I have to lean on her arm to be able to move forward at all... She points out all the different colours of the falling leaves, the mists between the mountains, the uniqueness of that very special autumn afternoon sun. I know that I will not see this again; that there will not be a 'next year' anymore. These are the most beautiful days of my life, more is not necessary…

She now lives with me in my room. She takes care of me, in as much as I cannot do it myself anymore. I feel her tears and try to comfort her with my total resignation to my fate. In the afternoon, when I should be sleeping, but am too unsettled due to the pain, she reads to me from her books by Steiner, Goethe... She reads to me in Dutch, she has a very sweet accent: French-Flemish. She doesn't always understand it herself, but if she reads in English or French, then I can't follow it. The only thing that weighs heavily on my heart is that we have to part, to say goodbye to each other. She is so lovely, so committed, so beautiful too... I warn her about the traps in life she could fall into, the 'wrong' men, those who do not know how to respect women. The nonsense about fame and fortune – as she might very well achieve both. She does, after all start out with riches ... she possesses half of my bank balance.

When we go to bed at night, we hold each other close and then she cries ... and I comfort her and cry inside.

In my work I was always silent. Discretion was an absolute necessity. The less you let out, the better. Even just thinking could be dangerous. In this place I had wanted to confess everything to Beato, to tell him all that I had done. But instead I had chosen to mention only a few sparse examples from that time ... so as not to empower the evil anew. It's because of that that I have learned to experience what 'conscience' actually is.

Sophie knows nothing about the details, I am taking my memories with me to the grave, and leaving her with her own memories. Her image of me will help me through. But what about her? How will she go on? Sometimes she tells me that she doesn't want to go on at all, that worries me... Then I tell her, that I am sure we will see each other again, we will then go on together. I don't doubt that anymore. I do feel death approaching, but at the same time with that death comes a real world, a real existence thereafter. That realisation grows stronger by the day and I imagine that soon, the realisation of that will push earthly reality out of the way, overcome it, overrule it. Then death will be here and I say once more: I am looking forward to it.

Johannes once said: "When the impulse to do evil is intentionally reversed to do good, then an inner power is released, similar to a nuclear explosion." That inner strength now lives within me. This shows that self-development does not always progress step by step; sometimes it is tempestuous and explosive. At first there was only a small point of light, that Beato planted within me while I was not aware. That grew and grew, very slowly, over fourteen years or so. Then the moment arrived when the light wanted to blossom, not just to keep growing, but to burst forth, to transform. That is what happened to me. I carry an enormous strength within me to want to change, to cut straight through every obstacle.

The body, the instrument for this work, has been used up, it cannot go on any longer, it never really had the necessary qualities for this work in the first place. I feel now, how I will have to die first, just as the flower has to wither away in order to bring forth new shoots – to be able to bear fruit.

Everything will need to die off and to rest in a different soil. A new body needs to be created from that soil, one that will have the right qualities to carry out such powerful intentions. That other soil, is not the grave, not the earth ... it is the spiritual world, hell and heaven.

First, a purification will need to take place, the beginning of which I have already witnessed here. Every detail, all the actions that have emanated from me have to be lived through; and out of each of the details and actions a new task will come forth. That will deliver a difficult and complicated life next time around. It won't be that long till I come back again. Due to the life that I have lived, there isn't much strength in my out-breath. Without the help of the powers-that-be the in-breath in the next life, may also be meagre. It will be a difficult life. But in the depths, Gerrit's strength will provide direction and courage to the impulse and the decisions I am making now.

They will be with me, those that brought me here, to this point: four men and a woman. I will be the least among them, and I will *know* it and also *want* it so. No, here, it isn't working any more. I am up against the impossible… I cannot go on … my breath is all gone. I want to breathe out as much as I can…

Epilogue ...

Gerrit's death and funeral were dramatic events, his death and his last days were intensely affecting. He died on the date of his birth, he had reached seventy. For the last two weeks of his life he never left his bed, but he did not want to return to the clinic. Sophie nursed him like the best of nurses; and I, as his doctor, visited him twice a day. The body, once so enormously strong, had become fragile and almost transparent. His steel blue eyes of earlier times had become mild and soft, in peace and almost smiling at the coming of death. I would have liked to have been able to cry, like a young boy. I would have burst into tears after every visit, his spirituality moved me deeply, shook me to my very foundations. He had unbearable pain, due to the metastases to his liver he was nauseous all the time and could no longer eat. His breathing was shallow and short ... his thinking, however, was clear and you could feel the Lord's Grace, how he was permitted to die with Him, in Him. His previously tempestuous and unscrupulous nature had already left him. He became increasingly gentle and intimate. He spoke little and listened much. And when he did speak, we were amazed at his wisdom, his ability to understand. He didn't regard his words as his own.

“Gerrit has no wisdom,” he said.

He had no need to see his children again. They belonged to another life from which he had taken his leave long ago. His money we could have. Sophie, and I for my children. Quite a shock I had when I saw the size of the amount: an indication of the nature of Gerrit’s life. In the end, he didn’t want to discuss it. I know that he did so want to confess everything – but, then decided to keep quiet about it, so as not to burden others. He so wanted to hear my life story, such a contrast to his. That didn’t get very far, either. But I resolved to write it all down for him and then read it to him... We were all able to say goodbye to him. Chiara, who is almost better now, kissed and embraced him. He ‘rescued’ her, we realise that quite well, though outwardly it seemed like an error in the laboratory – a wrong diagnosis.

I cared about Gerrit very much. I don’t think he realised how much I cared. From the time of our very first meeting a recognition was kindled, and I suffered much from his rejection and the years of separation. On the last day still I called him ‘my friend’. He could not imagine that he had ever been anyone’s ‘friend’. He was, after all, despite all his cunning, somewhat naive. That naivety came to the surface in the last weeks like a kind of holiness. He had become a lamb, filled with sacrifice for his fate.

In those last days he would sometimes be looking far into the distance with great intensity, a tragic look on his face. That’s when he was suffering, suffering about what he had to call his life. That suffering was something different from just being a bit uncomfortable about your own imperfections. He was looking within himself with the eyes of the Lord at what he had done. He had more or less to reject all his impulses, all his actions, everything he had ever done.

The only thing he was allowed to keep was what he had accomplished in this past year. That may sound meagre, on the other hand it is glorious and easily outranks what the average person achieves in a whole lifetime.

His suffering with himself was caused by the Lamb in him; at the same time, he was also comforted by Him.

My ability to view the invisible spirit world is much greater than I care to admit. He saw in me the perfect harmony and balance, but he could hardly imagine the abilities I possessed as a consequence thereof. His actions, the total aggressiveness that emanated from him, the brutal strength, with which he attacked me often, I caught these like catching a spear before they could hit me. That awoke his interest, made him unsure and, for the first time in his life, he experienced love within himself. There, almost fifteen years ago, the battle for Gerrit began, now completed by his death. I have observed, how he became more and more aware of the great all-encompassing Being, the one who has mercy for the sinner. He also began to experience the relationship of that Being with me, Beato, his friend.

Finally, he went to Him in death...

Sophie and I were with him when he died. There was no struggle for death, he wanted to go, he was not a frightened kind of person, had no fear of the unknown. He lay peacefully in his bed, his hands folded as if in holy prayer.

While he lay dying, he looked at me ... he looked at me till his gaze froze, and I could feel how his enormous will power, his newly born 'I', his life of feelings and his immature thinking freed itself, free, free ... to give himself over to the unity with God and His heavenly Hierarchies. To me his willpower was mightily felt, his *good-will* to develop himself, to change. Released from the ties to the physical body, that will, took on an impressive form. More impressive than the Gerrit the human being, with all his oppressive temperament, had ever been.

We watched over Gerrit's body, knowing about Gerrit's strong relationships with demons – in an attempt to protect him in the process of his liberation from his body. A person who has just died retains a connection to the spoken word, and therefore we read, out loud, passages from the New Testament. It was as if the enormous spreading out of his will was mirrored in the rapid shrinking of his body. By the hour it became less and less...

He was buried in the cemetery in the little town down the hill. Everything was simple, as he had wished it. A holy mass was organised, I gave an outline of his life, without details, obviously.

On his grave a bouquet of seven red roses, wilting...

One day a farmer at his toil
With his plough a hard stone struck,
And with his spade he cleared the soil,

Revealed a wondrous-shapen rock.

He called his neighbours to crowd round
But what it was they could not tell.
"Old wise grey beard – what have we found?"
The grizzled one looked, was stumped as well.

But, aware or not, it blessing stands
In timeless beauty in each breast;
Its seeds flower paths in every land:
It was a CROSS that had perplexed!

They see nor fight nor bloody gashes,
Only the conquest and the victor's dues;
They're blind to storm and lightning flashes,
View only the rainbows and their gentle hues.

The cross of stone they placed in a bower:
Mystery-filled history which merits renown;
On it roses abound,
And all kinds of flowers
Climb round and around.

So, stands the cross 'midst fulfilment and glowing
On Golgotha, glory-filled, meaningful, sure.
Long since enshrouded by dense roses growing,
Crowds sense roses only – no cross any more.